Goddess Chosen

Book One
of the
"Goddess Rising"
Series

Jay Hartlove

Cover design copyright © 2019 by Niki Lenhart
nikilen-designs.com

Author photo copyright © S. N. Jacobson

Published by Paper Angel Press
paperangelpress.com

ISBN 978-1-949139-58-7 (Trade Paperback)

10 9 8 7 6 5 4 3 2

DEDICATION

To my kids,
who keep me young enough to see it through.

Turning and turning in the widening gyre
The falcon cannot hear the falconer;
Things fall apart; the centre cannot hold;
Mere anarchy is loosed upon the world,
The blood-dimmed tide is loosed, and everywhere
The ceremony of innocence is drowned;
The best lack all conviction, while the worst
Are full of passionate intensity.
Surely some revelation is at hand;
Surely the Second Coming is at hand.
The Second Coming! Hardly are those words out
When a vast image out of Spiritus Mundi
Troubles my sight: somewhere in sands of the desert
A shape with lion body and the head of a man,
A gaze blank and pitiless as the sun,
Is moving its slow thighs, while all about it
Reel shadows of the indignant desert birds.
The darkness drops again; but now I know
That twenty centuries of stony sleep
Were vexed to nightmare by a rocking cradle,
And what rough beast, its hour come round at last,
Slouches towards Bethlehem to be born?

The Second Coming
William Butler Yeats, 1921

PROLOGUE

THE KEYS TO THE UNIVERSE

"WHAT DO YOU MEAN, HE GOT AWAY?"

Pharaoh Ramses II's bellowing voice still echoed in Royarna's ears as he walked toward the Sphinx at sundown. He was glad the avenue from his apartments was nearly empty of the Necropolis priests. The few he passed reverently dropped to their knees, which he found distracting. He did not need distraction now.

"Damn his eyes, I want your predecessor's head on a platter!" the pharaoh had railed back in his palace at Pi-Ramesse in the western delta. "A squad of my best men in my fastest chariots lost him above the Cataracts, with the idiot Kushites probably hiding him like some treasure. My armies are busy elsewhere; I cannot afford an invasion. Find him. Consult the Neters, personally. I don't want any answers third hand through some local god, and no signs or interpretations of nature!" his king had emphasized with a shake of his fist. "I may have just elevated you to High Priest of Amun, but I

1

know you can consult the gods directly, and this is what I want. Your predecessor, Nebwenanef, 'he-who-has-no-name', has disgraced both me and the Neters by sabotaging my conflict with … Moses," he spat.

Royarna breathed deeply the cool dry air and calmed himself. His king had given him a job to do, a nearly impossible job, to demand answers of the gods on his terms, not theirs. This was going to require heightened atonement and total concentration. He opened his senses. His body smelled of the spiced oils and silt with which the temple acolytes had bathed him. The rasping of his guards' heavy leather sandals behind him on the flagstone walkway was invigorating to hear, as was the scuffing of his own embroidered slippers. The edges of the carefully fitted flagstones of the walkway looked sharp and hard in the long deepening shadows. The feel of the gentle evening breeze fluttering his gossamer linen robes against his body was tantalizing. His whole-leopard pelt shawl felt massive and invigorating around his shoulders. His braided black wig swung around his neck with the rhythm of his stride.

The sun was just below the horizon and the Sphinx's enormous painted face cast a looming black silhouette on the darkening blue sky. The image of man's place in the universe, both master over, and yet only a part of the forces of nature: the human head of knowledge, the lion claws of courage, the bull body of will, and the falcon wings of patience. Here in Kemet, the center of the world. Royarna worked the images in his mind, letting them inspire him with confidence for what he was about to do.

Shawnut and Hertoc ran ahead of him and lit the torches ensconced on the inner sides of the statue's massive paws. This illuminated the enormous rectangular space walled by the forelegs and the Sphinx's chest. Royarna walked up between the paws to face a dark brown granite slab mounted against the Sphinx's chest. It was half again as tall and wide as a man, covered with deeply carved images of the afterlife.

The High Priest stood before the writings, raised his hands out to his sides, grew still and uttered the single word, "*Hu.*"

The guards looked away out of respect, and also to watch the surrounding grounds for intruders.

Hertoc, the younger of the soldiers, happened to glance back and let out a tight, startled gasp. Royarna had vanished, and an enormous black snake slithered away from where he had stood.

Shawnut admonished him with hand gestures to be silent and turn around. Remembering the sacred trust placed in him, the less experienced man forced himself to regain his composure and look away.

Shawnut knew where their master had gone. He didn't know the younger man had not been told what to expect. The snake, on the other hand, was a whole different matter. Had the High Priest left it to prevent anyone following him? Had he left it as an omen? Had he left it at all, or was it an omen from the gods? The guard kept an eye on the creature as it slowly crawled out of the range of the flickering torchlight and into the deepening darkness surrounding them.

After reading the blessings on the granite stele, Royarna stepped around it into a hidden niche in the Sphinx's chest. Pulling a secret lever, he opened a bronze door that swung silently open. This entrance was only used to initiate new priests, and he knew he would not be disturbed. Since this area of the subterranean temple complex was left vacant, he had to light and carry a torch with him to navigate the low ceiling of the narrow, undecorated stone corridors. Stairs down led to a short dead-end passage where he escaped through a hidden door. More stairs and more secret doors lead finally to the Approach Corridor which led to the Gallery of Mysteries.

The Approach Corridor was plain like the others leading to it, but it had been designed with one special feature: it took twenty-eight breaths to traverse it while walking normally. Not until long after a new postulate's initiation was this detail explained, but Royarna took full advantage of it on this momentous occasion. The air was oppressively warm, dry and stale, but this hardly caught his attention. Seven breaths each of Earth, Water, Air, and Fire left him infused with the raw power of the Universe. To mold that power, he stepped into the Gallery.

The Gallery was higher and wider than the corridors, and was made of white marble. He knew every detail of the twenty-two images painted on the two long facing walls, but being here crystallized their power in his mind like no simple recollection. He paused briefly in front of each one and let them stir in him the secrets of mastery over the elements. By the time he reached the end of the hall he was so keenly in tune with reality, he no longer needed the torch to light his way. He snuffed the torch against the floor and proceeded in inky blackness.

More stairs down connected to a long corridor under the plaza of the necropolis that led to the seven pyramids. In the darkness, he recalled these walls were painted with scenes of the afterlife, with people fishing and hunting and feasting with the gods. These scenes were of no concern to him now. A short distance down this tunnel, Royarna stopped and turned to face one particular, although unexceptional wall panel.

The Sanctuary of Isis was the most holy ground on Earth, with only a handful of adepts even aware of its exact location. He chose to enter this corridor from the backside, to avoid the temple priests who worked at the pyramids. He tapped further into his connection with reality and clairvoyantly moved his sight forward into the chamber. It was not empty. He smiled upon seeing that the only other two Magi of the Ninth Order had also seen fit to come consult the Neters.

Royarna tripped the lock, swung open the secret panel, and entered the temple. The cavernous room was a cube, as tall and as wide as five men, made entirely of smooth black granite, with a gray stone altar at the near side, a gold throne in front and to the side of the altar, and a colossal painted stone statue of Isis rising overhead, filling the rest of the chamber. Her hands were raised in welcoming beneficence. The room was illuminated by twelve torch standards mounted in the floor around the statue's feet. The air smelled warmly of torch oil, spices and flowers.

Apparently the Master of the Temple and the High Priestess of Isis foresaw his arrival, and prepared the altar and furnishings for him. Upon Royarna's entry, they greeted one another wordlessly with hand gestures. The Master of the Temple stood an entire head shorter than Royarna, and had the pasty-white skin of an indoor dweller. He was dressed the same as the High Priest, with the obvious difference of a yellow flaxen sash belt where Royarna's was purple silk.

The Priestess also was not tanned. Her light olive skin glowed richly in the torchlight and made her eyes look even darker than they already were. She wore a much slimmer-fitting robe than the men, bound up to her body with a yellow sash which wound around her three times, below the bust, at the waist and below the hips. On her black-braided wig, she wore a high gold tiara-like circlet.

The High Priest of Amun stepped up to the altar and regarded the items laid out for him, starting with the crown made of amulets of the seven planetary metals. There were three small copper mirrors, amulets and bowls made of blue-green faience, white marble and dark blue lapis lazuli. The pungent smell of herbs and flowers told him all had been properly anointed with magical condensing oils and was ready. He reached into his robes and produced a leather case, from which he withdrew a long dagger and a wand. He added these to the instruments on the altar.

Quietly reciting a prayer to himself, he untied his purple silk sash belt, held it aloft, and then retied it around his waist. Reciting another prayer, he placed the crown on his head. He presented his sword and rod to the Master of the Temple and to the High Priestess for them to kiss. The High Priestess then walked around to the side of the altar and sat in the gold throne from which she could act as intermediary to the Goddess. The shorter man stepped back behind Royarna, remaining close enough to assist or retrieve some implement for the High Priest if he needed it.

For the first time since he entered the chamber, Royarna looked up at the colossal statue of Isis that the altar faced. He dropped onto both knees and lowered his gaze reverently to her painted stone feet, holding the rod and sword in either hand down at his sides. He began quietly in a language known only to the highest orders of priests.

"Great Isis, Goddess of Life, Master of Magicks, Protector of Humanity, hear my summons." He swung the rod up in a broad arc to hold it aloft and spoke more forcefully. "I stand at the center. I am the Master. You must hear my summons." He then stood up and drew a symbol in the air with the end of the rod and stated, "I have the power. I now walk freely on your plane. You must come forward at my command."

5

The Priestess frowned at his bold gesture, but this was only his opening volley. He leaned back and looked the huge statue straight in the eye, pointed his sword at Isis and demanded, "I am Chosen. You must obey me. Tell me what I seek."

The Priestess abruptly stood up in what first appeared to be indignation. A second look revealed the truth. The Priestess' already dark eyes were now completely black. She raised her head proudly and one by one, twelve rays of light erupted from her forehead to form a wheel-like crown. She raised her hands and five more rays of light shot from each upturned palm. The High Priest's gambit had worked and Isis herself now occupied the priestess' body.

This wasn't right. Royarna looked at the amulet around her neck, the amulet of the seven-petaled flower-cross that all three of the High Adepts wore, and no light shone from it. Thinking the goddess was not yet sufficiently subjugated to his will, the High Priest commanded further.

"Do not dare to withhold your powers from me! I demand that you employ all your abilities to my task. I know of the last seven rays of enlightenment. I need them to strip away all deceit to find my enemy, our enemy! Reveal the last seven Arcana to me!"

Instead of the rays of light he demanded, a solitary tear welled up and spilled down the Priestess's face. The only other time Isis had wept was over the dead body of her husband Osiris. He was killed when he was the symbol of virility and that loss signaled the end of Earthly Paradise. What earth-shattering calamity could move the goddess to tears now? The thought terrified Royarna. For the first time in his life, he did not know what to do.

"Faen-ka."

In his sublime concentration, the High Priest had forgotten the other adept behind him. Clearly Faen-ka was the object of his search, but for the Master of the Temple to interrupt him by using the former High Priest's forbidden name was positively disrespectful. He whirled on the man, wig braids swinging wildly, but stopped short.

He was no longer facing a fellow priest. The eyes that literally glowed with knowledge regarded him over a long, thin, curved beak with patience and pity. Thoth was the one intelligence in the universe who could not be subjugated by man, for it was Thoth who gave man the keys with which to exert his will over nature. The ibis-headed god was also the only entity who could move about undetected by even the highest of adepts. Royarna was dumbfounded and powerless. His mouth went dry and he dropped to his knees.

"Son of Earth," the god addressed him paternally, "the twenty-two images at your disposal, those twenty-two rays of knowledge Isis is offering you now, are the only keys I have ever possessed for your use. The additional seven you seek, the Tablets of Aeth, reveal the powers of creation itself. In all my wisdom, I do not know how to convey such secrets to the minds of men."

The concept of knowledge beyond Thoth's ability to express it was too confusing to contemplate. "Great Teacher of Mankind," he humbly addressed the god, "if these keys are not yours, then from whence did they come? To whence did they go? Does Isis not command all the material, mental and spiritual realms?"

"These images were designed by the betrayer you now seek. My daughter Isis thought Faen-ka discovered them in a foreign land and brought them as a gift to the gods. Now he has taken them out of the temple."

Faen-ka had always been a mysterious man. There was no record of his life before Ramses appointed him High Priest of Amun. Faen-ka had forty years to introduce new magic to the temple. A whole new generation of priests, including Royarna and his fellow high adepts, had grown up assuming that all twenty-nine Arcana, like the rest of their magic, were centuries old.

He refused to believe such a theft was possible. "I have only watched my predecessor use these images. He used them just last month in our conflict with Moses. I was never given the opportunity to memorize them. I am certain neither of my fellow high adepts have ever even seen them. I may be the only person who has ever seen them, but I know they do exist. Is there no way for you to view them?"

"They are not of Our sphere."

Royarna was dumbstruck. Faen-ka used foreign magic to convince Ramses that Moses' magic was the same as Egyptian.

Moreover, this magic contained the power of creation itself. What manner of man could design such images?

"Can you help me find the traitor?"

"You will not find him in this lifetime."

The finality of the god's prediction gave him pause. The High Priest contemplated the prediction carefully before questioning further.

"The clairvoyance your keys have given me has never failed. If I will not succeed in my mission, is it because I will die, or is it because my adversary has the Tablets of Aeth and I do not?"

"You will not die an early or unnatural death."

As comforting as this might have been under other circumstances, the news was not encouraging.

Isis, through the High Priestess, spoke up. "If these Arcana are so powerful, then why didn't Faen-ka succeed in using them to defeat the Hebrews' magic?"

"Always the trusting one," Thoth commented lovingly at her, shaking his long beak back and forth slowly. "Why does the snake not fly through the air? It is against its nature. This man was never a son of Egypt. His intent was not to defeat Moses, but to lead Ramses into defeat."

Royarna had thought long and hard on how the High Priest could turn against his pharaoh. Doing so meant denying the god-king's rightful place at the top of nature's hierarchy. It meant denying the truths of everything they knew of the universe. That his old master had been a foreigner was shocking, but it explained a lot.

Finally coming to grips with the idea that there could be magic Thoth could not package for human consumption, that indeed Thoth was not omniscient, Royarna tried to explore the deeper consequences.

"If there are now powers on Earth that we cannot master, how will Egypt fare against those who have such power? We can blame the loss of the Hebrews to the treachery of one man, but if the traitor trains others and they attack us, we may not be able to defend ourselves."

The High Priestess stared at him with distracting intensity. It was as if the goddess was sizing him up for something.

Thoth ignored her and answered him. "Faen-ka will not attack Egypt, and he will never have any followers. Yet your thinking is correct. Although Moses was originally trained in this very temple, the secrets of power now at his command are not ours." The god raised his hands above his head and looked upward. "Seeker of Truth, know that the world is changing, and the truths I have given you, though immutable, will not always apply to the world of men. O Egypt, a time shall come when, instead of a pure religion and an intelligent cult, you shall have nothing left but ridiculous fables that posterity will find incredible. There shall be nothing left to you but words graven upon stone, dumb and almost indecipherable monuments to your ancient piety."

1

NIGHTMARES

"THANK YOU FOR SEEING ME ON SUCH SHORT NOTICE."
Charles Redmond's square shoulders slumped as he sat dejectedly in the psychiatrist's overstuffed armchair. He had a hard time maintaining eye contact, and only turned his handsome brown features up to speak. It was then that the dark circles under his eyes showed. He flashed a furtive smile, then turned his gaze back to his lap.

Doctor Sanantha Mauwad, seated in an identical chair across a coffee table from him, took note of his posture and his manicured fingers twitching uneasily in his lap. His dapper olive business suit and polished demeanor would normally have made the tall young black man a picture of confidence. She had no difficulty seeing that he used the practiced smile as a mask to hide a very troubled soul. "It's my pleasure to help out," she assured him in her lilting Caribbean accent. "Simon Carrera has been a close colleague of mine for years. I'm surprised he didn't make sure you had adequate supplies before he went on his two-month sailing trip."

"That's actually my own fault. I travel a lot and I lost track of when he was leaving Washington. I should have called him to get a refill."

As he spoke, she made notes on a pad in her lap without detracting her attention from her patient. "You're in the import-export business, yes? You juggle a lot of information, with shipments and payments coming and going all the time?"

"Yes, I handle a lot of information in my business," he said perking up a bit, clearly more comfortable talking about his business than his personal life.

Sanantha considered how distracted he must be if he was trained to keep track of volumes of information, yet forgot something as important as running out of his anti-depressants.

"Then obviously the date got lost in the shuffle," she said with a warm smile. She smiled with her whole face, crinkles around her eyes and deep dimples in her dark brown skin framing her ample show of teeth. "Your chart shows Doctor Carrera has you on Zoloft for depression from on-the-job stress. Have you run out yet, or are you just running low?"

"I think I've got two left."

"Is the Zoloft helping you cope with your stress?"

At this, his eyebrows twitched, and his gaze flitted around the burlwood tabletop between them. "Yeah, I guess."

She looked him earnestly in the eye. "If you're not getting the same relief you used to get, I can change the dosage or move you onto other remedies. Doctor Carrera comments in your chart that you had a very good result with this medication. Can you describe for me how your reaction is different now than when you first started with it?"

He frowned and looked around the room at the gaily colored watercolors of Haitian dancers on the walls. He leaned back in the armchair and nervously bounced his right heel on the thick carpet as he gathered his thoughts.

"It just seems like things get past me," he said, measuring his words carefully. "It's as if there's just too much going on, and it's too much for me to handle."

"This isn't typical of the depression you've had in the past?"

"No, I know what that feels like," he said with a nervous chuckle, raising a hand in a stop gesture. "I would get overwhelmed and just fog out. Everything seemed impossible and I would withdraw. I'd sleep for days at a time. No, this is like ... the opposite. I'll have everything under control, and then things will get more difficult, more demanding, more ... weird."

He paused between each sentence as if to make sure it was right, then said his words so quickly that Sanantha had to listen carefully.

"I'm not fogged out; I'm at the top of my game. Then the pressure goes up, almost as if to mock me." He rubbed his eyes tiredly with the fingertips of one hand. He glanced at his nails as he took his hand down. "Now it's affecting my sleep. I never used to have nightmares before."

"Well, depression affects people in different ways. You said you're not feeling 'fogged out' or disconnected from things. Do your co-workers agree that work pressures have increased recently?"

"I work almost entirely alone. Now that you mention it, no one at any of the agencies I work with here in D.C. has said anything about added workload." He shifted nervously in his chair. "I just can't shake this feeling that I'm always forgetting something, or that people aren't telling me the whole story."

A car horn blared suddenly on the street outside and Charles jerked around in his chair to look at the curtain-covered windows.

Sanantha took note of how he clutched the arms of the chair. "I'm sorry about that," she said earnestly. "This is usually a very quiet street."

He looked down and also noted his grip. He smiled weakly and commented, "I guess I had one cup too many this morning."

She absent-mindedly scratched her scalp with the eraser end of her pencil under the bun into which her frizzy gray-speckled hair was pulled. She looked at the notes she took and lingered on the last word she had written: 'paranoia.' "You used the word 'weird' a moment ago. Can you tell me more about that?"

He blinked rapidly as he thought about this. His foot bouncing got worse.

"There are times when I feel like I don't know what I'm doing. I mean, I've been in this business for six years, but then something will happen, and I'm left completely not knowing how to handle it."

"Has the nature of your work changed?"

"No, it's not the work." He paused in thought. "It's the people."

"Are you dealing with any new clients you don't know or trust?"

He laughed and shook his head without answering. He took a deep breath and let it out slowly, then met her gaze. "You're very good. I've been telling myself if I could just deal with the pressures of the job, then my suspicions about people would evaporate."

"You know anti-depressants don't help with this kind of anxiety."

"Being a little paranoid is a survival trait in my line of work," he explained frankly. "Everybody is looking for an angle. Cargo vanishes en route on a remarkably regular basis. The government always starts with the expectation that you're smuggling drugs. Everything has to be backed up with bank guarantees because nobody trusts anybody. So, when things started getting even more iffy, I figured, buckle down, push on through, close the deal and be done with them."

"Your suspicions have caused anxiety which is now affecting your ability to sleep and function. If you think you are in danger, why not call in the authorities?"

Charles looked away, raised his eyebrows and drew a noisy breath through exposed clenched teeth. "Because my suspicions ..." he began slowly, "are irrational. Well," he corrected himself, "at least part of them are. I strongly suspect one of my suppliers is CIA. That doesn't bother me that much. I've dealt with spooks before. The guy who's ordering the stuff, he's another matter." He looked her straight in the eye and declared, "I'm pretty sure he's a demon."

Without showing any surprise, she commented, "I can see why you haven't gone to law enforcement. The good news is you recognize this suspicion as irrational. I am glad you came to me today, because your Zoloft isn't going to help with this. I assume you have not talked to anyone about this."

"That's right."

"You last saw Doctor Carrera three months ago, and you weren't having this difficulty at that time. How long has this been going on?"

"The client contacted me a little over two months ago. I thought he was weird from the start, but my suspicions really took off about a month ago. The nightmares started about two weeks ago. What can you give me for … what? Paranoid delusion?"

"I'm afraid it's not as simple as taking a pill and I'm not prepared to reach any diagnosis at this point. I will need to have you answer a set of tests before I get to anything so specific. At the center will be your need to talk about this, to get it out and off your chest. I need to find what's at the root of your anxiety, and you need to find rational explanations for the things you fear. I can give you something to help with the nightmares so you can sleep. Normally, antidepressants are pretty good at breaking the cycle of obsessive dark visions and nightmares, but this is obviously something more intrusive. Beyond any pharmaceutical assistance, you and I have to open a dialogue so you can develop a comfort level. Intellectually you know this client of yours is just an odd person. Now you have to get comfortable with that fact on an emotional level as well. I need to make sure there isn't something else that's making you susceptible to this anxiety. You said you travel a lot. Are you going on any trips anytime soon?"

"No, not for at least another month. It sounds like you want to set up regular sessions."

"Yes, I think you need to get a handle on this as soon as possible. This sort of condition feeds on itself and gets worse if you leave it alone."

He shrugged his eyebrows and ran his hands over his short cropped curly hair. "Well, it certainly hasn't gotten any better in the last month. To be perfectly honest, the reason I ran out of the Zoloft is I've been doubling up on the dosage, trying to get this under control."

She nodded and commented, "I thought as much. Now I realize you did not come here today prepared to dig into the details of what's been bothering you …"

"Oh, believe me," he cut her off, "I'm glad you dragged it out of me."

"Okay, good. My point is, we have time today if you want to talk about it now."

"Sure, I guess so," he said with a shrug of his shoulders. "Where should I start?"

"Have you ever had periods where you found yourself irrationally suspicious of people around you?"

He thought about this for a second, then said, "No. Not irrationally."

"How about sudden bouts of anxiety where you couldn't calm yourself down?"

"No, not that I can recall."

"You've been seeing Doctor Carrera on and off for the last two years. Prior to that, did you ever seek help from a psychiatrist or psychologist?"

"No, Doctor Carrera was my first shrink," he said with a wry smile.

She wrote a note to herself: 'Not forthcoming.' "Okay, let's tackle this from another angle. Why don't you tell me about this customer of yours who has you worried."

"Right," he nodded. "Joseph. Joseph de Alverado, he calls himself, but I think the last name is a fake. He is always a little too demanding that I get the last name spelled right, with a 'v-e-r' in the middle and not the usual 'v-a-r.' In fact, that was the first thing which struck me as strange. He's extremely particular about minute details and he doesn't seem to care about big things, like cost."

"So he's eccentric."

"Oh, this guy takes eccentric to new heights. Every time I've ever seen him, he's always wearing the same steel-gray suit, no matter what the weather and he never takes his sunglasses off. He's got these semi-mirrored Italian looking wrap-arounds. They never leave his face, inside or out. When you're talking to him, he'll anticipate what you're going to say. At the same time, if what you were going to say was inaccurate, he'll correct you, even if you haven't finished yet. It's absolutely unnerving."

Sanantha took note of how Charles loosened up and became more animated as he spoke. He wasn't just describing the customer, he was trying to convince her that the customer was worthy of suspicion. She decided to let him hear the unreasonableness of his own words. "You're still describing an eccentric."

"That's what I thought for the first few weeks too. Then we started getting shipments in. He's ordering stuff from all over the world. We went down to the dock in Baltimore to check on the first shipment and he got all agitated. He said some of the boxes had the wrong stuff in them, even before we opened the first one. He went over to one of the crates and ripped open the top panel with his bare hands. Normally even the stevedores use steel pry bars. Sure enough, the box he picked had the wrong stuff. Not all of them were wrong, but the one he picked was."

"How big is this Joseph?"

"Not very. He's stocky, but he's not tall. Maybe five foot nine, one hundred and ninety pounds, tops. He's just this nondescript, balding, middle-aged white guy."

"What sort of stuff is he ordering?"

"Antiques mostly. A lot of it looks like religious temple furnishings of some kind." He waved his hands as if clearing smoke and launched back into his story. "So then things start getting really weird. He's got me setting up deliveries of these shipments to different buildings all over town, all days of the week, including weekends. At one point a delivery guy called me to say the destination building was locked and there's nobody there. I called Joseph and told him. When the delivery guy called, I noted the time. It was exactly one o'clock on Sunday afternoon. The next day, I got the receipt paperwork, and saw Joseph signed for the shipment, at the building, at one-o-five. Not more than a minute could have passed between the time I called him and the time he was at the building, letting the delivery guy in and signing for the shipment."

Sanantha raised a skeptical eyebrow.

"I know, the delivery guy's watch could have been off. But Joseph's office where I called him is across town from that building."

Sanantha noted how earnestly Charles was trying to convince her, and decided to take a bold step. "You think he can, what? Travel instantaneously? Let me ask you this question. If you're away from your office, how often do you call in to get your messages?"

"I don't. My office phone automatically forwards the call to my cell phone."

"You answer the call yourself?"

"Yeah."

"The caller doesn't know you aren't at your office."

Charles stopped, swallowed, and sheepishly looked down at the tabletop. He glanced at his fingernails as he collected his thoughts.

"All right, so there's a logical explanation. If you met this guy, you'd see he is not normal."

"No one said he was normal. You have to give him, and yourself, some slack. You have to stop feeding the fantasy that something is unexplainably wrong. Now you also said something about the CIA."

"Yeah, one of the suppliers Joseph orders from accidentally cleared a check through a Treasury department account. I say 'accidentally' because he then hurriedly reversed the transaction and ran it through a regular commercial bank. This happened to me a couple of years ago, and it turned out a new agent made the mistake and then quickly fixed it before his boss could see it. This check last month looked exactly the same."

"You also said that dealing with government agents doesn't bother you."

"No, not really. I just have to make sure I keep really good records in case they raid me. No, it's Joseph who shows up in my nightmares."

"Joseph, specifically?"

"Oh yes. Specifically and graphically, with horns and claws and a tail."

"Are you religious?"

"Not really. I was raised on a form of Catholicism, but I don't go to church. I don't normally worry about demons," he said with a weak laugh.

"I'm glad to hear it," she said, smiling back. "We're just about out of time for today. I want you to make some notes about the dreams you've had. I will want to talk about them next time." She got up and went to her desk and took out a form pad. "I'm writing you a prescription for trazodone that should help you sleep without the nightmares. It has a sedative effect, so do not take it during the day. I'm also refilling your Zoloft, but I want you to go back to taking the dosage Doctor Carrera originally prescribed. Taking more than that level is not doing you any good and it's just messing up your brain chemistry. It also wouldn't hurt to cut back on your coffee intake. Unfortunately, I am tied up all day tomorrow. Can you come back day after tomorrow, say any time after four?"

Charles stood up and came over to her desk. He reached into his inside jacket pocket and pulled out a billfold, which he set down of the desk as he continued looking through his pockets.

He smiled and explained, "The technology on these things has gotten to the point where everything feels like a wallet. There we go," he commented triumphantly as he produced his PDA.

As he punched away at the keypad, Sanantha was distracted by the symbol embossed on the leather billfold on the corner of her desk. She leaned forward to take a better look and he casually picked it up and put it back in his pocket. She wasn't sure if he had seen her looking, but she surely recognized the symbol.

"There." He finished typing. "Yes, Friday, January 26, 2001. 5 p.m. works for me," he announced.

She smiled politely and confirmed, "Good, five o'clock it is. Can I ask you one more question? Obviously from my accent I am from the Caribbean, and I'm always curious about other people's travels. You have a slight New England accent. Have you ever been to the islands, or do you do business there?"

"No. I have traveled all over the world, but I've never been to the Caribbean. I don't trade there either, but I do know a guy who does.

If you wanted to import something from home, I could get you his number."

"No, that's okay, I was just curious. Friday at five then," she said as she escorted him to the door.

"Yes. Thank you again."

She closed the door behind him and stopped herself. Had he lied about his contact with the Caribbean? The symbol on his wallet was the personal *veve* symbol for the Loa god Papa Legba, the protector Christ figure of the Voodou pantheon. It was possible that he believed in a type of Voodou without any contact with Haiti. Santeria was practiced by people who have never left New York City, and Haitian Voodou was widely practiced in New Orleans. He said he was not religious, and was raised a Catholic. She checked her notes. No, he said a 'form of Catholicism'.

From Catholicism to Santeria is quite a push, she thought. He had been evasive in general about his past, but that might have just been due to his paranoia. Yet he seemed almost too eager to tell her his stories about this Joseph character. She wondered how much she should trust of what he said.

She returned to her pad and documented the session.

2

THE VILLAGE

J OSEPH STEPPED OUT OF THE HAITIAN JUNGLE UNDERBRUSH and dusted the sweet-smelling pollen off his gray business suit. He looked down the dirt footpath into the village, and stopped, dumbfounded. A broad smile broke out across his stern features behind his semi-mirrored designer sunglasses as he looked into the center of town and saw the fifteen-foot tall assembly of wood and stone that was unmistakably an effigy of Horus.

As he walked into the hamlet, he beamed with pride and admiration at the hawk-headed statue. He also noticed several villagers looking at him with curious frowns from inside their rusting corrugated metal shacks. He realized they had probably never seen him smile like this before. He thought for a moment and recalled that he hadn't smiled like this since his master began converting this village some two years before. Maybe it was time to finally accept these people as believers and to ease off on his image of the tough enforcer. He met the villagers' looks with smiles and waves, which sent most of them scurrying about their business. *All in due time,* he thought.

He reached the bustling square and was thrilled again, this time by the sight of a similarly rustic statue of Isis on the opposite side of the square from Horus. Both statues were painted in joyous colors that shone brightly in the midday tropical sun, and both were generously adorned with wreaths of fragrant flowers. The women and children in the square went about their business undisturbed by the watchful gaze of the two gods. Clearly the images had stood for some time for people to accepting them so. How long had Joseph been gone? Two months? Joseph smiled again, this time in pride at his master for making such rapid progress.

Thinking of his master, he quickened his step. After wending his way through the vegetable and clothing carts of the square, he strode purposefully up the center street which connected the market with the temple complex. Here again Joseph saw significant improvements. The high outer fence of the communal gathering courtyard now had a pylon gate fashioned from sturdy bundles of logs. The courtyard itself was now lined in sapling palm trees. The large wooden porch of the temple which formed the public ceremonial platform now had stone stairs on all three sides. Most noticeably, the corrugated metal roof of the temple itself had been replaced with a beautifully crafted, high peaked, foot-thick palm frond thatch.

He entered the temple and was pleased to see a dozen villagers, praying quietly by candlelight at the various deity altars around the large square windowless room. The quiet inside from the ever-present buzzing of insects and squawking of birds in the jungle outside elevated the serenity of the temple. Joseph took a handkerchief from his pocket and mopped the sweat from his receding brow. He took note of how much more pleasantly cool the temple was with the new roof from how stifling it used to be under the tin one. As he walked toward the front of the room, he mentally probed past the main effigies of Ra, Horus and Isis into the private rooms which made up the back half of the building. At last he found the presence of his master, out in the central private courtyard.

Silas Alverado looked 65, but Joseph knew he was actually 82. He reclined in a rattan chaise, reading a book, his long, lanky form relaxed enough to show he had been sitting there for some time. At Joseph's approach, he looked up, turning his full head of pure white hair into the bright sun. His hair shone much brighter than the white shirt he wore. The halo effect it gave him did not escape Joseph's notice. This man was indeed powerful, and Joseph had less than good news.

"From the look on your face, I take it things are not going well in Washington."

The old man's voice rumbled across the gravel courtyard, cut through the continuous drone from the jungle around them and wrapped itself around Joseph.

As Joseph stepped up to him, he was further caught within the gaze of the old man's brilliant blue eyes. He removed his sunglasses and lowered his eyes so as not to offend his master. "Charles Redmond, the importer I found, is not just paranoid, but it seems he actually is under surveillance by the American Central Intelligence Agency. I am afraid I may have wasted the last three months establishing relations with him."

Silas raised an eyebrow, set his square jaw and pursed his lips. "Does he have the government contacts he claims?"

Joseph knew his master's bravery well, and anticipated his willingness to push ahead despite the dangers.

"Yes, Master, he does. He is capable of getting everything we need into the country. If the CIA is watching him, they will see me and what we are doing."

Silas smiled, bemused. "Who is being paranoid now? Do you really think the CIA will understand how all these disparate parts fit together? Very few of these things are illegal in the United States."

"That's true, Master. The greatest difficulty is in getting them out of their respective countries."

"The CIA won't care about that," Silas dismissed. "Do find out why the CIA is interested in Mister Redmond. You are right that their surveillance demands heightened caution, but that is not enough reason to start over looking for another importer."

Joseph blinked his bright yellow eyes and looked away, trying to hide his disappointment at being sent back to continue along the same path.

Silas saw it. "Joseph, I hope you realize how pleased I am with your work. I have given you great latitude to decide the details of how you accomplish my wishes."

Joseph stood up straight at attention. "Yes, Master. You have honored me greatly with your confidence."

Silas's tone was paternal and firm, not condescending. "I just want to make sure you understand this latitude I've given you has limits. Even if you think you're protecting me, you are not to circumvent my orders. Inform me if you think I've missed something, but do not assume I have. Is that clear?"

"Absolutely," he said, still at attention.

"I realize how frustrating this work I've given you is: dealing with government bureaucracies and petty businessmen. I know you would rather I send you off on some more heroic mission, like toppling some corrupt government. You'll only have to do this for another three months."

Joseph's forward-locked gaze faltered in his surprise. He didn't know there was an endpoint set.

"Yes. Tonight is the first full moon of the new year, the night I put into motion the final phase of my plan. In three months, it won't matter what the CIA thinks. I will be traveling most of that time, and I won't be reachable by electronic means."

"I understand, Master."

Silas sighed and smiled up at him. "Joseph, the respect is appropriate, but I actually prefer you use my name in conversation."

A local youth appeared at the door to the courtyard holding a drink tray and hesitated. He was bald and wore a white linen sarong around his waist. Silas waved for him to approach. Joseph casually but swiftly replaced his sunglasses. The boy knelt down and lowered his gaze as he set the tray on the small table next to Silas's chair. Silas then dismissed him, saying, "*Merci, mon petit.*"

When the boy was gone, Joseph continued. "I understand, Mister Alverado. May I refresh myself before returning to Washington? I also have some things to take care of on the ship."

Silas picked up the drink with the steel prosthetic that was his right hand. The fingers were long enough to wrap around the glass, but appeared stubby next to the rather oversized bulbous body of the mechanical hand. He sipped at the tall, orange drink, then said, "Yes, of course. I assumed that it would take you the afternoon to recover, given the distance."

"Yes, sir. It will make the crossing a lot easier."

With a wide sweep of his flesh and blood left hand, Silas added, "Besides, the day will give you a chance to take in all the changes we've made around here."

Joseph involuntarily stiffened when he caught view of the large silver ring on Silas' hand — the ring which bound Joseph to his master. He took a breath and finally relaxed his posture. He smiled at the ground between them. "Yes, the village's conversion is most impressive."

Silas looked up at him with a compassion that took Joseph by surprise. "I know you've had doubts about the fealty of these people from the beginning. What you have to understand is how closely they are in touch with their feelings. They were easily smart enough to recognize the old gods as the original truth behind their Loa deities. It just took time for me to put it into their cultural context." His jowls, the bags under his eyes, even the usually stern bushy white eyebrows, all took on a gentleness Joseph had rarely seen. He clearly had come to care for these people.

"You have the ability to see the unwashed truth. Walk around town. Look into their faces. They have accepted the gift of the Neters' counsel and protection. They are willing to give their devotion to get it. You saw the statues in the square. They have accepted that Legba and Erzulie are shadows of Horus and Isis." Silas smiled at him reassuringly. "Our work is almost done here. I have only saved back the Dark Lord."

Joseph frowned in silent question. *Why leave the pantheon incomplete?*

"I will replace their worship of Samedi with Osiris when the rest of my plans come together," Silas supplied.

Joseph hoped for more details of his master's plans, but he recognized this was all the explanation he would get today. Joseph bowed and said, "Thank you, Mister Alverado, for sharing your time and thoughts with me."

"I will contact you with further instructions as I complete my work overseas. Good luck with Mister Redmond."

Joseph stepped back to leave and bowed again. "I will do my best, Mas ... Mister Alverado." That was going to take some getting used to.

When he walked back through the main temple hall, he stopped in the shadows and watched the villagers praying to the gods. He slipped his glasses off and searched their dark features as they earnestly hoped for guidance and assistance. A few were filled with joy and thankfulness. Most brought fruit, alcohol or some personal token as offerings. He knew how desperately poor these people were. Even meager gifts were a lot for them.

Joseph appreciated what a hard life these people led, in this poverty-stricken country the rest of the world had abandoned. He recalled how his homeland of ancient Egypt started alone, with nothing but the favor of the gods, and how it came to be the longest lasting civilization of all time.

He also recalled how he spent the millennia since chained away, labeled a demon, a political prisoner of his fellow deities. That was until four years ago, when this mysterious visionary, his master, freed him and brought him to the land of the living.

The devotion in the villagers' faces filled him with deep warmth. By showing them that their gods were just diluted versions of the original Neters, his master gave them a fresh start. These villagers had a renewed pride in themselves, a renewed work ethic, and renewed hope for the future. This truly was a land of new beginnings, both for the people of Haiti and for Joseph.

As he stepped out onto the wide front landing of the temple, he looked up at the clear blue sky and breathed deep the jungle air fragrant of tropical flowers and rotting vegetation. He slipped his glasses back on. *Paradise,* he thought. He would do anything for this man who had brought him here.

3

THE MEETING

S ANANTHA MAUWAD PUSHED THE FRONT DOOR of her apartment open with her knee as she struggled to keep control of the plastic bags of groceries she had looped in her fingers. She flipped on the lights and reached to retrieve her keys that dangled from the knob, but couldn't get them and still maneuver the swinging bags. She sighed and walked the five steps across her tiny dining area into her even smaller efficiency kitchen. When she looked around for a place to put the groceries down, there was none. What little counter space the kitchen had was filled with appliances, cookbooks and the clutter of always having something more important to do than tidy the kitchen.

"*Merde,*" she muttered under her breath, and set the bags on the floor. As she stood up, she checked her tall, bright orange turban with one hand.

She pulled the keys from the door and closed it, slipped off her long tan mohair coat and draped it over a dining room chair. The phone rang. She shot it a skeptical, raised-eyebrow look as she went back into the kitchen and began putting away her food. After the third ring, the machine picked it up. The screening speaker blurted alive with the utterly panic-stricken voice of Charles Redmond.

"Doctor, you've got to call me back at 586-8490. Don't use my cell number — he can probably hear that. Please make it quick. I don't know what else to do. Believe me, this is an emergency."

She frowned at the phone and picked up the receiver.

"Yes, Charles?"

"Yeah, doc, is that you?"

"Yes. How did you get my home number?"

"Yeah, I'm really sorry about that; your service said you were out. Listen, you've got to help me here. I'm really out of options. He's got me cornered in this restaurant, and I just don't know what to do."

"Wait a second," she interrupted him. "Are you in danger? If someone is attacking you, call the police."

"Well ... I ..." he struggled. "That's just it. I don't know how much of this is in my head. I mean, I'm pretty sure he pinned me down here, but I don't want to accuse him with the cops and all if he didn't."

"Who are you talking about?"

"Joseph," he whispered.

"So he's in the restaurant with you now?"

"Yeah, he's right out front. I can see him from here."

She glanced at her watch and saw it was 7:25 p.m. "Is the restaurant crowded?"

"Not crowded. I'd say maybe half full."

"Then why can't you just walk out? Do you think he will attack you with all those people around?"

"I don't know, probably not. What if he sees me? The place is long and narrow. There's no way I could walk out without him seeing me."

"What's wrong with him seeing you?"

"He could follow me out."

She rolled her eyes and sighed away from the receiver. "Charles, may I make an observation? If he doesn't know you're there now, then how can you say he has you cornered? He doesn't know you're there, does he? He just happened to walk in while you were there, didn't he?"

"I don't know, he must have followed me. I was only here for a couple of minutes before I saw him come in."

She noted that logic just made him more agitated. "Do you agree that this threat might not be real? That this might be a panic attack and not a real danger?"

"Yeah, but the panic is real enough," he shot back. "I mean this place doesn't even have a back door I can use. Doctor, you're the only grip I've got. You've got to help me."

She envisioned him standing in the back of a restaurant cowered over a public phone, frozen with fear. "Do you have the sedatives I prescribed?"

"Yeah, you mean the sleeping pills?"

"Yes. I want you to take one of those. Now it's going to take maybe fifteen minutes for the medicine to calm you down. Can you take a table at the back of the restaurant and just sit quietly until the pill takes effect?"

"I've already got a table, but it's up front, dammit! There's no way I'm going to hide out in the men's room. He'd get me in there in a heartbeat. Look, I need you to come here and just walk me out of this place. Can you do that, please?"

She furrowed her brow but restrained her voice. "No, Charles, you do not need me to come there."

"Look, it's Philly's Cafe on Vermont. You're only five minutes away from here."

This time she failed to restrain her upset. "How do you know where I live?"

"That doesn't matter," he insisted with some belligerence. "You've got to come down here, even if it's just to stand by the door so I can leave." His tone shifted to pleading. "I know this is way off base. I'll take the pill now, and I'll hang on as best I can. But you've got to walk me out of here." He hung up.

She blinked several times at the receiver in her hand. She pushed the rewind button on her machine to get the number he said before it had picked up. The display on her answering machine printed out "Start of messages." She hit the play button, and got "No messages."

"*Merde,*" she muttered. She punched in "∗-69".

"We're sorry, recall service is not available to the previous caller's number."

"*Merde,*" she said out loud. "Damn payphone." She started to call information for the restaurant's number, and realized what a tailspin Charles would go into if the *maitre d'* called out his name for a phone call. "*Merde!*" she said and slammed down the phone. She grabbed her keys and coat and headed for the door.

•   •   •

Sanantha pulled the lapels of her coat closed against the cold February night air as she looked through the front door glass to size up the situation before entering the restaurant. She didn't see anyone who fit Charles' description of Joseph, and she didn't see Charles anywhere. She pushed the door open and the odor of stale cooking oil lingering in the air hit her, such a change from the crisp smell of fresh snow outside, it made her blink and wrinkle her broad nose. She sidestepped the host's counter and walked straight to the back. As Charles had described, the seating area was long and narrow, with the kitchen and restrooms in the back. Trying to look at each patron as she walked without arousing suspicion, she finally found Charles in a booth at the back of the cafe. He was hunkered down behind a magazine, trying to hide, but looking conspicuous and pathetic in his attempt.

He lit up at her approach. He kept his voice down but could barely contain his enthusiasm. "You came!"

"You gave me no choice," she accused flatly as she sat down across from him. "Did you take the sedative?"

"Yes, I did. Thank you so much for coming," he said earnestly. "Did you see him when you came in?"

"Never mind about Joseph for the moment. Let's focus on you first. Sit up. You look ridiculous slouched down like that. How do you feel? Are you still feeling overwhelmed?"

He sat up and smoothed his blue suit jacket, but still kept his head low. "Well, I am a lot calmer. But I'm still stuck back here." As he spoke his eyes kept darting to a spot at the front of the restaurant.

"You wanted me to help you walk out of here. We can do that any time you're ready."

"Okay. Give me a minute."

"Take as long as you like," she assured him calmly. "Rather than getting yourself all worked up about walking past Joseph, how about if you focus on your schedule for tomorrow."

He frowned at her odd reference.

"What time you can come see me so we can start working together," she added with gravity.

He took a deep breath and raised his eyebrows at the table between them. He glanced at his fingernails, then admitted, "You're right. I'll be in whenever you want me. I owe you that much, at least."

"Ten o'clock."

He nodded. "Okay, ten it is." He looked back toward the front of the restaurant and became agitated all over again. "How did he look when you came in?"

Sanantha was disappointed with how quickly he slipped back into his fear. "To tell the truth, I didn't even see him." Acting as if nothing was wrong, she scooted to the edge of her bench seat and smiled. "Shall we go?"

He shook his head and flashed her that boyish smile she recognized as nervous defense. "I'm not so sure about this."

"Sure, come on, there's nothing to it," she said playfully as she got up. "Here, take my arm, and we'll just walk right out."

He looked at her offered arm, took another deep breath, and got to his feet. As they walked to the door, Sanantha saw that Charles couldn't keep from glancing at a particular table they were approaching. She followed his gaze and found a booth with empty plates and no occupant.

When Charles saw it was empty, he froze.

Sanantha gave his arm a little squeeze and said quietly, "It looks like he left."

Charles turned to face her when they were both startled by a man who stepped up right in front of them.

Joseph fit Charles' description exactly, balding, broad shoulders, grey suit, all the way down to the mirrored sunglasses. He smiled politely and nodded to Charles. "I apologize if I startled you. How are you Charles? I've been trying to reach you all day."

Charles just stood there and sucked in a slow deep breath through flaring nostrils.

Joseph's smile remained unchanged as he turned to Sanantha. He extended his hand and said, "Please excuse my manners. I am Joseph de Alverado."

His handshake was among the most gentle and polite she had ever felt. "I'm Sanantha Mauwad. I take it you two are in business together. Charles is always so mysterious about his business," she said playfully. "It's nice to see he actually has real clients." She indicated the booth and added, "I see we've interrupted your meal. Please excuse us."

"Oh, not at all, I'm done. I was just up paying the bill." He reached over and put a five-dollar bill on the table before turning back with that same polite smile. "I'll walk you two out."

Sanantha heard Charles swallow, but made a point of not reacting or looking at him. "Thank you. Don't you have a coat? It's freezing out there."

Joseph stopped and thought about her question for a second. "No, I parked right outside."

As Joseph headed for the front door, Sanantha gave Charles' arm another squeeze and a tug to follow along. When he resisted, she looked up at him. He shook his head with the smallest, tightest motion possible. Even without that, his eyes told her everything she needed to know.

She collected her thoughts, then called after Joseph. "Mister de Alverado. I'm sorry, I left my scarf at our table. You go on without us."

Joseph turned around and frowned at her. She felt as though he were staring right through her. "Oh. All right, then. It was nice meeting you. Charles, we can talk tomorrow."

"It was nice meeting you as well," she said with a flash of her big smile and a nod of her turbaned head.

As he turned and opened the door, the cold night air swept in. "Good night, doctor."

Sanantha could only blink as the door swung shut.

4

THE ANGEL ISLE

M AJOR GREGORY BAILEY locked the side entrance door behind himself and walked down the front service driveway of the British Museum. When he reached the unoccupied guard booth on Great Russell Street, he took a deep lungful of the freezing, late night air, steeped in the warm aroma of wood burning in fireplaces. He spread his arms wide and stretched his tired six-foot, three-inch, heavily muscled frame, straining against his business suit and fur-lined topcoat, before blowing out a huge cloud of foggy breath past his bushy mustache. He began to walk to his car when he was surprised to hear the soft crunching of footsteps on the snow-covered sidewalk, already very close to him. He turned to find a tall, white haired gentleman walking up to him.

"Excuse me," the man said cheerfully in a deep voice and a clearly American accent. "So sorry to bother you, but I seem to have gotten turned around. I'm looking for the Virginia Woolf pub. I was told it was on Russell Square, which I think is only a couple of blocks from here. I've been all the way down here and back and I can't find it anywhere."

Bailey couldn't help but notice the man's metal right hand as he pointed down the street with it. From the man's advanced age, he assumed he lost the hand in WW II.

Bailey smiled graciously and supplied in his rich Cockney, "Oh, well, that would explain it. To get to Russell Square you've got to turn left up Montague or Bedford Place," he explained pointing the other direction.

"Really?" the old man said disbelievingly as he took out a map. He stepped closer and showed it to Bailey, insisting, "I found a Bedford, and it led to a Bedford Square."

"Oh, of course you're confused, you have the map upside down."

"How silly of me," the white-haired man conceded and handed Bailey the map.

The Major left his gloves on against the bitter cold and had to manipulate the paper carefully through the wool. As he turned it over and pointed out the square's location, he thought he caught a fleeting look of unexplained disappointment in the old man's kindly bright blue eyes. "Oh, don't feel badly," Bailey explained. "You can hardly blame yourself when we went and put streets named Bedford on both sides of the museum."

"Well, thank you so much. I might have never figured it out if you hadn't come by." The man took off his left mitten and extended his hand in thanks.

Bailey was impressed with this American's manners and gladly removed his own left glove and shook his hand. "Lordy, your hand is cold."

"Sorry," he said replacing it in his mitten. "A little circulation problem I have. Age, you know. Well, thank you again."

Silas Alverado got halfway back to his car before looking over his shoulder to see Bailey rubbing his eyes and shaking his head as if to clear cobwebs. By the time he returned to face the Major, the tall man had stopped moving. He looked closely at the man's hazel eyes and saw they had glazed over.

"Good," he commented quietly. "I can drop this moronic, degrading charade. You had to be a martial arts expert, didn't you?" he added sarcastically. "Major Bailey, I know you can hear me, even if the drug has sapped your will. You're a big man so you won't lose consciousness for another minute. Since I'm not about to drag your body, you will now walk to that black Jaguar and lie down in the back seat."

As he followed his prisoner across the street, he saw the Major's glove, out of the corner of his eye, on the sidewalk where he had dropped it. Silas glanced admonishingly at the man's back and walked over to retrieve it. As he bent down to pick it up, a Bobby turned the corner onto the street, not thirty paces away, obviously walking his rounds. Without wanting to arouse suspicion, Silas resisted the urge to look back at Bailey to make sure he was still headed for the car. Hesitating as he picked up the glove, Silas held his breath for a moment and listened to both Bailey's and the policeman's footsteps. When he heard the car door open, he knew he was safe. He exhaled slowly, slipped the glove into his coat pocket, smiled and nodded politely to the policeman, then returned to the car.

•   •   •

Silas took his time driving the rented car across central London. Not only did he know that Major Bailey would be out for some time, but being stopped for a traffic violation was the last thing he needed now. As he neared his destination, the lights within the row houses he passed were going out. He pulled up in front of the small three-story office building, which was his objective, and was pleased to see no lights on except in the lobby. He drove around the block and parked in the alley at the back of the building.

He left Bailey in the car while he unlocked the back door and went in, only to return a moment later with a wheelchair. It took all the strength he could muster to get the Major's massive limp body out of the car and into the chair.

After he took the freight lift to the top floor, Silas stopped at his own rented office. He flicked on the light and wheeled Bailey's unconscious body into the small front waiting room of the sparsely decorated doctor's suite. Silas stepped into the back office, rolled up his left sleeve with his metal right hand, grabbed the edge of the latex skin that covered his flesh hand and carefully turned it inside out as he removed the form fitting rubber glove. He threw away both the latex wad and the drug soaked woolen mitten.

He then went to the dentist's office across the hall and picked the lock.

By the time Major Bailey recovered consciousness, Silas had finished his preparations. His patient was bound into the dentist's exam chair with leather straps, naked except for an assortment of glittering gold jewelry around his legs, arms, shoulders and head. The room was filled with the sweet-smelling smoke of burning incense.

"Ah, Major," Silas greeted him as he looked into the man's eyes. He checked his watch and concluded with mild good cheer, "Right on time."

Bailey blinked and squinted as he looked around at his naked body, the jewelry, and the dentist's office with its white Formica counters, pale green cabinets and black linoleum floor.

He focused on Silas, who wore a buttoned up white lab coat, and blurted out in his thick Cockney accent, "Who the fuck are you, why am I naked, and why the bloody hell can't I move my arms and legs?!"

"Ah, hostility," Silas observed calmly. "That's good. It will improve your circulation and keep you clear headed. I am Silas Alverado. I am ushering in a new Age of Man. And you, Gregory Bailey, being the Chief of Security for the British Museum, have something I want."

"You're gonna try to hit the museum? Ha! Forget it!" he spat. "You'll get nothin' from me. I don't care what you do to me."

"Oh, but I think you do care," he insisted with controlled intensity and a slight squint of his expressive blue eyes. "I knocked you out with extracts of curare sap and puffer fish livers in a DMSO vehicle. But that's the least of your troubles. You are now what biologists call a 'spinal animal.' You can't move your body because I severed your spinal cord at the base of your neck." He retrieved a bloodied scalpel from a nearby metal tray and held it up for Bailey to see. "With this. I left your cranial nerves intact, which is why your heart and lungs still work, your facial senses are still operative, and you can still hold up your head." The old man did not gloat, but rather proceeded clinically, as if instructing a student. "In case the names are unfamiliar to you, I'll explain the jewelry in plain English. The ankh bracelets I've placed on your wrists and ankles as well as the vulture necklace around your shoulders are keeping your life force from taking flight. The incense helps with that too. That way your tissues don't die now that they are no longer monitored by your brain."

The terror that consumed the man left him staring speechlessly wide eyed at his body and the shiny gold jewelry inlaid with red, blue and black stones. Despite the chilly room and his unclothed state, sweat broke out over his whole face.

"No," he said breathlessly. "You're lying. You're just trying to scare me," he denied vehemently.

Silas continued in his calm serious tone. "With your military training in human anatomy, I'm sure you can appreciate that I am deadly serious in what I am describing. I also realize the hopelessness of your condition doesn't leave me any bargaining room, so I won't bother. You probably wish I would just kill you and be done with it."

Bailey shot him a look of such pathetic alarm Silas was almost affected by it.

"I assure you I will let you die very soon. At no point will I let you feel any pain. I am not a barbarian," he insisted. He pointed to the gold band around Bailey's head, sculpted with intertwined snakes supporting the head of a jackass. "In fact, that Seth circlet is already keeping pain away from you. Now stick out your tongue."

Bailey defiantly pressed his lips tight together.

Holding up his steel hand he asked with a sigh, "Do you really want me to force your mouth open?" Just as patronizingly, he then added, "Just think of me as your confessor."

"I don't believe in confession," he spat.

Silas smiled at him approvingly. "Anglican?" he asked with raised white eyebrows.

"Damn straight," the major confirmed proudly.

"Good, then we have a common enemy in Rome," he commented aside. Dipping a swab stick into a small bottle of white powder, he again instructed, "Now open up."

Distracted by the old man's comment, he did as he was told. As soon as he tasted the powder, though, he recoiled and gasped. "Shit! That's awful! What the hell is that?"

"Just a little something to help your concentrate," Silas explained as he put the powder bottle back on the counter that was filled with an array of supplies and tools Silas had brought from his own office.

"Ha! You're going to try to hypnotize me," he laughed. "I've been counter-conditioned. You won't get anything out of me even if you do get me under," he stated resolutely.

"Let me worry about that." Silas held the top of Bailey's head still with his metal right hand and put his left hand up to Bailey's face too close for him to be able to focus on it or look around it. He began curling and uncurling his fingers in a rhythmic, wavelike motion. "Your only concern is how heavy your eyelids are getting … how you're feeling sleepy and relaxed, despite all that's happened. Think of how good it will feel to be free of your ruined body, to be whole again."

Bailey looked past the hand in his face and shot Silas a frown of confusion.

"Oh yes, there is an afterlife," he assured him. "Let your cares flow out of you and let the motion of my hand become the center of your universe. You feel warm and comfortable. You're getting sleepy."

Silas could see the strong-willed man trying to resist, darting his eyes around the office past Silas' hand, trying to think of other things. Undaunted, the old man continued to weave his spell with his soothing deep voice.

"The ancient Egyptian priest doctors would focus their patient's own ability to heal themselves by recounting the stories of Gods that had suffered with the patient's malady, and how the Gods had overcome and survived their ordeals. Unfortunately, you've never been shown the beauty of my view of nature, and stories about my Gods would do little to comfort you. Thankfully the drug is stripping away your anxieties, helping to make my words more soothing. Your universe is shrinking and becoming simpler. The only thing you can think about is the movement of my hand. The only sound you can hear is my voice. You are very sleepy. You can barely keep your eyes open now. Your eyelids are too heavy to hold open at all. Let them close." When they did close, Silas followed up with, "Continue to think only of the motion of my hand."

Silas withdrew and massaged his left hand with his mechanical right and allowed himself a momentary assessment. He had known hypnotizing such a traumatized, highly resistant person would be difficult. Now he faced the tricky, delicate task of getting past the barriers of the Major's counter-conditioning.

"State your complete name," he ordered calmly.

"Major Gregory Alan Bailey, R.A.F. retired," came the clear, immediate answer.

"Are you married?"

"Divorced."

"What is her name?"

"Cynthia Anne Bushnell."

"What is your mother's maiden name?

"Atkinson."

Silas was interrupted by the sound of footfalls from the hall. "Hello!" came a young man's voice. "Doctor Henrick? Is that you?"

"Yes," Silas called back. "I'm quite busy. Please leave me alone."

This clearly did not deter the night watchman, as Silas could hear him entering the front waiting room. "What are you doing up here so late, doctor?"

Silas quickly assessed the array of tools on the counter and grabbed up a long cardiac needle he had prepared. With his metal right hand, he snatched a lit incense burner off the instrument tray of the exam chair and ducked behind the door. When the uniformed young man stepped into the exam room, he was taken aback at seeing the naked bejeweled man strapped into the dentist's chair. He hesitated just long enough for Silas to whirl around from his hiding place and dash the smoldering ashes into his eyes. As the young man howled and recoiled across the room, Silas followed closely but silently. When the guard slammed his back into the cabinets on the far side of the room, Silas planted the needle in his victim's chest.

The blinded man flailed at his assailant but missed. Silas dispassionately stood back as the guard ripped the needle out of his chest, then clutched viciously at the wound, fell to the floor, and began spasming violently. With his eyes and chest in so much pain, he gasped desperately for breath as he writhed on the cold, black linoleum floor. As the epinephrine overloaded the young man's heart into full arrest, the magician in a lab coat left the room.

He returned a moment later with a paper cup of water. Silas knelt next to the dying man, who was slipping out of consciousness. He frowned with his gentle blue eyes and shook his head.

"How unfortunate for you that I have yet to re-enshrine His Dark Majesty," he began quietly. "You could have been his first new follower. The only fair place to send you is to He who is next to be replaced. That way at least you'll have the choice to join Osiris when He is victorious."

Silas reached under the man, pulled his wallet out of his back trousers pocket, and glanced at his identification. Working quickly, he passed his hand over the cup of water, saying, "I call upon thee, Loas of light and darkness, bless this water so it may cleanse the unholy." He dipped his left thumb in the water and drew a cross on the man's forehead. "In the eyes of Guede Ni Bo, Lord of Death, I do sanctify and prepare your soul." He held the paper cup aloft and poured the water over the guard's head, saying, "With this blessing I give onto you the name of Lawrence, so that Maitresse Erzulie may embrace you, and you may dwell in the House of the Lord, forever and ever." Drawing another cross on his forehead he concluded, "In the name of the Father Danbhalah, the Son Legba, and the Holy Virgin Aida Wedo, Amen."

He checked the man's pulse, found he was quite dead, and returned to Major Bailey.

The Major, deep in trance, hadn't reacted to the incident in any way. Silas rechecked the bracelets and other jewelry, then checked Bailey's pulse. He noticed that urine had leaked out of Bailey's derelict body, down over the chrome and leather chair onto the floor, and mixed with the pool of blood and cerebrospinal fluid that had run down his back from where Silas had operated on his spine. The urine was no surprise since Bailey's brain was separated from his bladder.

Proceeding as if nothing had interrupted him, Silas continued with his questions. "What is your immediate supervisor's name and title at the museum?"

"Bradley Rutherford, Director of Internal Affairs."

"What company manufactured the video cameras used to monitor the hallways of the museum?"

"Sony."

Silas considered how unprotected that information was and pushed further. "How many photocell beams cross the main lobby floor of the Egyptian wing of the museum?"

"My name is Gregory Bailey and you are wasting your time."

The old man's eyebrows lifted, and he tried a different tact. "What is the name of the psychiatrist who conditioned you?"

"Doctor Eichorn."

Silas was about to continue with that line when he frowned at his subject and interrupted himself. "By what name did you call the psychiatrist when you saw him?"

"Doctor Eichorn."

"What is Doctor Eichorn's first name?"

"My name is Gregory Bailey and you are wasting your time."

Silas leaned against the counter and stroked his heavy chin as he worked this puzzle in his mind. After only a few seconds, though, the deep-thinking squint was replaced by a small but triumphant grin.

"Has anyone ever spoken Doctor Eichorn's first name to you?"

"No."

"What does your wife look like?"

"My name is Gregory Bailey and you are wasting your time."

Silas's smile widened. "About how tall would you say I am?"

"My name is Gregory Bailey and you are wasting your time."

"Visual information," Silas confirmed quietly to himself. "Fascinating."

He frowned when he realized how much more work this would involve. He shrugged and got started. At least visual information fired nerves on the surface of the cortex, which he could reach.

He turned to the assortment of tools he had brought from his own office across the hall. He selected an instrument that looked like a barber's electric shaver, except where a razor would have comb teeth, this tool had a small, finely toothed circular saw blade mounted on a shaft. He turned the bone saw over in his hand to find the proper grip.

Silas set it down and retrieved a large roll of gauze bandage. "In your present state you are in complete control of all sensations that you feel. You can prevent any sensation from being painful. Focus on the warm, comfortable sensation that bathes your whole body and do not allow any discomfort or pain to disturb you." He stepped up to Bailey, ignored the puddle of urine, and removed the snake image crown from his head. Silas then wound the gauze around his cranium making a circle from high on his forehead, covering the tops of his ears, and around the base of his skull. He then retrieved one last leather strap and secured Bailey's head to the upright headrest of the dentist's chair.

"You can see, hear and feel anything I tell you. Until you hear my voice again you will not hear or feel anything. You are sinking into a deep sleep where you will think of nothing but warmth, peace, and the motion of my hand. When you awake you will still feel nothing, no pain, no hot nor cold, no tactile sensation at all. Now sleep until you hear me call you. Sink deeper and deeper."

When Silas saw Bailey's face go slack, he pulled the swing arm exam light around over Bailey's head. He put on a rubber apron, and reached for the electric saw.

After carefully peeling away the last layer of meninges from Bailey's exposed brain, Silas checked his watch and verified he was still within schedule. His surgical gloves were covered with so much blood, he had to wipe his wrist clean on his right arm sleeve to see the watch through the latex. He surveyed his work to make sure the forceps clamps were holding as they squeezed off the blood vessels all the way around the edge of the sawed open skull. The long handles of the forceps, with their round finger holes, radiated out from his head to form a flower-like chrome crown that glistened in the intense white light of the swing arm exam lamp. The pinkish-gray brain had collapsed slightly since most of its usually supportive cerebrospinal fluid had spilled out. Silas pushed back the now gore-soaked gauze headband and verified that the flesh below the opening was still engorged and alive.

He stepped to the sink and rinsed the blood off his gloved hands before exiting to the front office. He returned with a blank sheet of typing paper and a large marker. He drew a single wide black line down the middle of the page and set it aside.

Then he peeled off his right latex glove and opened his mechanical hand. A sour, yet slightly floral, smell filled the air as he undid the locks and cracked open the large, bulbous center body of the prosthesis, exposing his normal sized, flesh and blood right hand cradled inside. As he lifted his hand out, the soft, form fitting plastic liner glistened with the wetness of low pH saline. So did the electrodes that filled the wrist area and, when closed, operated the mechanical hand from Silas's nerve impulses without the need of moving his fingers. He inhaled sharply when the cool air hit his oversensitive skin. With his skin continuously treated by the ancient recipe of herbal solutions that circulated within the metal glove, and with no physical sensation allowed to raise the trigger thresholds of his nerves, his pink, print-less hand was a direct open link to his nervous system. He smiled at the wisdom of purposely handicapping himself to gain this unique tool. He thought of the times he had used his hand in magical divinations. Clearly, this would be the best use of it yet.

After running the water in the sink until it felt warm to his left hand, he gently rinsed the herbal solution from his right. He left the deactivated metal hand on the counter and stepped to a spot behind and slightly to the left of the dentist's chair. He ignored the squishing sound his Vibram-soled wingtips made as he walked in the now enormous sticky pool of fluids and gore that had run down Bailey's naked body and onto the black linoleum floor.

"Major Bailey, this is Silas Alverado. Return now to your previous state of perfect concentration. You still feel no pain and no physical sensation and you are mentally alert." With his left hand he held the sheet of paper up about a foot in front of Bailey's face with the line vertical. "Open your eyes and focus on the line."

Silas very gently set his right hand down over the left rear portion of the Major's brain. He closed his eyes and calibrated the mental image of the vertical line to the pattern of nerve impulses he was feeling on Bailey's visual cortex. When this image was clear, he rotated the page so the line was diagonal, readjusted the image, and finally moved it to horizontal and did the same.

"Continue looking straight ahead," was Silas's command as he dropped the page out of Bailey's sight. It took a moment to sort out the deluge of signals and visualize individual edges and shapes. With his eyes still closed, little by little Silas made out the patterns of the countertops and cabinets that Bailey faced. Fine tuning the calibration, he began filling in textures, shades and shadows. Lawrence's dead body slumped on the floor came into focus. Hints of color surfaced in the image.

"Without moving your head, look around and describe to me what you see."

"My name is Gregory Bailey and you are wasting your time."

Silas laughed a quiet, gravelly chuckle as he, standing there with his eyes closed, watched through his victim's eyes and saw every detail of the room in front of them.

"Now close your eyes and imagine yourself standing in front of the British Museum."

After an hour of having the Major walk him through all the parts of the security system he needed to know, Silas sighed and allowed himself a moment to run it all through his mind again.

Silas had clairvoyantly walked through the museum earlier that evening. For some reason that he could not explain, there had been large parts of the security plan that he couldn't fathom through astral inspection. This session had been a lot more work than he had hoped, but Major Bailey had filled in all the gaps.

He was about to lift his hand off the man's brain when he was seized by a startling realization. In all his lifelong study of the occult, in all his learning of mankind's beliefs and fears, never had he found a better opportunity to experience the most elusive process of all: death.

Not wanting to break the finely tuned connection between his right palm and Bailey's brain, Silas opened his eyes and looked around to see what was within reach of his left hand. The assortment of instruments on the counter was too far away so he had to settle for the blood covered scalpel sitting in the chair's ceramic rinse bowl. Silas considered his options and decided oxygen deprivation to the brain would give him the most controlled situation. He realized that even under deep hypnosis the heart's rapid beating response to raised levels of carbon dioxide would be difficult to control. He needed to prevent a runaway heartbeat. His target was clear.

"Major Bailey, you are now back in the room with me. You will continue to feel nothing, but concentrate on seeing everything that passes before you with objective, crystal clarity. Keep your eyes closed and think only of the images that appear to you."

Silas regretted not having time to do anything for the man's soul, he was after all an enemy of Rome and Israel. He was glad Bailey had such a strong spirit, and he wished the Major well in the upcoming war in heaven.

When he "saw" Bailey had properly emptied his mind and was waiting for visual stimuli, he reached around in front of his victim and plunged the scalpel directly into the man's heart. With his left hand he felt the big man's powerful heart muscle on the other end of the knife spasm deeply once, twice, and then go still. He was pleased to feel no indication that the pain of this fatal wound had made it past the lower brain centers up to the hypnotically controlled cortex under his right hand.

At first the mental vision remained blank. Despite all the dispassionate science and method he had employed to get to this point, Silas couldn't help but feel awash in giddy anticipation at what he was about to witness. He had treated this man's body like meat to get the information he wanted, but now this stranger he had butchered was going to take him on a trip no one had ever traveled without tempting their own mortality.

Silas had spiritually voyaged beyond his body many times, including visits to the Land of the Dead. But the nature of the final one-way trip, the path of the severed life thread, the voyage of the Ka unfettered, was something he could only dream of, until now. Sweat broke out all over Silas' body and his lips trembled in a nervous, blissful smile. His excitement was so complete that, for the first time in years, his loins warmed and swelled. He waited and waited for the man to die.

Just as he was growing concerned that something was amiss, he caught a glimpse of a view of the room, but from a point high above Major Bailey, looking back down at the two of them. Since this was the typical start for an out-of-body experience, Silas waited for what would come next.

Then the image faded and nothing took its place. He pressed his hand harder onto the surface of the brain, fearful that somehow the connection had slipped. When this didn't help, he opened his eyes and checked it.

Cold, ugly, disappointment swept his joy away and left him feeling cheated. There was nothing wrong with the Major's cortex, it was his hand. He pushed down with a pressure that surely should have inflicted great pain on his oversensitive skin and it only hurt mildly. He had been touching the cortex too long and his nerves had fired too much, which raised their triggering thresholds too high for him to be able to sense the impulses of Bailey's brain.

He arrested the raging temptation to vent his anger and dash the Major's brains across the room with his left fist. Instead, he lifted his now desensitized hand off the brain and quietly sighed while surveying the carnage of his dead victim. It was as if he were seeing the hideous scene, with its stench of stale incense, urine, blood, and flowery herbs for the first time. The brilliant white light from the swing arm lamp that had helped him so much in his surgery, now glistened off every blood smeared surface and brought every detail into gruesome clarity.

None of this bothered him as much as his disappointment at the failed death viewing. He calmed himself with the assurance that the knowledge he had gained from this session was ultimately much more valuable than even witnessing death second hand. He could, after all, always try it on someone else some other time.

He did nothing by way of hiding evidence; there was none to implicate him. In fact, he would be on his way back to the Caribbean by the time the bodies were discovered. When he washed his right hand and put it back in its metal surrogate, he was disappointed to find some blood had gotten past the rubber apron and stained his yellow silk tie.

5

GHOSTS

"THANK YOU SO MUCH FOR BRINGING THIS BY, Mister Redmond, and on a Sunday morning no less." The expensively dressed young Asian woman beamed up at Charles as they stood in the marble entry hall of her home.

"You said you needed it as quickly as possible. It arrived by FedEx last evening."

She hefted the small blue and white box and smiled at it. "My father will be so pleased you could get this out of Indonesia. I will call my brothers and we will present it to him tonight."

"Believe me, it was my pleasure." Charles turned to go, but hesitated. He flashed his easy-going smile and added, "Just remember me next time you need any other family heirlooms brought to safety."

The woman cradled the box in one arm and held out her other hand to Charles. "You need not worry about that," she said with a smile.

As Charles walked down the front steps and across the small walled garden to the street, he pulled his coat closed against the chill air. The sun shone brightly but generated very little heat. The acrid pine scent of the juniper trees that flanked the gate added to the crispness of the morning air. The sidewalk outside the gate was layered with snow from the night before, almost undisturbed from the lack of foot traffic in this upscale Georgetown neighborhood. He looked back at the large brick house and smiled. Another satisfied customer, he thought.

As he got into his car, his cell phone rang. "This is Charles."

"Yeah, this is Rocket Delivery. Is this Charles Redmond?"

"Yes, it is."

"I've gotta delivery goin' out to 405 Delany, and the bill here says to call you for access."

"Good. I can be there in about twenty minutes. I'll meet your man there."

"Twenty minutes. I'll tell him. Thank you." The dispatcher hung up.

After driving across town for about fifteen minutes, Charles was taken by an idea that he knew could not come to any good. He struggled to dismiss the notion. He even turned on the radio to drown it out. But it persisted.

He turned off the radio and picked up his cell phone.

"Rocket Delivery."

"Yes, this is Charles Redmond calling back. I'm not going to be able to make it over to Delany Street. Do you have a second contact number on your invoice?"

"Lemme see. Yeah, I gotta Joseph De Alverado. You want me to call him instead?"

"Yes, that would be great."

"All right. Will do."

Charles pressed his lips tightly together and pressed down on the accelerator. He was only a few blocks away. He knew he would regret this, but he had to know. He parked half a block away where he could see the building entrance. He saw the delivery truck, already arrived, with the driver doing paperwork in the cab. Charles looked up and down the block, and saw no trace of Joseph. He checked his watch. It had been three minutes since he called. He checked his nails and found them clean. He thought about calling the dispatcher to see if he had gotten through to Joseph. He felt his heart starting to race. He knew this had been a bad idea, but what was he to do now?

Another minute crawled by as his regret at attempting this stunt grew and grew. He checked his watch again. As much as he had wanted before to catch Joseph in the act, now he wished Joseph would not show up, so he wouldn't look like he had set a trap. He was reaching for his phone when he was startled by someone in a gray suit walking from behind him, right by the passenger side of his car.

It was Joseph.

Amazed though he was at Joseph's appearance, he was far more worried about getting caught. He turned away and busied himself with his brief case in the passenger's seat, praying to vanish into anonymity. When he glanced back out the windshield, Joseph had spotted him and was walking back toward the car, frowning.

Charles fought down the sudden hollow ache in his stomach, lit up his smile and stepped out of the car. "Joseph! Good morning! I take it the dispatcher called you too."

The stout, balding man cocked an eyebrow behind his sunglasses. "Yes. On your instruction, after you told him you couldn't make it."

"How's that? Oh, he must have misunderstood me."

It was all Charles could do to act natural. His heart was pounding so hard he thought it was going to interrupt his speech. He stuffed his hands into his overcoat pockets for fear that his twitching fingers would give him away. He poured on the smooth and prayed it was seamless.

"I told him to call you *if* I couldn't make it in time. I thought I was going to get stuck in traffic, and he said his guy was already on his way over here."

Joseph's face didn't move for a long second while he just stared at Charles. Despite the frigid air around them, Charles could feel the sweat rising on his scalp. Finally, the raised eyebrow came down and Joseph nodded slightly.

"All right. He may have made a mistake."

Charles could feel his lungs give way under the relief, and he coughed to cover his involuntary sigh. He pointed across the street and said, "So, do you want to take care of this, or shall I?"

Joseph didn't move his gaze off Charles' face. "I can get it. May I ask you a personal question?"

Charles hadn't expected this. He smiled and said, "Sure."

"Are you well?"

He blinked and chuckled nervously. "Am I well?"

"Yes. I understand that I make you nervous. But lately you have become so stressed that you can barely function. I am depending on you to handle these arrangements. I need to know if you are going to be well enough to perform."

He took a sobering breath. He looked over and saw that the delivery man in the truck was watching them. Maybe this was as good a time as any. He was awfully tired of being afraid. Maybe it was now or never.

"Physically, I'm fine. Our working relationship, on the other hand, is not fine. To say you make me nervous is an enormous understatement. I've worked with a lot of quirky people before, but this has gotten out of hand. You do things that genuinely frighten me. I mean, how is it that you can get here in four minutes, regardless of when the dispatcher calls you? I mean, you did this last month too. Don't tell me you live around here. This area is crime-ridden and nothing but warehouses and businesses for miles."

Joseph's face softened and he shook his head. "But I do live about three blocks from here. I rent a room over a delicatessen on Worthington," he said pointing behind Charles. "Surely that isn't cause for fear. Do the items I'm importing bother you?"

"No, I've handled spookier stuff than yours. I can't pin down why you make me so uncomfortable. I wish I could."

"Is this why you introduced me to your psychiatrist the other night?"

"Yeah, that's an excellent example." He pointed accusingly, barely able to contain himself. "How in the hell did you figure out who she was?"

Joseph frowned and folded his arms. His normally loose cut suit jacket pulled snug and Charles noticed that Joseph had very well-muscled shoulders and arms. This did not help Charles' composure. "I don't recall having to figure out anything. She introduced herself, and everything seemed pretty clear."

Charles blinked and shook his head. "It was not clear at all. Look, I'm not going to argue minutiae out here in the middle of the street. I just want you to understand that I don't think I can trust you anymore. As soon as I can, I'm going to find another importer to give your account to."

Joseph's lips parted and he visibly took a deep breath. Charles could see his eyes go wide behind the sunglass lenses. His usually smooth voice took on a depth of strain that Charles had never heard before. "You question my honesty?"

Charles fought down the wave of fear that shook him. "I apologize. I don't mean to insult you. I don't want this to get personal at all. I just want out of this contract."

Joseph stared at him so intently, Charles thought he felt pressure on his face. "No," he stated flatly. "There isn't time to establish new contacts. I only have two months to finish collecting everything I need."

"Look, we can work something out. All of your big items are already *en route*. I'll make the transition smooth for you. But I've got to hand this over to somebody else." He opened his car door. "Please don't take this as an insult. Just satisfy yourself that I'm a fruitcake. But I'm severing our relations."

He got in his car. His hands were shaking so badly he had to try a couple of times to get the key in the ignition. As he pulled away from the curb, he saw Joseph standing there in the street watching him, arms folded, frowning intently, slowly shaking his head back and forth.

•　　　•　　　•

"I'll tell you, I thought I was going to wet my pants." Charles slouched back in Sanantha's overstuffed chair with a limp spine posture borne equally of relief and exhaustion. His fashionably oversized dark brown suit puddled around him and added to the collapsed effect.

"I'm proud of you for having faced him," she said encouragingly from the facing chair. "And you survived."

"Yeah. I don't know what I thought he would do to me, but he didn't do anything. I still drove to get away. I mean, I hit the highway and drove the rest of the day. I finally turned around at Niagara Falls. I didn't get home until 2 a.m."

"So how do you feel about this turn of events?"

He took a deep breath and blinked a few times, assessing his feelings. She noticed that he bounced his heel on the carpet, but only a couple of times. "Relief, mostly. He still frightens me. But at least now I can start unwinding my ties to him."

"Do you feel any differently about yourself now that you faced him?"

Charles chuckled. "You mean do I feel courageous or more self-confident? Not really. I was just tired of being afraid. When I look back on it rationally, it was a pretty stupid thing to do. I mean, I still don't know how dangerous he is. I only had the one witness. Any courage I had at the time I will gladly attribute to divine intervention, and I'll thank Guedes later, if this all works out."

Sanantha's eyebrows shot up involuntarily at his slip. She covered by adjusting the light blue fabric of the turban across her forehead. She then made a note on her pad: Guedes not God. She also decided to change the subject. "Do you think Joseph will sue you for breach of contract?"

"Lawsuits I can handle." He smiled at the thought. "I'd frankly be relieved if he did file a suit. Demons don't sue, humans do."

"I'd like you to continue to keep track of your dreams. If your nightmares taper off, or if your dreams change in any way, I'd like to know."

"I'll let you know."

She looked over her notes in her lap and pursed her full lips in thought. "There's a side to this that we haven't talked about openly, and maybe now, with your confrontation, we can move onto this." She looked him in the eye and chose her words very carefully. "Do you feel that you were just unlucky to have fallen into doing business with this man who may be a demon? Or do you feel that this demon sought you out, and showed up in your life looking like a businessman?"

Charles sat up straighter in his chair. His gaze danced around the top of the coffee table between them as he collected his thoughts. In a motion Sanantha was starting to expect, he checked his nails. "I guess that begs the question of whether my cutting off business with him will really make any difference. He may just move to more overt aggression."

"Or he may file suit," she countered. "Or he may just go with whatever other importer you set him up with. I'll be frank with you. Based on my meeting him last week, and on how your meeting went with him yesterday, I am not convinced he is a demon. I think we should explore why you feel a demon would want to come after you."

"So you feel this was all in my head." The note of disappointment in his voice was unmistakable. "And you feel I just threw away a lucrative contract for no reason."

"Not at all. This guy creeped you out. He provoked all kinds of unhealthy thoughts and feelings in you. That alone is reason enough to end the contract. Do not think your feelings are inconsequential. But I'm here to help you sort out why such destructive thoughts came to you in the first place. Now you are a religious man."

He started to object, but she cut him off. "I know, you gave me a line about Catholicism. But you have Papa Legba on your wallet, and you thank Guedes for your courage." The Caribbean lilt of her accent was especially strong when she spoke the names of Voodou gods. "I'm from Haiti. I've practiced Voodou all my life. You can't get those things past me." She noted him stiffen up, clearly uncomfortable with where she was going. "Having faith in the Loas is nothing to be ashamed of, not within these walls. I think you're very fortunate to have randomly found a believer to help you through this."

He raised his eyebrows and sighed with resignation. Then he smiled and nodded. "When I first walked in here and saw your dancer paintings I wondered if I should just tell you right off."

She flashed her big smile and nodded, but then moved back to the subject. "My point is, the question is not whether Joseph is a demon. Whether he is or is not, why do you think a *l'alouby* would come for you?"

"You mean, what have I done?" Sanantha noted that he looked away and blinked several times. He then steadied himself with an intent frown. He shook his head and declared, "Nothing that should warrant this."

"Then how can you be sure he's after you specifically? Might he be after someone else, and he's only doing business with you towards some other end?"

Charles thought about this for a moment, but he seemed unconvinced. "Then what about the nightmares? Those are definitely coming from somewhere."

"Maybe you are a sensitive. You could be picking up bad vibes just being around him."

"So you're saying he might not be after me. But that doesn't mean I don't have reason to fear him."

"If you don't want to be around him, for whatever reason, then you don't have to. You've already taken the first step in getting away from him. If you can't show he is after you specifically, then you shouldn't let your fear of him rule your life. There is a big difference between crossing evil's path and having evil come hunting you."

Charles took a deep breath and let it out slowly. It was the first time she had seen him look genuinely at ease.

He nodded and looked her in the eye. "Thank you. You still don't think he's a demon, do you?"

"That doesn't matter," she chuckled. "But honestly, no I don't."

"I'm still going to pray for protection."

"Good," she said soberly. "You do that."

6

THE LAND OF THE DEAD

S TEPPING CAREFULLY OVER where he knew the last electric eye
beam lay in his path, Silas walked confidently into Salon 90 on
the fourth floor of the British Museum. The wide rectangular room
had a plain brown linoleum floor, plain white walls, and high
windows that filled the far wall. He set down his black leather bag
and looked with a wry smile at his objective. Widespread terrorist
bombings and rapidly worsening civil unrest had finally forced the
Egyptian government to lend, on an indefinite basis, many of its
most valuable national treasures to museums in ally countries.

The room was filled with ancient Egyptian furniture, chariots,
statuary and display cases of jewelry. The faint smells of sawdust and
furniture polish spoke of the newness of the installation. At the
collection's center front, the shriveled brown mummy of Ramses II
lay serenely within its temperature and humidity-controlled glass

casket. The only illumination in the room was the cold white light that flooded the display cases.

The tall old man glanced at his watch as he undid his tie with his metal hand. Ignoring the frigid museum air, he undressed completely, opened his bag and withdrew a long, gossamer-thin, white linen caftan. As he slipped it over his head, he whispered to himself, "With this garment I shield the microcosm from all unwanted influences."

He took out a long purple silk sash belt and held it up with both hands in front of him. He looked at each of the hieroglyphic icons embroidered on it in various colored metal thread, and allowed each symbol to stir within him the emotions and attitudes he would need. Tying it around his waist, he said softly, "With this belt I confine and balance the energies of the microcosm."

Next, he retrieved a crown made of the same variety of metals as the belt embroidery. It carried a solitary symbol on its front: the all-seeing eye. Placing this on his head he whispered, "With this band I announce my presence and claim dominion over the forces of the macrocosm."

Next out of the bag was a box of seven colored sticks of chalk. He drew a large red circle on the brown linoleum floor in front of Ramses' body and a large yellow triangle around the mummy case with one side of the triangle facing the circle. While he drew, he recited in his mind the powers each line symbolized until he worked himself into a deep, clear meditative state. Last out of the bag was a set of three small copper mirrors, each of which he placed at a corner of the triangle.

He stepped inside the circle and placed all of his baggage behind him, also within the line's protective confines. He withdrew two final items from the bag, both of which were wrapped in pale red silk, one in each hand, and turned to face the eerie white light of his subject.

The magician didn't allow his low, resonant voice to rise above a whisper, yet the force of his words reached far across dimensions. "Within this infinite circle I am the embodiment of Highest Divinity. All I do is in the name of Divine Providence, and all must obey my word as the word of Destiny itself." He dropped the cloth off the item in his metal-encased right hand and held aloft a deeply carved cylindrical rod, over an inch in diameter and a foot long, of solid amber. "With this wand my absolute will is manifest and is one with the holy Akasha light of the universe." He dropped the other cloth and held up a copper handled dagger with an eleven-inch meteorite-steel kris blade that twisted back and forth to form seven snakelike curves. "Let any who resist my will feel the wrath of my magic sword as he may feel the wrath of Fate itself."

Having thus transformed the hall into his own personal cathedral, Silas closed his eyes and grew still. His breathing slowed to a near stop and his mind floated up and out of this plane of existence, abandoning his standing body but taking with him the essence of his preparations and implements. He did not travel far, only to the Earth Zone Barrier, to the shores of the River Nile in the Land of the Dead.

"Ramses Usimaare Setepenrat Titenre, son of Sethos, Greatest King of Mortal Men!" he cried into the dense fog that hung low over the black, calm water. "He whose body I now visit on the Physical Plane, appear to me now!" he commanded. He waited but got no response.

He wondered what could be wrong. His wand and sword both glowed brightly with the light of the spheres, so it was clear his power was fully with him. He noticed the river didn't smell sweetly of flowers as it should, but rather sourly of rotting vegetation.

He was about to call again when he heard a movement on the water. He stood steadfastly on the gray pebble shore and held his sword up, ready to subjugate whatever demon was swimming towards him. His usually gentle blue eyes squinted down and became menacingly bright. He relaxed when he saw the prow of Sobek's long reed sloop emerge from the fog.

The ferryman brought no passenger. Moreover, the tall, crocodile-headed man-god was so emaciated he was little more than a skeleton, with every bone and string-like tendon visible through his thin, dried skin. As the boat touched shore, Silas fought down his shock. He had expected the Neters to be reduced from their previous glory with so few believers in the world, but such a decayed manifestation reflected a much greater loss of power than he ever imagined. Maintaining the upper hand, the old man boldly demanded, "What is the meaning of this? Where is Ramses?"

Sobek's only answer was to slowly shake his bony head from side to side.

"No? You dare deny me?" he accused angrily and raised his sword against the boatman.

The god fixed his hollow stare on the weapon and it was clear the magician's threat was understood. He spoke quietly, with the sorrow of one in deep mourning. "I am sorry I cannot bring Pharaoh across the river. The Master lies still, and all who died following Him are beyond reach."

"But I am evoking Ramses from his own physical form. That should be sufficient to contact him regardless of any divine intervention," he insisted.

The ferryman cupped his hands above his lowered reptilian head and simply repeated, "I am sorry."

The god's meaning finally hit him. "That's not possible," Silas quietly breathed his shocked denial. "Osiris cannot have died the Second Death. And Anubis with him?"

The crocodile god closed his eyes and slowly tilted his skeletal face up and down.

"I was reincarnated from this Land only eighty-two years ago. Osiris must have lived then." he insisted over his own despair.

The god's sadness was almost tangible. "Yours may well have been the last ka to make the flight back."

Irony nearly overwhelmed the magician. He had purposely avoided introducing the Dark Lord to his new believers, wanting to secure the Tablets of Aeth and prepare a truly glorious reception into a world of faithful. Had he waited too long? His gaze drifted down the misty shore, and he watched the black water lapping at the gray pebble beach as he thought. Was there no one left on Earth who believed in Osiris? Apparently the pagans and cultists who honor Osiris didn't give him the kind of faith he needed. "But *I* believe in Osiris!" the human declared. "If I have to use my power to revive the Dread Master, then I will! Thank you, Great Lord of the River."

The crocodile-man frowned and tilted his head. "I sense great power in you, the power to bring new life out of the Nu. The power I once had," he added with much melancholy.

Silas smiled warmly. "My power is but a shadow of yours, great Seb-Sobek. But I am the one who shall restore your power to you."

The magician spread his arms and his mind flew into the next further plane of existence, the plane of imagination, the Mental Sphere. He alighted on an open field of the same plain brown linoleum as in the museum. It stretched endlessly into a white haze that obscured horizon and sky alike. The only things on this flat expanse were the glass mummy display case, his chalk diagrams and his clothes, all exactly as they were back in England. All except for one detail: the body in the case wasn't Ramses, it was Osiris. His body was wrapped from foot to neck in clean white cloth, his smooth white face looked like alabaster, and on his head was the tall rounded conical crown of Lower Egypt, also in white. Only his rigidly woven, spike shaped beard was black.

Satisfied with the probability configuration he had sampled, he went immediately to work. "I do hereby strip away the ignorance of your Holy Presence that has accumulated entropically over the eons!" He thrust his sword toward the case and blue-white lightning flashed from its tip, instantly, explosively annihilating the glass and metal box into tiny, spinning fragments. The sound of the thunderclap rolling away across the infinite flatness lasted for minutes. So did the stench of ozone in the air.

He knew this would attract the attention of many spirits, but that was part of his plan.

A myriad of shadowy forms began crowding up to the edge of the mist. He lowered the sword and raised his mechanical hand, presenting the amber wand for all to see. He slowly turned as he spoke, addressing the cautious crowd of onlookers. "In the name of the all that is Holy, I ask for your voluntary assistance in raising this noble being who has expired ignominiously of neglect. I will not force any of you to help me. We are all comrades in the Cycle of Life. I appeal to your sense of propriety and justice. Come, join me in helping this unjustly wronged Child of Providence."

Though he could see several of the gray outlines stir, none of the spirits stepped forward.

"Will none of you help me?" he entreated.

Still he got no reply.

"Very well," he resigned with evident disappointment. Then through clenched teeth he added quietly, but clearly, "Woe be to any who try to stop me."

Staying within his red chalk circle, Silas turned back to the mummified god lying in the remains of the now shattered display case. He held the wand up in front of his face and looked past it at Osiris. He stood statue-still for a long moment as he concentrated and forced, by sheer willpower, the energies of the universe to obey. The copper mirrors on the floor began to glow as they focused the Akasha light of the spheres up onto the prone figure, dimly at first, then brighter and brighter.

The light they threw did not illuminate Osiris's body, but revealed a ghostlike image of Osiris's life energy *djed* pillar lying within the god's body. The skin on the magician's forehead pulled back smooth, his expressive blue eyes tightened, and his jaw muscles bulged rock hard as he concentrated every fiber of his will into his task. The pillar glowed brighter and its details, its flared base and capital, the four stacked rings above the two closed eyes of Horus, all became distinct through the white fabric wrappings.

Silas fleetingly realized what he was doing. Isis herself raised Osiris after his murder, using these same magicks, secrets revealed to her by Anubis and Ra. She was the first to perfect the formula. Though she was elevated to godhood for her knowledge and acts, she was originally only a mortal human. How far he had come to follow so closely in the footsteps of his patron goddess.

Satisfied with the energy shining onto the body, he turned his wand to what he knew was North, and commanded the appearance and opening of the door of the North Wind. He then turned to each of the other cardinal points and opened these doors as well. Lastly, he focused his willpower through the wand and formed a *meskhetiu* pry adze, and with this ceremonial lever, he telekinetically opened Osiris's mouth.

Sweeping his sword in a huge circle about his head, he subjugated the winds of the cardinal points and made them do his bidding. As the winds roared in across the plain, they punched holes in the mist and scattered the shadow-hidden witnesses. The North Wind smelled sweetly of ice and pine, the South Wind smelled sourly of sun-baked grasses and animal dung, the West wind smelled richly of salt and the sea, and the East Wind smelled pungently of spices and incense. The four converged and interacted, becoming a tornado mixture of fire, earth, air and water, which he then commanded to enter the god's open mouth.

When they entered, the *djed* pillar ignited with so much light, the carved details of its surface could no longer be distinguished. The light lanced out across the plane, stripping away the fog to the horizon. Those spirits that had not already left now fled in sheer panic.

Through squinting, tearing eyes, Silas finally saw what he had come for. Osiris stirred. The mummy wrappings burned away to reveal a well-muscled body in kingly garb. The god opened his eyes and held up the crook and flail in his hands, stretching his arms from where they had been folded over his chest. As the god got up from the table, the pillar within him righted, the eyes of Horus on the pillar opened, and the glow spread to fill Osiris's entire form. The broken glass from the exploded display case crunched under his leather sandals. Silas lowered the wand and sword, allowing the spell to dissolve as he wiped his eyes on his sleeve.

The glow from the god's body persisted for several seconds after the magic mirrors had gone dark. As the glow faded, his skin grew progressively darker until it was coal black. Silas noticed how his subject had grown much taller in the revivification.

Now eight feet tall, his massive frame was draped as a pharaoh at court, in a white sarong, tall white helmet crown, beaded pectoral necklace over his broad, bare chest, girdle sash, bracers and sandals. Osiris surveyed the empty expanse around them before addressing the human.

"Magician, where are the legions of believers who brought you the faith to revive me?"

His voice was inhumanly deep and had an almost liquid sounding resonance.

"Nowhere," he answered flatly. "I acted alone." Since Osiris was the magician's prisoner within the yellow chalk triangle, Silas resisted the urge to drop prostrate before the god. Out of respect, though, he never let his gaze rise above Osiris' waist.

The god's brow furrowed deeply over his solid black eyes. Silas knew the god could sense the truth in his words. Grasping the implications was another matter entirely. "Who are you that your will alone can change the destiny of a god?"

"Destiny is my trade. I am one of nature's agents of change. I am Chosen." Silas let the word hang in the air. He needed to develop Osiris's trust before making any demands, so he let the god ask all the questions.

"So, Chosen One," the Egyptian started with obvious resignation. "What do I owe you for your kindness?"

"Only your seal, that I may call you ally."

Osiris raised a doubting eyebrow. "My true written name? Are you planning on dying soon and wish my intervention to reprieve you?"

"No, nothing of the sort."

"You wish only to be able to contact me at any time?" The raised eyebrow did not come down. "No special favors?"

"Only the sort one might ask of an ally. My intention in reviving you was as much the righting of a despicable wrong as it was a personal favor to you. When you fell dormant the gates of your underworld closed, trapping the souls of all who had been buried in your name. For a thing of such enormity to occur out of sheer apathy seemed an absurd injustice."

"You speak like a philosopher. Philosophers are dangerous," the god observed coolly.

"Would you trust me more if I gave you my seal in return for yours, so that you may call on me freely?"

"Why would I want to do that?" Osiris nearly scoffed.

"I am the only living creature who knows you exist," Silas stated pointedly. Seeing that this only made the god more defensive and suspicious, he added, "Although there is an island near my home in a sea called the Caribbean where people worship many African gods. I will put you at the head of their pantheon."

Osiris was visibly pleased with this. He smiled slightly and asked, "If you are to be my ally, what is your name?"

"Silas Alverado, and my seal is thus." With the tip of his wand he drew a complex jagged symbol in the air. Light poured out of the wand like ink and hung in the air until he finished the diagram.

"Are you not concerned that someone in the spheres will see such an openly demonstrated seal?"

"Not to worry," the old man assured him. With an expansive sweep of his wand he indicated the utterly vacant brown linoleum plain around them. "Every spirit who even knows this spot exists fled the instant you awoke. I'm afraid you're not very popular."

"Your seal looks familiar to me, yet it has been a long time since I have seen it," the god observed curiously.

"You are correct. I died one hundred generations ago under your care, bearing the name of Royarna. I was the High Priest of Amun at the end of the reign of Pharaoh Ramses Usimaare Setepenrat Titenre Meryamun."

"And you are risen without my intervention?" Osiris was incredulous.

The only explanation Silas offered was, "As I said, I am Chosen."

Osiris sized him up and down again. Then he sniffed. "I sense about you the presence of another's assistance." He sniffed again, and smiled broadly. "It has been eons since I enjoyed that perfume." He nodded and said, "You are indeed Chosen, and I approve of my wife's choice. Why did Isis bring you back?"

Silas wanted to change the subject, to get back to his objective. He dared not upset the god, he needed his cooperation too much. "It is not my place to question my goddess's plans. I know my motives, and I am left to assume She approves, since She has cleared my way many times."

Osiris seemed as much amused as curious. "Very well, you may see my seal. Just the same, I will think of my seal and allow you to view it with your inner eye."

"Very well," the human agreed. Even though he only had to make the most superficial telepathic contact to find the symbol, a rush of freezing cold washed over Silas as he touched Osiris' consciousness. He quickly memorized the complicated looping pattern and broke the contact. Giving no hint of his discomfort, he graciously said, "Thank you. Now that we share this confidence, I would ask your indulgence in one small matter. I discovered your former predicament when I tried to visit one of your subjects. I very much need to speak with my former Pharaoh Ramses."

"What could he know that I do not?"

"He knew someone in his lifetime who has never walked your lands."

"A foreigner?"

"No, if that were the case I could go to the appropriate land of the dead," Silas explained patiently. "No, this individual is an immortal."

The god pondered this, clearly trying to deduce Silas' true intent. "Do you seek a demon?" he asked tentatively.

"Yes."

"I do not like demons," Osiris stated flatly.

"Neither do I," the old man agreed. "I intend to subjugate this one mercilessly. Will you help me?"

"Yes, gladly. Besides, what you ask is trivial."

"However far you can bring him will surely be ample," the magician added graciously.

Despite his tone, the god took offense. "You mean to question my power?" he demanded tersely.

"I meant only to save you embarrassment, Great Lord," Silas explained without humbling himself. "Your power comes from your followers. Right now, I am the only one. When I convert the Haitians, you will have as much power as you ever enjoyed in Egypt. In the meantime, I am prepared to speak with Pharaoh using whatever clairvoyance is necessary."

The deity eyed him suspiciously then looked down at his own body. "I do seem considerably shorter than I should be," he admitted quietly. He cocked an eyebrow wryly at the human and concluded, "I am beginning to like you, Silas Alverado, formerly Royarna. Under other circumstances such insolence would gain you an immediate and painful trip to my underworld. You have my admiration for engineering this situation where I need you as much as you need me. I will do as you ask."

"Thank you, Your Highmess," Silas said with a little bow.

"There is one thing that troubles me about you, Chosen One," the god added somewhat to Silas' surprise. "I remember you when you were Royarna. You clearly have regained your Mastery, but you are changed. How can you have such understanding of Nature, and yet have no trace of love in your heart?"

Silas had hoped to keep Osiris off the subject of his own soul. He considered not giving him an answer, but decided his new ally deserved one. "I am on a vengeance quest. I cannot afford to have room in my heart for love."

The god apparently realized this was all the answer he was going to get, because he didn't press the point further.

Without either of them ever having broached the subject, Silas pointed his wand at the triangle that held Osiris his prisoner and willed the chalk line to break. Continuing to ignore this action, they both nodded goodbye and flew off to their respective planes of existence.

A long, cautious moment after they were gone, the empty silence was broken by the footsteps of a lone man walking up to the tableau from beyond the edge of the now clear horizon. His leather sandals crunched the broken glass from the exploded display case on the brown linoleum. He stroked his long curly black beard as he sternly regarded the chalk drawings and Silas' discarded shadow clothing with his bright violet eyes. He lowered and shook his head in resignation, when he noticed his long simple robes had fallen open, revealing the gold studded polished black leather body armor he wore underneath. He quickly pulled the cloth shut and casually glanced around to see if any spirits had noticed, then strode unassumingly away.

When Silas' mind returned to his body, he checked his watch and shook his head at how little time he had left. He left the circle to repair the yellow chalk triangle around the mummy display case which had been broken by analogy when he broke its counterpart when he released Osiris. Since the glass case on the Mental Plane had represented the ignorance surrounding Osiris, and no such ignorance applied to Ramses, the case on the Physical Plane remained intact.

Snatching up his wand and sword, he returned to face the mummy from inside his circle. The magician took a breath and fought back a wave of fatigue. He then started again by concentrating on his implements, and mentally repeated his oath of faith and purpose. Then, tracing the outlines with his wand held at arm's length, he restated the value of the chalk drawings, charging them anew with their magical qualities and allowing their symbolism to work his mind into a trance of oneness with the universe.

He looked up at the mummy and caught himself. The moment had arrived when he would speak with his beloved king. He took a breath and set aside his reverence. He was the master of this contact. It would only work if he kept control. He pointed his wand at the preserved body and began in a quiet but forceful tone. "Ramses, son of gods, king of mortal men, hear my voice, see the might of my will and understand the righteousness of my commands. Step forward into view of my inner eye that we may discuss your memories of the days when you trod the earth in this body before me."

•   •   •

Four floors below him, the cold that had slowly leeched the heat from the water pipes running within the outside wall of the basement finally managed to fill in the last layer of ice inside the water main and choke it off.

•   •   •

Silas hoped with all his might for a strong contact. He simply could not afford the time to do a lengthy interpretation if all Ramses could manage were vague images.

He only had to wait a few seconds before he felt the pharaoh's presence. Osiris had kept his word. Unfortunately, the old man had to reach all the way across the Mental Plane to the ephemeral Astral Plane before he made contact. He sighed out loud before setting aside his enormous disappointment.

Oblivious to the freezing linoleum, he sat down in the middle of the circle, set aside his sword, and working with his left hand, took one of the two Tarot decks from their box. He continued to hold his wand aloft in his steel-gloved right hand. He separated out the Major Arcana and court cards and set the rest of the deck in his lap. He spread the deck's red silk wrapping scarf on the floor before him, then fanned the cards out on the scarf. "Welcome Great Pharaoh Ramses. I was your humble servant when you walked among the living. I was your High Priest of Amun and I was called Royarna. I am seeking another man who used to work for you. He was the High Priest of Amun and your chief magician during your conflict with Moses. He was my predecessor. He has come to be remembered by the name Nebwenanef, which I believe meant, 'Name not spoken.' Do you recall this man?"

Silas separated his spiritual left hand from his material one and held it up toward the mummy case. Reaching through dimensions he at last felt the pharaoh's touch. Using his material left hand as a conduit for the dead king's will, he pawed through the cards and pulled one out. It was The Sun.

"So you remember him well. Good. Did you ever see his personal seal, his spiritual emblem?"

The Moon was the answering card.

"No, he kept it a secret. I thought as much. I know you didn't kill him after he failed you. To where did you exile him?"

Again he sifted. This time the card was The Fool.

"Confusion," he interpreted. "Wrong question. You didn't exile him at all. Did he run away?"

The Chariot was the answer.

"Yes. Do you know to where he escaped?"

Strength.

"The answer requires more effort," Silas mused. "We'll have to do something a little more subtle." The pharaoh guided his left hand to pick out seven cards and place them in a row. They were, in order, The Emperor, The Page of Rods, The Magician, The Hierophant, The Page of Swords, The Chariot, and lastly The Page of Pentacles.

The white-haired man quickly combined their meanings to form a conclusion. "You don't know, but someone close to you might." Pointing to The Page of Rods, he asked, "Who is this other person?"

Much to his surprise, he felt the rush of a very strong message. Going with the impulse, he scooped up the entire deck, then fanned the cards and selected one, guided by Ramses. The card was The Magician.

He smiled and looked up at the mummy. "Your Highness, I know I was there in my previous life, but I have searched my life as your servant Royarna, and I have found nothing."

•   •   •

Once sealed, the ice inside the water pipe grew with unnatural speed until it swelled and split the steel pipe. Half a dozen scrawny rats, their eyes glinting violet in the darkness, fought over the remains of a long-forgotten, dropped candy bar. The water that squeezed past the ice dripped from the split pipe and splashed on the floor, scattering the scavengers.

•   •   •

Appropriate to the complexity of the situation, Silas shuffled the entire deck together except for The Magician, which he turned sideways in the center of the cloth. With practiced fluidity he laid out four cards around the Page of Rods in a cross, four cards in a vertical column to the side, and placed one card, face down, across The Magician.

He sorted out their implications without touching the downturned card and deduced, "When I was Royarna, I kept extensive records." Turning up the last card revealed Death. "I'm going to have to start a new venture to find those records." Muttering under his breath he complained, "This wasn't supposed to be this complicated." Looking up to the mummy again, he asked, "Did the man I seek ever personally oversee the interment of any of the royal family?"

The king guided him to sift through the deck again and pulled out the Wheel of Fortune, inverted.

"No, but pull another card."

The Seven of Wands, inverted.

"Curiosity? You want to know why I ask. He may have signed the stress lintel of the burial sanctum," Silas explained to the ghost.

He was about to ask another question when he got the nagging suspicion that Ramses wanted to ask him a question. Not knowing anything about the inquiry he began to lay out a large spread that would allow him lots of card interrelationships from which to work. He didn't have to go past the first few cards to realize what was on the king's mind.

"You are shocked and outraged that your priest may have put his name on the resting place of one of your relatives. Let me relieve your concern. Very few scholars today know of the ceremony, but I didn't realize it was a secret even in your time," he interjected. Continuing patiently, he said, "The officiating High Priest put his seal there to take responsibility if anything should happen to the structure. In the pyramids, the signature went on the angled stress vaulting in the chambers above the sanctum. Since royal burials in your time were done in hillsides, the main support beam was used instead.

"My liege, since you feel I may have written of this man when I was your High Priest, where might I find such writings now?"

Again he used a large spread for such an open ended question. The answer was simpler than he had expected. "You forbade anyone from writing anything about this man as long as you lived." The old man smiled, nodded and shared his deduction with the king's remains. "On the walls of the tombs of any royalty I buried, *after* you died. Hence the new journey. I have to go to Egypt."

.   .   .

In their frenzied feeding on the candy bar, the rats blithely chewed on anything their ravenous teeth passed over, including the hastily run electrical cables for the extra lights that had to be installed for the new Egyptian displays in the fourth and fifth floor salons.

.   .   .

He put away the cards and opened another wooden box. From it he unrolled a mat on which were embroidered the letters of the English alphabet, the words 'yes' and 'no,' several Greek letters, the Arabic numerals zero through nine, as well as the twelve symbols of the zodiac, all in a circle. Lastly, he removed a long thin white metal chain on the end of which hung an ivory and gold, teardrop-shaped plumb bob pointer. He held the end of the chain over the center of the planchette mat with his flesh left hand and set the pointer swinging in a circle around its center.

"Great Ramses, I have one last favor to ask of you. In fact, it is the most important of all. Since I am now looking for what is probably the only written record of your old High Priest's name, I need to know how I might have written it in my previous life. I appreciate that you forbade his name to ever be spoken, but I need you to break that edict now. I need to at least know how it sounded. Think only of the sounds used to say it out loud. Concentrate on one sound at a time until I feel it."

As his hand wavered in its unsupported posture, his subconscious, guided by Ramses, slowly changed the plumb bob's swing until it crossed the center of the pattern rather than circling over the symbols. Thus two possibilities for the first sound appeared, and since one of them was a number, he knew the sound was 'F'.

•   •   •

The dripping icy water pooled and flowed over the chewed cable, and all the lights in the new Egyptian display rooms went dead.

It was all Silas could do not to let the sudden pitch darkness distract him from the concentration needed to maintain his tenuous link with the long dead pharaoh. But through that open contact, the king was still feeding the phonemes of the name to his wavering aloft arm. In his desperation he considered fire as a light source. Stopping himself short of such a potentially disastrous move, he took his only remaining option. In the total blackness he snatched up his sword with his right hand and threw it through the glass of the mummy case.

Sirens blared, klaxons pealed, and the floodlights of the alarm system showed Silas Alverado exactly what he had come for. As soon as he secured the last syllable of the name, he replaced his psychical arm into his physical one, grabbed up his tools, sword and clothes, stuffed them in his bag and ran for the door. He only hesitated long enough to release the pharaoh's spirit by scuffing the yellow chalk triangle. "Thank you, my liege."

As he dropped into a snowbank from a second story window, he smiled at what he had done and learned. He had hoped to discover more than he had, but now he had at least taken the first step forward in his quest, the quest to capture a demon who once masqueraded as an Egyptian High Priest of Amun named Faen-ka.

7

THE PACT

CHARLES REDMOND LOVED HOW PREPARING FOR RITUAL both focused and excited him. He had already traded his daytime uniform of Armani, Gucci and Rolex for baggy white linen pants and a white short sleeved cotton shirt. He stood barefoot in the middle of his bedroom and stretched and shook his lanky limbs, trying to limber up some of the tension in his six-foot one frame.

He checked to make sure his cell phone was turned off. He stood on a chair and disconnected the ceiling mounted smoke detector. He stepped to his stereo where he put on a set of wireless headphones, inserted a CD, and slipped the remote into his shirt pocket. He walked around the room and lit half a dozen candles on nightstands and dressers, before turning off the overhead light.

He then turned to a double-doored armoire made of rough-hewn dark wood. He opened it and was engulfed by the rich, sweet smell of incense. He withdrew a woven grass mat which he unrolled on the floor in front of the armoire. He knelt down on the mat and continued withdrawing objects: a gourd rattle, human shaped candles in red, black and white, a dagger, bundles of herbs, a bottle of white rum, and a glass. Remaining within the cabinet was a large white pillar candle, and a large, flat-topped gray stone with a hole in the front. The stone also had a wooden pole stuck in the top that was affixed to the top inside of the armoire. The pole was painted with two intertwining snakes, one black and one white. The inside of the cabinet was painted black and decorated with white *veves*, the elaborate curlicue designs that were the personal seals of the Loa gods. On the insides of the doors, which now faced forward, were hung two banners painstakingly covered in shiny sequins that formed a pink heart on one, and a green cup on the other.

Satisfied with the arrangement of the objects around himself on the mat, he turned on the CD player. The music started with a lone drummer beating a simple rhythm. Charles let the sound focus and relax him as he stared at the snakes painted on the pole. He lit the large pillar candle inside the cabinet and focused on the flame. By now the lone drummer had been joined by others, each beating out a simple rhythm, but together they formed an increasingly complex pattern. When a chorus began singing praises to gods in Haitian Creole, Charles began quietly singing along with them.

"Praise to Danbhalah ati Wedo, Lord over All. Praise to Papa Legba, Savior of Mankind." At this point he stroked the flag with the heart on it. "Praise to Madame Erzulie, Queen of Compassion." He then stroked the cup flag. "Praise to Dread Ougu, Lord of Might. Praise to Baron Samedi, Lord of the Graveyard ..."

As he focused on the icons and implements, his mind slipped away from his daily worries and became more and more immersed in the spiritual world the objects represented. He gained confidence, through familiarity and a sense of belonging, and it felt good.

While the singers continued, Charles lit one of the bundles of herbs from the white pillar candle, let it burn for a moment, then blew it out. Billowing white smoke wriggled up from the glowing embers. Holding the incense between his praying hands, Charles bowed to the altar and began his own entreaties. "Lord Danbhalah,

Highest of the High, Mightiest of the Mighty, Great Serpent of Creation who graced mankind with the gift of the world, hear my plea. I have greatly wronged your people, and I have become your devoted servant in hopes that you would show me the way to repent for my sins. I bear the blood of many souls and many ruined lives on my hands, and I am sorry. I send great sums of money to Haitian charities. I give huge breaks to Haitian exporters. I live my life according to your creed. I am ever vigilant for your signs, and I follow them unerringly.

"Now a *l'alouby* has come for me. I know I deserve his wrath. How can I continue to be your faithful servant if this demon kills me? I beg of you, protect me from this misguided instrument of vengeance, that I may redouble my efforts to serve you."

Through the smoke curling up from the incense in his hands, he looked up at the pole and the two intertwined snakes, Legba and Erzulie, the male and female principles that made up the Serpent of Creation. Though the rising, twisting smoke, he saw the snakes slither past one another around the pole. His eyes went wide. He was amazed, and not sure if he should be afraid or overjoyed. He stared more intently. Maybe it was a trick of the smoke. Maybe it was a sign.

•   •   •

Far away in a jungle thicker than any ever seen on Earth, an enormous black forked tongue flicked out from a crack between two rows of smooth green boulders. It flicked again, questing for more of the smell it had tasted the first time. A huge green stone atop a hill behind the boulders stirred and rolled opened to reveal a giant yellow eye. The vertical slit of its pupil widened, and the tongue flicked again.

•   •   •

He set the incense down on the gray altar stone and poured a glass of the rum. By now the musicians in his headphones were chanting and drumming in such a dizzying fury that Charles found his hands trembling to the rhythms. The heady sweetness of the incense was having its way with him too. Fighting his growing giddiness, he steadied himself and set the glass down in the hole in the stone. "O Great Lord, accept my humble offering. Feel at ease in the comforts of my home. Come rest here and grace my pitiful life with your magnificent presence."

The incense sitting on the stone had filled the cabinet with swirling smoke. The plume of smoke did not disperse, but wound around the central pole and the glass of rum in an unmistakably snake-like coil. Charles sat stunned by what he saw, grinning uncontrollably at what it could mean.

•   •   •

A boulder rolled open on the other side of the hill to reveal another eye, and a shudder ran through the ground for a hundred yards behind. A thousand birds and insects all noisily took flight as the ground buckled, the trees swayed, and the terrain undulated as the Serpent of Creation slid through the jungle floor.

A man in simple flaxen robes with a long curly black beard was walking through the jungle and felt the ground tremble. His thick black eyebrows furrowed over his bright violet eyes and he searched through the layers of canopy and undergrowth for the source. The escaping cloud of birds and insects showed him the way. He flashed a mischievous smile.

He ran towards the commotion, his sandaled feet quietly munching the carpet of fallen leaves as he deftly sidestepped outcroppings of brush and vines. His robes untied and flapped aside to reveal his gold studded black leather armor, but he didn't care. The wind whistled past his ears as he flew through the dense greenery, laughing to himself all the way.

As he approached, he saw the trees swaying wildly to and fro as the earth buckled up and then back down as the serpent shape slid by. He stopped and sniffed the air repeatedly. Finally he caught the smell of incense and rum among the myriad rotting vegetable smells of the jungle. His curious frown slowly pulled back, as his face stretched into a self-satisfied grin.

•   •   •

Spurred by the possibility that he had gotten the god's attention, Charles heightened his fervor. He picked up a white man-shaped candle, lit it from the white pillar inside the cabinet, and held it up in front of himself with both hands. "You who designed order out of chaos, you who conceived of justice, I give myself over to you for your protection." He prayed with all his might, clutching the candle tight, pressing his eyes closed with the effort. "I devote myself to your greatness, and all I ask is your watchful eye to keep me safe so I may continue to serve you."

•   •   •

The bearded man heard a faint voice coming from nearby. He stepped to a pool of water and peered into it. He saw reflections of images and could hear echoes of a voice, pleading for help. He sniffed and verified this pool as the source of the incense and rum odors. He knelt down on all fours at the water's edge, closed his eyes, and pushed his face into the water.

He opened his eyes and found his view of the world turned sideways. He was in a large black box, apparently wrapped around the side of a pole, looking out through wreaths of smoke at a young black man who was holding up a burning, man-shaped candle. He grinned at how unexpectedly interesting this was.

Charles opened his eyes and recoiled in a gasp so violent he nearly dropped the candle. The painted white snake on the central pole had opened its eyes and they now glowed bright purple. He sat wide-eyed and paralyzed for a whole second before realizing what he must do. Still holding the man-shaped candle in front of him in one hand, he grabbed up the painted rattle of command in the other hand and held it above his head. Any joy he had felt was now washed aside by the fear of the unknown. He bowed his head but kept his gaze on the painted snake. One could not be too careful when dealing with the fickle gods. "Great Madame Erzulie, welcome and thank you for gracing my humble altar. I sought only that you might smile upon me if I become endangered by this demon I fear. I am overwhelmed by the honor of your actual appearance."

The bearded man twisted his snake head free of the wooden pole so he could see the world level. He could see this had a rather startling effect on the young man. The man scooted back on his knees and held the rattle up in a clearly threatening, bent elbow stance. The bearded man was unimpressed and unconcerned. The young man had said something about fearing a demon. He flicked out his snake tongue to smell more details.

Charles considered how much of this vision could be due to the drugs Sanantha had him taking. All the same, he had to stand his ground. He shook the rattle and declared as forcefully as he could through the shaking in his voice, "Please stay where you are. I am not prepared to welcome you any further into this plane of existence. I am not inviting you to mount me. I can only make you comfortable on the altar."

The now half-painted, half-sculpted snake acknowledged his request with a nod.

Charles could barely think between the pounding of his heart and the pounding of the drums in the headphones. Using a finger of the rattle hand, he dragged the headphones down around his neck. He assumed he needed to still hear the drums to maintain the connection to the god. He gathered his thoughts and decided to state his case and then end this session before things got further out of control. "I specifically need protection from a demon who calls himself Joseph de Alverado. I don't know who sent him, and I'm not sure he's after me personally, but he'd have plenty of reason to be if he were."

The snake pointed its head straight at him and flicked its tongue many times rapidly.

"I am ending my business relations with him, and I'm hoping to never see him again in person. But if he is after me, then he will probably move soon to openly attack me. That's why I need your help."

The snake flicked its tongue one last time, and pulled its head back as if it had smelled something bad.

Charles didn't know what to make of that response. "Does my request disgust you? Is my request too trivial or demeaning for one of your stature?"

The snake shook its head no.

Charles fought back a wave of enthusiasm that surged at the possibility. In his overly excited state, his emotions raced from one extreme to the other. He tried to contain himself but still ended up smiling ear to ear. "So you will help me?"

The snake nodded yes.

The sheer joy of being not only graced with a visitation, but granted protection from his gods was too much for him. His face bunched up and tears filled his eyes. "Thank you," he blurted out. "Thank you from the bottom of my soul! How can I ever thank you enough?" He gathered himself and declared earnestly, "I will never fail you. I will be your servant, and I will spread the glory or your name forever."

The snake nodded one more time, then withdrew into its original flat, painted form.

Charles was left shaking. He sat staring for a long moment, waiting to see if the vision was really over. He was greatly relieved that the god had left on its own, since he had no idea how to end such a visit. He looked at the last wafts of smoke in the cabinet and the man-shaped candle still burning in his hand. He blew out the candle, then took an enormous breath and let it out slowly through flaccid lips.

•　　•　　•

The bearded man pulled his head out of the pond and shook the water from his long curly black hair. He chewed on his bottom lip as he frowned and stroked the end of his broad hooked nose with the knuckles of his fist. What had started as a curiosity, an idle amusement, had turned into something much more important. There was no mistaking the stench he had smelled. Egyptians.

His thoughts were interrupted by the horrendous sound of the earth tearing open and the pitiful sound of lambs bleating in terror in the distance. The Danbhalah manifestation had found the decoy the man had set. Half a dozen lambs soaked in rum and chained to bushels of smoldering sage incense embers mirrored the evocational smells Charles had sent, but a thousand times stronger. The living earthen serpent reared up out of the jungle floor and pounced on the offering, swallowing the entire tableau in one mouthful as it then passed through back into the earth.

The bearded man smiled wryly.

8

EGYPT

"WELL, SIR, HERE WE ARE," the dark-skinned taxi driver said over his shoulder in Arabic. "Again, I'm sorry about the time. The riot was bigger than I thought."

"That's all right," Silas forgave him in the man's own tongue. "You said it could take as much as two hours to go around, and it took considerably less. How much do I owe you?"

"Sixteen pounds Egyptian. I charge you only for the regular distance."

"That's very kind of you," he said handing the man a handful of bills. "That should cover it." He picked up his black leather bag and got out. "Praise be to Allah."

The driver, having quickly counted the money, smiled at Silas' tip and called back through the open windows, "Praise be to Allah, and enjoy your stay in Cairo!"

As the cab drove off, the white suited old man quickly sized up his new environment. The Egyptian capitol at the beginning of the twenty-first century carried the fruits of a modern educated nation in one hand, while in the other it clung to the baggage of an underdeveloped backward one. Along the narrow street Silas saw peddlers in traditional Bedouin rags selling their wares to the infrequent passersby in business suits. He noticed a half-naked child had fallen asleep against the post of a mercury vapor street lamp. The buildings were mostly decaying one and two-story offices with an occasional, very conspicuous, new four or five story unit. As if to add to the contrasts, everyone behaved as if there was nothing wrong, despite the deepening economic depression and increasingly militant religious fanaticism that spawned the almost daily riots just a few blocks away. The assaulting sulfurous smell of burning tires corrupted the breeze that blew dry dust down the street.

"O, Kemet," he sighed. Silas wondered what Pharaoh Ramses would think if he saw how stumbling a step his kingdom had made into the modern age.

The short, very thin, olive skinned man answered the door of his second story office with a big smile on his face. "You must be Mister Alverado," he said in English with only a slight trace of accent. "I saw you from the window. Come in, come in."

He closed the door behind Silas and turned to face him. Silas noticed the man's double take when he saw Silas' bright blue eyes. Silas understood the superstitions about blue eyes and divinity among Islamic people. The man blinked, kept up his smile, and reached to shake Silas' hand. When he felt the metal prosthesis through the black cloth glove Silas wore, he hesitated again but then graciously passed it over without mention.

"I am Hameel al Qabek," he introduced himself. "Very nice to meet you in person."

"The pleasure is mine," the white-haired man said. "You come highly recommended."

"Thank you for saying so," the Egyptian smiled as he stepped around behind his dark wooden desk.

The office was one large room with windows across the far wall, gray metal filing cabinets stacked across one end, and al Qabek's desk and chairs at the other. The windows were open, and two ceiling fans blew the warm air around to very little cooling effect. The white plaster walls under the windows had the dinginess of always being exposed to dusty outside air.

"Please, have a seat. When I received your fax two days ago, I went to work on it right away. I had some photographs taken yesterday of paintings that may be what you're looking for. Before I show them to you, though, I have to mention that we have not discussed any terms. You said in your cable that you would pay more if I found what you wanted quickly."

"That's correct. I'm surprised you didn't have a photo already in your files. Your counterpart in England spoke glowingly of your portfolio."

"I must remember to thank him for such a complement. Alas, I had only notes as to what is said on these wall sections. But, as you will see, my photographer did an excellent job of correcting that deficiency."

"I'm glad to hear that. You will also remember in my wire I said I was only paying you for the expedience of not having to go to the dig myself. The photographs must be that good."

"Not a problem. That quality is what I have," al Qabek said positively. He began figuring with a pad and pencil on his desk. "Let's see, my finder's fee, plus what I had to pay the photographer, plus, shall we say," he looked up at Silas, "10% for the rush job?"

"That will be fine," came the gravelly agreement.

"That comes to 7,600 Egyptian," he said finishing his calculations. "That's 3,000 American."

Silas looked him straight in the eye and let his breath out slowly in disappointment. "No it isn't," he said in a low flat tone. "It's 2,920."

"Oh, is it?" Hameel said innocently looking back at his pad. "Oh, so it is. I'm sorry, you're right, 2,920 American."

Silas did not release his iron gaze. For a long tense moment, the only sound was the quiet whirring of the ceiling fan which did nothing but redistribute the smell of nervous sweat. "Let me make one thing absolutely clear to you. No one has ever successfully cheated me. A bargain made with me is as binding as an oath to the Almighty. I am just as relentless if you should go back on it."

The antiquities dealer chuckled as innocently as he could muster, insisting, "But Mister Alverado, it was just a simple mistake."

"The eighty dollars means very little to me. I would have gladly paid the full 3,000 American, if that had been your honest quote. You will deal with me fairly or not at all. As good as your catalog may be, there are many other brokers in Cairo who would love to please me."

"I wouldn't have it any other way," al Qabek smiled nervously. "Let me show you what I have." He took a large manila envelope out of a desk drawer and handed it to Silas.

The six 8-x-10 photos were obviously taken with a flash inside dark tomb corridors. He quickly glanced over each one, checking names and key phrases.

"These were definitely written by Royarna," he conceded with a slight nod. "This one wall panel appears to be what I want."

As he scrutinized it more closely, al Qabek inquired greedily, "Then you are satisfied?"

Silas's brow furrowed as his eyes danced back and forth across the photograph. Ignoring the dealer's question, he asked one of his own. "Are you sure there hasn't been any restoration done on this tomb?"

Surprised and alarmed, Hameel asked, "What do you mean?"

"It appears that someone has attempted to repair part of the painting."

The dealer was on his feet reaching across the desk. "Let me see." Silas handed it to him, and he turned to the window to examine it in the daylight. "It looks all right to me," he said while still looking at the picture.

"Oh, it's a good job, and undoubtedly done with only the best intentions. Some overzealous scholar probably thought he was doing the right thing." The old man did not try to hide the disdain in his voice.

"But how can you tell?" the Egyptian asked, completely baffled.

"The meter of the language changes suddenly on the seventh line. It's grammatically correct, but it sounds stiff, like a non-speaker was using a dictionary to write it. The writing stays that way down to the fifteenth line where it changes back to Royarna's fluent speech."

The raised-eyebrow, wide-eyed look of resigned confusion on Hameel's face would have been comical if Alverado were not so genuinely disappointed.

"If you say so," the dealer sighed, shaking his head slightly. "But you must appreciate that it is not my fault the tomb has been tampered with." He handed the picture back to Silas and sat down.

"That is true," the older man admitted unemotionally. "We agreed to a price for a product which you have delivered."

With that point settled, al Qabek couldn't help but ask, "Is it not at all useable?"

"No," Silas sighed, looking at the photo. "My misfortune in this case is quite complete. From what is said before and after, it is clear that the altered passages did contain the information I require. What is written here now is essentially idle filler, nothing more than expansion and repetition of what came before." Reaching inside his white suit jacket, he quickly counted out fifteen 500 Egyptian pound notes and a 100. "I assume cash will suffice."

The man's face lit up. "Oh yes, that will be fine." Catching himself on the edge of a conspicuous display of greed, he added in a more subdued tone, "I am sorry you couldn't find exactly what you seek."

"I appreciate the sentiment," Silas gave him a small gracious smile as he stood up to leave.

"I do know an archivist who might be able to find drawings made by the people who discovered the tomb," the dealer offered. "That wall may have still been intact then."

"No, I have a feeling the painting disintegrated centuries ago," he said, bending down to pick up his bag.

Having put the money in a desk drawer, al Qabek moved to see him to the door. "So your cause is lost?"

"Oh no, I'll keep looking. I may go look at these ruins myself to see if there are other panels I can use."

"No, you mustn't," Hameel said a little too quickly. "I mean, it's much too dangerous," he covered more calmly. "My photographer said the stonework was in very bad condition. He feared for his safety the whole time he was inside, and there are guards. My man had to sneak in and risk arrest as well."

Silas acted as though he hadn't noticed al Qabek's clumsy apprehensions and decided to play along. "Thank you for the warning. I'll be sure to keep it in mind. Now if you'll excuse me, it seems I have much work to do." He held out his gloved steel hand and al Qabek shook it.

"Good luck to you, sir," he concluded, sounding relieved by Silas's agreeability.

·   ·   ·

The white-haired magician sighed and rubbed his temples. Sitting at the desk in his hotel room, he looked with tired disappointment from one item before him to the next. The photograph of Royarna's writing had been faked. Hameel al Qabek, whose business card sat next to the photograph, was a man forced to act against his will. Lastly, he looked at the map of the tomb digs, a place that would be a trap if he went there. He sighed again and, with practiced fluidity, scooped up the Tarot card spread and put the deck away.

To think clearly and get away from the maddening three pieces of paper, he walked out onto the balcony and looked up at the moon and stars. A deep chestful of the cool desert air did nothing but assault him with the smell of burning wood that hung over the city from the day's violence. "O Egypt!" he said softly to himself. "How I long to bring you back to your former glory."

Why had he not foreseen the obstacles his adversary had put in his path since he began this quest? Clearly his precautions to keep his research and preparations secret all these many years had worked. But now, with the visit to Osiris, his enemy knew without a doubt what he was after. Still, he should have seen these stumbling blocks coming. Was Faen-ka capable of putting obstacles in his path that even the cards could not see? Now he was being led into the petty personal entanglements of a slimy little art dealer. Unfortunately, knowing who was responsible did nothing to help him overcome the barriers.

He looked at his watch and, knowing sleep would not come easily this evening, decided to retire early. He didn't know what might try to stop him tomorrow, but surely he could face it better with a few hours of sleep.

•   •   •

The next incline sent the rear of the Land Cruiser fishtailing around like a one-oared rowboat despite the clawing attack the knobbed tires made on the sand to find traction. Turning the wheels into the side-slip and downshifting even further, Silas brought the jeep under control halfway down the slope. When he reached the bottom, he considered how easy it would be to characterize the 120-degree heat and the unforgiving arid terrain as a version of hell. The notion of having to travel to hell to pursue a demon struck him as amusingly appropriate.

An hour east of the ancient city of Thebes he found his destination. The tomb was closer than the map had led him to expect. He slammed on the brakes as he crested the edge of the rocky canyon and furtively looked around to see if he had been spotted. But there were no guards. As he drove up to the chain link and barbed wire fence, he wondered how much more of what al Qabek had told him was false.

After making short work of the padlocks with meter-long bolt cutters, Silas retrieved from the car his black bag and a tool he had once thought he'd never use again: a Weatherby hunting rifle. He paused and surveyed the landscape again but found no trace of human company.

The gaping maw of the excavated opening narrowed quickly to the dark, low-ceilinged throat of the outer corridor. The blue-white light of his neon lantern threw out a sphere of light that he moved down the square, smooth-walled painted hallway, step by step, while he examined the walls and ceiling for clues left for him by his own previous incarnation three thousand years before.

He cared little about the distant cousin of Ramses who once laid here. Section after section he read of the illustrated hieroglyphic text, ignoring the details of the man's boring life of luxury, looking for the reference he knew once was here.

Around a corner, in the hall to the long-ago looted treasure annex, he found the panel in al Qabek's photograph. Rather, he found what was left of it. The top layer of plaster just below the paint had been mixed improperly and had separated and peeled off, tearing the center of the text away. He compared it to the photo and realized the forgery had been expertly crafted in a darkroom.

Relieved to find the original unmolested, he opened his bag. He turned on a small voice-activated tape recorder and slipped it into his shirt pocket. Then he pulled out his Magus Crown, with its multi-colored metals and all-seeing eye. He kissed its crest and put it on. Lastly, he unclipped a canteen from his belt and opened it. After extracting his right hand from its metal case, he rinsed it with the sun warmed water. Facing the damaged text, he closed his eyes.

Silas stood there for a long moment, working his mind deeper and deeper into the sympathetic trance. He imagined himself as Royarna, working with his scribes, watching himself meticulously paint one glyph after another. He opened his eyes, but he did not see the neon-illuminated wall. He reached up and gently began tracing the missing symbols with his hypersensitive hand, speaking aloud what he felt without allowing his consciousness to interfere with the words that flowed from his lips in the ancient Egyptian language. When he was done, he began the long walk back to consciousness, through the centuries, until he again saw himself standing by his electric light.

Something was wrong. He heard nothing, but he clairvoyantly felt the presence of another. He unslung the rifle from his shoulder as he ran around to the main corridor.

Looking out the length of the main entrance corridor, Silas instantly understood the man's intention as he crouched down over a small metal box on the far side of the narrow canyon. To steady the barrel of the left-handed rifle, Silas had to grab the gun with his naked hypersensitive right hand. It took every ounce of self-denying concentration Silas could summon to ignore the staggering, searing pain that lanced all the way up his arm. In the brilliant sunlight outside, the glint of purple in the man's eyes was unmistakable.

His forehead exploded long before the sound of Silas' shot reached him, but not before the message had already left the man's brain and depressed his thumb on the detonator.

Silas's view of the world vanished in a deafening torrent of dust. He ran back into the recesses of the tomb ahead of the billowing cave-in cloud. He grabbed a kerchief and pressed it over his nose and mouth. Rounding the corner, the cloud overtook him, and he had to stand there with his eyes closed in the dark, waiting for the air to clear. The sounds of falling rock behind him went on for a dishearteningly long time. When he ventured a glimpse, and saw the dust had settled enough to see and breathe, he sat down and sighed.

He arrested the growing anger and frustration that threatened to choke off his objectivity. He was convinced that only through strict adherence to his quest could he see the opportunities to succeed. He decided the task of escaping was a lower priority, and returned to his work. He tied the kerchief around his face and tried to ignore the taste of dirt that filled his every breath. He took off his Magus Crown and dropped it into his bag. He replaced the metal glove on his still throbbing hand before rewinding the tape recorder. Translating from the ancient Egyptian, he pieced together the entire panel's text:

May the Ka of Nocutautan fly freely to and from this place, may the Ba of Nocutautan be seen and heard by men, may Nocutautan always speak clear and true that he may be admitted through all the gates of heaven. The body of Nocutautan is made ready for his visitation in this the fifth year since Great Horus-Ramses has shed his wings and become Great Osiris-Ramses. In this year the condemned one whose name may not be written has still not been found in the lands above the Cataracts to where he fled after his betrayal. Royarna, High Priest of Amun to Great Horus-Ramses, has given Nocutautan what keys are remembered of Aeth, that he may command greater mastery in the Land of the Dead. May Nocutautan, in whom flowed the blood of the gods, rejoice with his cousin, Great Osiris-Ramses, and may he always be welcome in the Great Hall.

Silas beamed. Though disappointed at having to extend his quest on yet another leg, finding that he had, as Royarna, actually seen the Tablets meant he would recognize them, maybe even remember them, as soon as Faen-ka's barriers were broken. This put Silas closer to his objective than he had thought. With renewed enthusiasm he got to his feet and reached for his bag.

Dressed in his complete evocational attire, Silas Alverado stood barefoot within his chalk-drawn circle on the sealed tomb's stone floor and smiled a pleasant greeting at the coalesced spirit held within the summoning triangle.

"It is good to see you again, Bebait," he said telepathically.

"The honor is mine, Your Grace." The man-sized praying mantis tilted her head down and swiveled forward on her four hip joints to bow to the human. "If I may say so, I find it most delightful that I may be able to serve our Highest Priest after such a long respite, and on consecrated ground, no less!"

"I had a feeling you would appreciate the beauty of this circumstance, o Guider into the House of the King, given your love of orderly things."

She bowed again, saying, "Your Holiness flatters me with titles. What may I do for you?"

"Kheprera scarabs." Silas pointed past the summoned god at the cave-in at the end of the hall. "I need some earth moved."

As Bebait shuffled her feet to turn around in the triangle, the magician noted how her shiny, green plated body and wings glistened, not from the light of Silas's lantern, but from the unseen light source above the apparition, the Akasha light of heaven.

"More elegant yet!" the god intoned mentally. She turned back to the old man with a grandiose flourish of her huge serrated claws and insisted, "It will be a pleasure to do such a thing."

She then folded them in front of her thorax and lowered her head, which made her look even more like she was praying. Bebait stood motionless for several seconds while she did her work on the astral and mental planes. At last she requested, "I will need your will power to bring them across."

"Of course," Silas agreed knowingly and held out his sculpted amber wand.

The wand was carved to form two snakes wrapped around one another, eating the tail of the other at the ends. He concentrated and smiled with his kind blue eyes and a single shiny black dung beetle solidified within the translucent wand, floated to its surface, broke the surface, pulled free, and dropped to the floor, leaving the wand unmarked. As soon as the first one cleared the wand's surface, another appeared to take its place. Silas concentrated harder and soon there were two appearing at a time, then three, and so on, until the entire foot length of the carved rod was continuously covered with them. Within minutes they were falling to his feet in a steady stream. Most of them scuttled around aimlessly while some found Silas's feet interesting. He ignored the pricking sensation of their spiny little claws as they poked among his toes and clawed up around his ankles. He pushed harder and formed a flood of the hard, black bodies. They piled up around his legs and out over his hand and arm. Soon they were climbing on the fabric of his robe, both inside and out.

When Silas had brought in a sufficient army, the mantis god opened her huge green claws and made a sweeping gesture toward the cave-in. As one, the horde swept down off the human's body and back out from the interior of the tomb to where they had wandered. With an audibly violent scrabbling, the beetles attacked the mound like hundreds of tiny drill bits.

Silas lowered his wand, and Bebait turned back to face him, awaiting his next command.

"I think I shall let them be when I am done with them," the magician announced.

"A most wise decision, o Highest Priest. Let them die a natural death here in the desert and return to the Land of the Dead from whence I retrieved them." The rationale was given with an undeniably maternal tone.

"It pleases me that you agree. You have done me a great favor, one which I will not forget."

"Nor will I forget your kindness." She bowed again, offering formally, "We move together in the same cycle."

"Yes, we do. Return now to the fields of Sekhet-Hetepu. The triangle no longer binds you."

Out of long practice, Silas's grip automatically tightened around the dagger in his left hand in case something went wrong as the dimensional barriers opened and the spirit faded away. He relaxed when he felt he was alone.

Within the hour the tiny black army reduced the blockage enough to allow spears of sunlight and trickles of fresh air into Silas' prison. Seeing how tirelessly they obeyed the god's command and not wanting to confuse the mindless creatures by intervening, he decided not to help them. He passed the time reviewing the entirety of his plan.

As the space above the rubble grew, though, his thoughts turned more and more to settling his differences with Hameel al Qabek. He had warned the Egyptian, yet he had acted against Silas anyway. This was a matter of honor. Even though he was far behind schedule, it was still unthinkable not to punish such insolence. His position as a Master of Creation demanded it. An hour later, when Silas stepped out into the fading twilight, his eyes flashed blue fire and his face was painted with the shadows of anger and grim determination.

•   •   •

The magician's face remained coolly expressionless as he surveyed his ransacked hotel room. He knew he'd get no help from the hotel. He had very little luggage to go through, so the thieves had probably only been here a few minutes. The police would be a waste of time. In such a strife ridden city, a case like this wouldn't rate a high enough priority for them to even take a report. Besides, Silas already knew who had robbed him.

He walked directly to the bathroom and examined his shaving kit. Indeed, the false bottom had been discovered and his cash was gone. His passionless mask cracked as the muscles of his jaw knotted. Murdering a man and then robbing him was as low as a creature could get in this world. If he had harbored any reservations about pursuing revenge, they were gone now.

He picked up the phone and dialed a familiar series of numbers.

The call didn't go through, and after a series of clicks a voice came of the line. "International operator," the bland female voice said in English.

Silas' voice was businesslike and pleasant, and showed no trace of the storm raging within him. "I'd like to place a call to Switzerland. Thank you."

While he awaited the connection, he pulled the two-year old telephone directory out of the desk drawer and flipped to "Photographers."

"Hello, Switzerland? Please connect me to the Royal Bank in Berne. No, just station to station will be fine. Thank you."

He glanced through the listings until he found one claiming surveying capability.

"*Allo, Banque Royal? Directeur, s'il vous plait.*"

"Samir Dallafa," he read to himself. "Do I have a job for you."

•   •   •

Hameel al Qabek broke into a cold sweat when he saw the silver Rolls Royce pull up outside his office. For once he had the money, but that didn't stop his nerves from dancing on edge. He loathed everything about Raghashi, and tonight he was taking the first step toward ridding himself of the drug pusher's awful influence. The art dealer was halfway to his door when the knock came. Before he could reach it, though, the tall, extremely thin, pale skinned Arab arrogantly let himself in. He was accompanied by a man of equal height, but who must have weighed 300 pounds, all of it muscle.

"Ah, Mister Raghashi," he said with purposely strained courtesy. "Why don't you come on in?"

The tall man walked right past him. "I believe you have something for me," he said in a very low, very quiet rasping croak. He lowered his six-foot four frame straight down into one of the chairs without being asked.

The little man quickly stepped behind his desk but remained standing, trying to regain control of the situation.

"Yes I do. In fact, business has been very good. Not only do I have this week's payment, I have most of what I owe you from before."

The visitor reached up with one very long bony finger and stroked the humped blade of his nose that jutted out between his small, dark, close-set sunken eyes. "Where would such a payoff leave you?"

The loaded question didn't escape Hameel. He jumped at the opportunity.

"Free of you!" he sneered openly, leaning forward on his desk with straight arms.

"Oh," came the almost inaudible, totally unemotional response. "How is your lovely wife, anyway?"

"You know very well she's still hooked on your poison," he hissed.

"Yet you want to end our business?"

"Business is business," he stated flatly. "What I do about my wife's addiction after I've paid you off is none of your concern."

Raghashi held up a skeletal hand. "There is no need to raise your voice. As you said, business is business, and ours is private," he added, indicating the open window behind al Qabek.

The broker turned to it absentmindedly, insisting, "There's no one out there; we're on the second floor."

His attention was caught momentarily when he saw a man with a camera on a tripod across the street photographing Hameel's building. He dismissed it as inconsequential and turned back to his unwelcome guest.

"Say whatever you like. Money talks louder than any of your words." He took an envelope out of a drawer and slapped it down on the desk. "Go ahead, count it. It's all there — save fifteen hundred pounds and I'll have that by the weekend," he stated indignantly.

The tall, thin man slid the envelope off the desk and looked through its contents.

"You never thought you'd see that, did you?" Hameel gloated.

"One doesn't get over a heroin addiction like a bad cold," Raghashi rumbled without looking up from the cash. "Just because you get current with your payments doesn't mean our business is over."

"The hell it doesn't," the short man said through gritted teeth.

"We shall see," the pusher said as he slipped the money into his inside coat pocket and stood up. He turned at the door as he left and said, in all earnestness, "Allah be with you."

"May Allah piss on your grave!" Hameel called after him.

For the first time the art dealer had ever seen, Raghashi smiled a mouthful of perfect white teeth before his silent bodyguard closed the door behind them. It was not a pretty sight.

●   ●   ●

Seated at his hotel room desk, Silas looked up from his maps of East Africa and glanced at his watch when he heard the wailing evening prayers echoing from a nearby mosque. He hoped Samir Dallafa wasn't devout and hadn't stopped to bow to Mecca. Time was running short. Almost as if on cue, someone knocked on the door.

"Yes, who is it?" he called out in English.

"Uh, Mister Avadado?" came a very youthful, very unsure voice.

He opened the door and the bright faced young porter struggled to explain himself in extremely broken English. "Man … wanted … bring …"

"Yes, yes, is that for me?" Silas demanded in perfect Egyptian.

"Yes!" he said, obviously relieved. He handed the large envelope to Silas and continued. "The man wanted to bring it to you himself, but said you had told him not to come here, and so he gave it to me to bring to you."

Silas didn't know if the youth's prattling was an attempt to fatten the tip or just exuberance, nor did he care. He snatched the package from the boy, shoved a five-pound note into his hand and slammed the door in his face.

He cleared away the maps and went immediately to work setting up an array of items he had spent most of the day gathering: a smooth, hand-blown, lead crystal bowl, a matching platter, a small bag of plaster, a tin of denatured alcohol, a bottle of purified water, and an artist's precision knife. He slipped the stack of enlarged photographs from the envelope and read Dallafa's note.

Thank you for what must be the most demanding, yet fascinating job I've ever done. I didn't think my equipment was accurate enough to enlarge or reduce all the views to exactly the same scale, but I think you'll be pleased with the results. All in all, I think hiring the airplane for the top shot on such short notice was the most difficult. Thank you again. I enjoyed the challenge, not to mention the chance to earn such a generous fee. If you ever have any other jobs in Cairo, please remember me.

Silas looked at the five photographs and smiled. They were perfect. One of them even had al Qabek looking out of his window. Silas took up the knife and started cutting.

When he had trimmed the images down to the edges of the building, he lightly taped the pictures together, edge to edge, to form a box. He then took this model and the plaster into the bathroom and sealed the edges on the inside. Once the plaster was hard, he gingerly pulled the tape off the image faces. All the while he worked, he quietly recited litanies to himself, charging his simulacrum with the essence of the original building.

A few minutes later his preparations were done. The model sat on the platter, the pure water was in the bowl, the lights were out, and each of the two glass vessels were surrounded on the desktop by four lit black candles.

Silas began a different kind of work. He withdrew a small vial from his black bag and dripped four drops of pungently floral smelling yellow liquid into the water. He then withdrew his magical dagger and pricked the end of his left thumb and dripped four drops of his own blood into the bowl. Sitting down to face the bowl, he dipped in his left index finger, stirred it, and then ran his finger around the lip until it sang. He closed his eyes and let the clear ringing sound permeate his mind, let his mind become tuned to the vibration. He continued the dipping and stroking for several minutes before he opened his eyes. He tore open a small envelope of dirt he had collected from in front of Hameel's building late the night before, upon his return to Cairo. He poured the soil onto the platter around the photographic model and the candles flared.

The magician resumed sounding the bowl but this time he concentrated deeply on the surface of the water. The microscopic ripples threw reflections into his eyes, reflections that congealed to become images. As the images clarified, the harmonics of the bowl's tone wavered and became voices.

Hameel was in his office, walking quickly to his door, looking at his watch, a confused look on his face. He stepped back apprehensively as two very tall men, one sickly thin, the other built like an ox, moved commandingly into the room.

"Raghashi," al Qabek nearly gasped. "What are you doing here?"

"I've considered the offer you made me this morning. I'm here to renegotiate."

"And," the little man hesitated and looked furtively at the huge man, "Is he part of the new deal?"

At first Silas was apprehensive about killing these other men, but now it was obvious they were ultimately responsible for Hameel's deceit. He decided to watch further.

As the art dealer retreated behind his desk, the phone rang. He grabbed up the receiver like an escape hatch. "Hello, yes. Oh, hi. What!?" His face blanched and his eyes shot wide. "No, it can't be. How? Oh God, no." He slumped into his chair and grabbed his forehead with his free hand. "Oh God, what have I done?" he asked no one in particular. "Yes, yes," he returned to the person on the phone. "No, I don't know what to do next," he barked, his voice cracking. "Yes, all right. Goodbye."

"What's that all about?" Raghashi asked dispassionately.

Hameel pulled out a handkerchief and mopped his glistening brow. "Nothing, family business," he dismissed, muttering at his desktop. Looking up at his would-be assailants, he asked in an honestly pathetic voice, "Could we discuss this later? I really have to be alone for a while."

"Absolutely not," he stated flatly. "How do I know that call wasn't planned to get me out of here?"

The little man frowned indignantly. "Because I had no idea you were coming by."

"Not good enough. You either tell me what that call was, or we get back to business."

"All right," he said, screwing in his courage. "All right, I'll tell you. That money I gave you today? It belongs to a man I cheated yesterday. I sent my brother-in-law to stop him from uncovering my fraud, but apparently he got carried away and tried to kill my customer. Well guess what? My wife's brother is now dead, and this man is free. You don't have to worry about doing business with me anymore. You're talking to a dead man," he spat passionately.

"Just how dangerous is this man? I could kill him for you, for a price," the drug dealer offered with characteristic coolness.

"Ha!" Hameel blurted out nervously. "Akbar buried him under a mountainside, and he still got out! He told me that if I crossed him he would hit me like the wrath of God. Go ahead, stay here," he insisted broadly. "I'd love for you to meet him."

"What's that ringing sound?" the giant muscled man spoke up.

"What? I don't hear anything," Raghashi dismissed him.

"No, wait," the big man insisted. "It sounds like an air raid."

"I hear it too," Hameel agreed. "Only it's too high pitched for an air raid." He turned to the open window and listened. "It's getting louder."

"I hear it now also," the thin man commented. He started to waive his hand as if to get back to business, but he halted when the sound grew much louder. "It's coming from all around the building," he observed, worry creeping into his usually overcomposed voice.

Silas continued circling the bowl with his left hand while he popped open the tin of alcohol with his mechanical right and poured it into the platter.

The sound was now so loud the men had to yell to hear one another. "Let's get out of here!" Raghashi demanded and headed for the door.

Silas lit a match and dropped it on the platter.

The thin man howled as his palm seared and stuck to the suddenly red-hot doorknob. He ripped it free of the smoking flesh and shot Hameel a look of terror that made the little man squeal with joy.

"It's him! It's Silas!" he screamed with glee.

An instant later, though, his expression matched his enemy's. The entire outside of the building exploded spontaneously into flames.

"Don't just stand there!" Raghashi yelled at his man. "Kill him and kick open the door!"

But before anyone could move, their zippers, watches and rings all flashed white hot and ignited clothing or melted into flesh. The bullets in the gun the thug pulled out exploded inside the weapon, sending shrapnel into his face and chest. The metal buttons on Raghashi's linen suit sent a burst of flames up his front, setting his hair on fire.

Apparently so thrilled to see his tormentor in such agony, Hameel acted as if his own pain were insignificant. "Go ahead Alverado!" he screamed out. "Kill me! I welcome Allah's judgment!"

In an instant, the floor, walls and ceiling were all consumed in flames. Hameel just laughed maniacally as he watched Raghashi rolling about, futilely trying to put himself out.

Soon, Silas could hear the laughter no more, and all he could see was the reflection of the burning crumpled mass in the plate next to him. He stopped stroking the bowl and drowned the fire with the water.

That night he slept soundly.

9

FLIGHT

J OSEPH WAITED IN HIS RENTED WHITE FERRARI for the patient to leave Sanantha Mauwad's office. He assumed that her four o'clock session would be the last of the day, and that she would stay in her office for at least a few minutes past five to write up the session.

He had to force himself to sit calmly and contain the anger that had brought him to her office. He had the heater turned on to make himself more comfortable. The snow was coming down lightly but steadily outside. He had no trouble ignoring the cold, and he didn't like the restriction of an overcoat. But he definitely preferred heat.

He also calmed himself with the distraction of getting in some reading. Having only been in this modern era for four years, he consumed news and information whenever he could. As much as his master eschewed electronic communications for security reasons, Joseph loved the access the Internet provided him. Wireless technology and subscriptions to every major news source and magazine in the world meant he could continue to fill in his understanding of his new world wherever and whenever he had a moment. His ability to see the truth of whatever he looked at also meant he could read articles as fast as they could be downloaded.

He had just finished a news story about a mysterious fire in an office building in Cairo when he heard the front door open across the street. He watched a petite blonde in a fox-trimmed leather coat walk down the three stairs from the small porch to the snow dusted sidewalk in front of the brick row building. Four fifty-six. He closed his laptop.

He made himself wait another five minutes to be sure no other patient was going to arrive, and to give the doctor time to organize herself. As he stepped up to the door, he could see it was locked. He rang the doorbell and faced the intercom box.

"Yes?" came her staticky answer.

"Hello. This is Joseph de Alverado. I was hoping I might have a moment of your time."

There was a meaningfully long silence. He had realized that a face-to-face meeting might make her uncomfortable. He also knew she would be more likely to speak with him if he were standing in the cold outside her door than if he left her a phone message. At least that's what he'd hoped.

"Mister de Alverado ... sure ... come on in," she finally said, and the lock buzzed open.

He stepped into the outer waiting room and brushed off the snow that had fallen on the shoulders of his steel gray suit. He noticed a small security camera in the corner of the ceiling.

She opened the door to her inner office and asked, "Is it snowing again?"

"Yes, it's been doing that right around sundown every day this week." As he crossed the room, he took note of how her yellow and brown striped turban matched the butter yellow of her business suit. "Thank you for seeing me unannounced like this. I was hoping this would be a good time for you."

They shook hands at her office door, but she did not invite him in. "Yes, I have a few minutes to spare."

"This may take more than just a moment," he suggested graciously.

Her eyebrows twitched and she pursed her full lips ever so slightly. "Oh, all right." She stepped back into her office and added, "Then won't you come in and have a seat." She seated herself behind her desk and Joseph took a facing chair. She rested her folded hands on the edge of her desk and smiled politely. "What can I do for you?"

"If you don't mind, I'll be blunt. Charles Redmond has decided he can no longer conduct business with me, for apparently personal reasons, and he is handing over my account to a group of importers. He has assured me that these gentlemen can accommodate my needs, but I have reason to believe that Charles has already tainted my relationship with this new group by sharing his feelings about me with them. I cannot very well ask these gentlemen what he has been saying about me, so I have come to you."

She frowned and shook her head slightly. "What do you think I could tell you about Charles?"

"I need to know what presumptions he harbors about me that would drive him to risk breach of contract. I have tried to talk to him about it, and he has become irrational, accusing me of preposterous acts and insulting my integrity. I appreciate that you maintain a professional confidence as to matters of his mental health. Frankly I don't care about his mental health. I need to know what he has been telling people about me."

She shook her head again and said, "I'm afraid patient confidentiality prevents me from repeating a single word of what Charles has told me. I appreciate your predicament, but you're going to have to get your information from some other source."

"You do understand that unless I get some comfort that my reputation has not been impugned, I will be forced to bring legal action against Charles for breach?"

"That's between you and Charles and his lawyers."

"I'm hoping it doesn't come to that. Whether as his counselor or as his counsel, I suggest you advise him to not share his irrational imaginings about me with anyone else."

The phone on her desk rang. "Will you excuse me? That's my front door." She picked up the receiver and punched a button. "Yes?" she asked the caller.

Her face went slack and had her skin not been such a dark shade of brown, Joseph was sure she would have blanched. He noted that she turned away from him and her eyes darted around on the floor next to her desk.

"Sure," she said. "Stay right there and I'll come and get it."

She hung up and started to get up. "I have a delivery," she said flatly. "Please excuse me for a moment."

Her reaction was so severe he thought to ask whether the caller had bad news, but her excusing herself was so controlled, it was clear she didn't want to share. "Of course. I'll wait here."

"Thank you," she said as she left her office and closed the door behind her.

This was not going well. Joseph folded his arms and wondered how he could convince her to influence Charles to not ruin anything further. Charles was dangerously close to figuring out that Joseph was not human, but as long as Charles kept it to himself, that information shouldn't interfere with Joseph's business. Surely the psychiatrist believed Charles' conclusions were irrational. Giving Charles rational explanations had failed to assuage him. Doctor Mauwad didn't seem to be able to contain him either. Maybe Charles was just too great a liability to keep around.

Joseph looked around her office and couldn't help but notice the brightly colored paintings of Haitian native dancers. He had seen on that first night in the restaurant that she was from the Caribbean, but he was a little taken aback at the coincidence of her being from Haiti.

He listened for her return and heard nothing, so he got up to better view the paintings. As he moved about the room, he noticed the glow of a television monitor on a shelf next to her desk. He recognized the bird's eye view of the outer waiting room from the security camera. He stepped closer.

Sanantha was at the front door, talking to a man in an overcoat who was standing on the front porch. The man's arm movements were agitated, and he wanted to come in. Sanantha clearly did not want him to. When he pushed past her, Joseph could see why. It was Charles. She shot a furtive look over her shoulder at the security camera, shook her head in resignation, and closed the door against the cold.

Lip reading came naturally to Joseph.

"Charles, I'm glad that your prayers have given you confidence, but that's no reason to act recklessly."

"This isn't reckless, this is righteous," he declared flatly. "I'm telling you Madame Erzulie agreed to protect me from Joseph. If he wasn't a demon, she wouldn't have agreed — she would have told me he wasn't a demon. With her protection, I can do more than just hide from him. I can take steps to ensure that whatever demonic plan he has fails. It is the duty of the righteous to take action against evil."

Sanantha glanced at the inner office door and stiffened her arms in growing impatience. "You came here for advice. I am advising you to step away from this. Protection from a god means you don't have to worry about a demon attacking you. Have you ever heard the phrase 'God helps them who help themselves?' If you take action against Joseph, then you will change the rules of the game. Did you tell Erzulie you were planning on attacking Joseph? No. You asked her for protection and in her grace, she granted it to you. Be thankful. Be jubilant. But don't go looking for trouble."

The fact that he didn't even take a breath to consider her words made it clear that he didn't want to be talked out of this. "I've got other evidence too. I just got word that one of my contacts in Egypt died under very suspicious circumstances over the weekend. Everyone is convinced that he had been dealing with supernatural forces."

"Egypt is in the midst of civil war," she countered. "The Middle East is full of superstitions. You have contacts all over the world. Just because someone you know died doesn't mean a thing. What does Egypt have to do with you or Joseph anyway?"

"Don't you get it? I guess I never mentioned that part. All of the artifacts that Joseph has me collecting from around the world are privately held items from ancient Egypt."

"I'll admit that is an interesting coincidence, but nothing more." She shook her head and shrugged her shoulders. "Clearly nothing I'm saying is having any impact, is it?"

"How can I convince you that I've got this figured out?" he fired back.

"I guess neither of us is going to convince the other of anything tonight." She again glanced at the inner door. She took Charles' arm and led him to the outer door. "You have got to go now. I told you I've got someone waiting in the other room."

"But you said it's not a patient, right?"

She frowned at him and insisted, "That doesn't matter. We can resume this tomorrow. I'll move your appointment up and see you tomorrow afternoon."

"If you'd seen the things I've seen in the last twenty-four hours ..." he lamented.

She opened the front door and escorted him into it. "We can talk about this tomorrow," she insisted. "I'm sorry to cut you off like this, but I've got to get back to my guest."

"Don't bother," Joseph said ominously from the open inner office door.

Sanantha and Charles turned to look down the barrel of the silenced nine-millimeter pistol Joseph had leveled at them. Charles was stunned stock still. Sanantha turned and plowed into Charles' chest as the gun went off with three quick tight pops. The first bullet tore through Sanantha's high turban. Charles had his hand on the doorknob as the two of them fell through the doorway, and the other two bullets slammed into the edge of the closing door.

The two of them stumbled down the front stairs and ran across the street to hide behind a white Ferrari parked there. Charles pulled out his cell phone and punched in 911. As he waited for it to connect, he blurted at her, "Why the hell didn't you tell me Joseph was in there?"

She shook her head as she peeked over the car's hood at her still closed office door. "I didn't want to upset you that I was talking to the enemy, and I didn't want to tip him off that you were outside."

She turned back to Charles and was terrified to see Joseph standing on the sidewalk not fifteen feet away from them, bringing up his pistol to fire. Before she could scream an alarm, Joseph's aim was ruined as two bullets ripped into his chest from somewhere behind the car.

She and Charles dove around in front of the car to maintain cover. She looked past the car and saw two men in dark glasses and black parkas closing on Joseph with pistols drawn. "Central Intelligence, stand down where you are!" one of them yelled.

Joseph didn't seem affected by his wounds, and he returned fire on the men at close range, which didn't seem to slow them down either. Joseph sprang on the man closest to him, knocking the man's gun away, but this left Joseph wide open. The other man stepped in and delivered a bone crushing high kick to Joseph's throat.

To the amazement of both the onlookers and the CIA agents, this did not faze Joseph in the least, but only knocked his sunglasses off.

As if stunned by some paralysis, the kicker's arms fell defenselessly limp at his sides as Joseph hauled back and launched a roundhouse left that annihilated his head and sent bloody bone fragments, brains and teeth spraying across the snow-covered sidewalk. The body arched up off the ground as if trying to follow its head and landed on its back with a limp thud next to Sanantha and Charles.

The other man had retrieved his pistol and opened fire on Joseph. Unfortunately, the five bullets he put into Joseph's back did little to slow him down. He spun on his assailant and fired one very accurately placed round right in the man's forehead.

To Sanantha's wide-eyed horror, Charles picked up the decapitated man's gun and advanced on Joseph. As Joseph turned back to finish the job, he was finally caught off guard. Charles fired the revolver at point blank range into Joseph's face. The .38 slug threw him back, but Charles kept firing, following his backward stagger, scoring as many head shots as he could manage.

The two of them were out in the street when the gun ran out. By then Joseph's face was mostly torn off, with only one eye and a piece of jaw still intact, yet he was still on his feet! Sanantha saw Charles go stiff when he realized how defenseless he was, and how he couldn't be sure his attack had done any good.

Finally, Joseph stumbled, paused, and shook his gore dripping head as if to clear it. He then turned and stomped to the white Ferrari and climbed in. Sanantha jumped up onto the sidewalk as he drove off.

The car was completely out of view before Sanantha's breathing slowed from its ragged racing. She hastily said a prayer of thanks and crossed herself several times. She looked over at Charles who was standing in the middle of the street looking at the empty revolver in his hand.

Then she saw the old woman standing across the street. She hardly noticed her, except that it seemed odd that she hadn't run away from all the gunfire. She made eye contact just as the woman turned to walk casually away. It must have been a trick of the light, but Sanantha could have sworn she had a purple glint in her eye.

Charles staggered over to Sanantha with a giddy half-smile on his face. "I thought I was a goner," he said between heaving breaths.

Sanantha surveyed the scene and had to look away from the headless man. She shook her head, not able to take it all in. "I never would have believed it. You were right all along."

The sound of approaching sirens grabbed their attention. "We've got to get out of here," Charles instantly decided.

Sanantha was shocked. "I don't understand. We haven't done anything wrong. Don't you want to give Joseph's description to the police? You can't just leave the scene of a crime like this."

"The police can't stop Joseph. He just proved that. We don't know how long those wounds are going to slow him down, but I'd rather not have him recover while you and I are tied up filling out police reports. We got lucky with these CIA agents tailing me. Joseph only failed this time because he was acting on the fly with no plan. He'll have a plan next time. We need to get some real help, and real fast."

She was taken aback by how easily Charles handled such combat strategy. "What do you have in mind?"

"Do you know a *houngan* locally?"

Her eyebrows shot up again. She started to object, but then thought better of it. Maybe a priest was what they needed. "No, I don't belong to an *oumphor* here in Washington."

He shook his head. "Neither do I. We may have to travel." By now the sirens were very close. "What we really need to do is leave here now. That's my car," he said pointing to the blue BMW across the street.

· · ·

Silas Alverado pocketed his change from the hotel check-out counter, picked up his bags, turned toward the door, and stopped dead in his tracks. He dropped his suitcase and whipped his flesh and blood left hand up to closely inspect his silver pinky ring. The stone in the ring was still red, but it was cold, and getting colder by the second. His jaw and lips tightened as he snatched up the fallen case and strode across the tile lobby floor to the pay phone.

After withdrawing one of the polished copper mirrors from his black bag and setting it on the writing ledge, Silas propped the receiver against his ear with his shoulder but held the hook down inconspicuously with his hand. He focused on the shiny metal surface and calmed himself of his anxiety. Though he tried to ignore it, the ring stayed very cold.

A long moment passed and still he felt no contact, no reception of the thoughts he poured into the mirror. Finally, he sensed the slightest give and he pushed even harder. When he was sure he felt a grasp on the other end, he held the mirror up to the number on the front of the phone. "Cairo," he said softly. "Call this number in Cairo, Egypt."

Joseph, parked in an alley in Washington DC, felt a familiar ping in his mind and struggled to become alert. He blinked furiously until he could see, then straightened himself in the blood drenched leather car seat. He concentrated as best he could to hear the message he knew would follow. When he heard nothing, he assumed it was due to his own condition. Hoping his master had chosen to make it easier for him, Joseph tilted the rear-view mirror at himself and tried to concentrate on that. Much to his relief, the image wavered and became a phone number. It was accompanied by a distant, though recognizable deep voice telling him the city. He grabbed his cell phone and dialed.

Silas peripherally noticed someone standing behind him. He glanced back and the man stepped up, asking politely, "Will you be long?"

"I'm on hold," the old man answered tersely. As he turned back to the phone, it rang. The man gave him a confused look and wandered out of the lobby. Silas ignored him except to be sure he was gone. "Joseph? What's wrong?"

"I underestimated the enemy, Master, on several counts." His usually controlled manner was deliriously conversational, and he was barely able to form words with his mouth ripped open. "I've been shot, but I'll recover. I guess I overestimated this human body you chose for me," he added groggily.

"You sound terrible," Silas observed with great concern. "Just how badly did you damage it?"

"My biggest problem seems to be lack of mental coherence. Lack of oxygen to the brain from blood loss, I guess. The lungs probably aren't working very well, either, given how much blood is in them. I soon as I get my ... focus back ... I'll heal the body straight away."

"Who shot you?" Silas asked dispassionately.

"Charles Redmond!" Joseph blurted drunkenly. "Sorry, I didn't mean to raise my voice." He paused a moment as if to gather his composure, but didn't succeed. "He and his psychiatrist both turn out to be Voodou practitioners, and they figured out I'm not human," he cackled. "When they made the connection to Egypt, I figured, enough is enough. I tried to kill them, but somehow, and I haven't figured out how, he managed to get the drop on me. Blew my whole face off!"

Silas ignored his servant's demeanor, and analyzed what must have transpired. "You said they made the connection to Egypt. Have they learned of my efforts to convert the Haitians?"

"Oh, no, no, no. I mean they know *I'm* Egyptian." He interrupted himself and added uncertainly, "Or maybe not. I'm not sure how much they know, but I can assure you they know nothing of your activities in Haiti. In fact, they know nothing of you at all. I can't express how sorry I am for losing control of the situation."

"I'll think of an appropriate punishment when the time comes," he said calmly. "Your predicament may not be forgivable, but it is understandable." His usually kind blue eyes squinted down as his gaze wandered across the hotel lobby to the morning sun out on the street. "You see, I too have met with greater resistance than anticipated. My senses and my guides have all shown me a clear path, yet time after time I have had to improvise and take longer than expected." He paused to decide on the right words to use. "I am certain this is due to intervention. My adversary in this matter has clearly deduced my objective. This means he will stand in your way as well, Joseph. You must be prepared for the unexpected."

"An adversary," Joseph repeated quietly to himself. "Master, I didn't know we had an adversary."

"I know that, Joseph. I'm telling you now so you will be better prepared. Is there anything else to report?"

"Only that in a month you're going to get a very large billing on your credit card for the upholstery in this rented car. It seems blood stains leather very effectively."

"In two months, we won't have to concern ourselves with such petty matters. With any luck, I will wrap up my work here in about two weeks. Meet me on the *Purgatory* at that time. Goodbye until then."

"Goodbye Mas—" Joseph caught himself. "… Mister Alverado."

Silas rolled his eyes as he hung up the phone

•   •   •

Sanantha paced up and down the length of Charles' living room while he made a series of phone calls. "I am still not convinced this is a good idea," she insisted. "We flee the scene of a crime, you're being shadowed by the CIA, and now you're making arrangements for us to leave the country under cover of darkness before the authorities connect us to the shooting. Why do I feel like a criminal here? I'm the one with the bullet hole in my turban," she indicated by poking her finger in the hole.

Throughout her tirade, Charles listened while continuing to make calls. He was on hold at the moment.

"I am not happy about having my entire life uprooted like this," she continued. "I mean, I can't even go back to my house for clothes or my passport. It's a good thing I'm single, but I can't even call my friends and tell them where I'm going."

He put his hand over the receiver. "Not unless you want them to call the authorities we are trying to elude."

"When did you stop being my patient and become my cohort in crime?" she added.

"Right about the time the bullets began flying and you realized I've been delirious, not delusional."

She stopped pacing and turned to face him with one eyebrow pushed down and her fists on her hips.

"Don't give me that look. You know I'm very sorry I dragged you into this. But the fact is, we know he's a demon, and he doesn't want us to live with that knowledge. I'm afraid you don't get to walk away from this." He checked the phone again. "Hello? Still on hold. We went through this. Neither of us has belonged to an *oumphor* in years, and the only *houngan* either of us trusts with this is your old priest in Haiti. Believe me, if there was anywhere else we could go for help, I'd be the first to endorse it." He then returned to his phone conversation, and Sanantha returned to her pacing.

Her attention wandered to a couple of photographs he had displayed on top of his television. They showed Charles posing with various black men she didn't recognize. On the other hand, she did recognize the building in one background and the dockside in the other as being in Port au Prince, Haiti. So much for Charles' original claim of having not traveled there.

Charles had hung up. "Well, we're all set," he announced tiredly. "We've got a cargo plane out of BMI in an hour that will take us to Miami. Your traveling papers will be ready for us when we arrive. From there we take the local carrier to Port au Prince."

She sat down in the chair next to the couch where he sat. "Okay, so I'm supposed to believe all this cloak-and-dagger is just part of being in the import-export business. That just because you work with people who move cargo around the globe, you can pick up the phone and spirit someone out of the country with fake ID. Ditto for why the CIA follows you around."

He pressed his lips together and frowned at her for a second. "Isn't it more important that I can do these things, that I can get us safely away from Joseph and to somewhere we can get the kind of help we need? I admit I haven't completely leveled with you about my past." Almost reflexively, he checked his fingernails. "But the truth is, and I mean the whole truth, is that I work with people who have very shady connections. I am calling in all the favors I have to be able to do this. I agree it looks bad, but I can assure you my ability to do this should not be a reason to distrust me."

She looked at him for a long, thoughtful moment. Then her gaze wandered around the black contemporary rug that covered most of the hardwood floor of his living room. She blinked a few times, shook her head and sighed. "I'm sorry to take this out on you." She squinted at him. "I can deal with your past. You certainly aren't the first patient to hide things from me. But you need to realize how much trust I am being forced to put in you. I have to suddenly abandon my whole life to go take care of this."

She frowned at him with renewed intensity. "Before this went down, I was hoping that, even if he was evil, that maybe he had just crossed your path, that he wasn't necessarily after you. But now it looks like, whatever you did in the past, it has prompted someone to send a demon to exact revenge on you."

She rolled her eyes, sighed and shook her head. "I'm having a hard enough time wrapping my mind around what we're seeing here. I mean, seriously, an incarnate demon? I have always taken comfort that the Loas were watching over me. I'm actually a big believer in the grand design of coincidences. I left Haiti convinced that Psychology would show me why people believe in the supernatural so completely that they act to fulfill their own worst fears. I thought you were the perfect example. And now Joseph turns out to be the real thing!" She held her cheeks with her hands. "This goes way beyond thanking a god for a lucky break. We're talking about breaking the laws of physics. He had what, seven or eight bullets in him? How is that possible?"

Charles raised his eyebrows high on his forehead. "So, the scientist in you is having an ecclesiastical crisis?"

"You're damned right I am."

"Well, you said you believe in divine intervention in coincidences. How about the fact that I, who happened to be chased by a *l'alouby*, accidentally ended up with you as my doctor, you who have a lifelong faith in Voodou?"

She chuckled nervously and shook her head. "You're right. It looks like the gods have been working on us all along."

"When you were in Haiti, did you hold a religious position that we can leverage when we get back there?"

"You mean my post in the village *oumphor*? I don't know how much mileage we can get out of it, but by the time I left my village at age seventeen, I was the Head Flag Mistress."

"That's nothing to scoff at. Where is your village?"

"North coast, about thirty miles inland from Cap Haiten, little place called Seranada. I haven't been there in twenty-five years."

"Well, I hope your priest can figure out who created Joseph."

"Only the most powerful magicians can create *l'aloubies*, so there can't be that many candidates. The whole point of sending a *l'alouby* is for the victim to know who is inflicting the punishment. You still have no idea who could have sent Joseph after you?"

He looked her square in the eye and said, "No. I wish I did."

•   •   •

Charles found himself standing waist deep in a calm warm lagoon. The sun shone down hot from a clear blue sky, and a soft breeze blew in from the dark blue-green sea. The palm trees beyond the narrow white sand beach and the dense jungle brush beneath the trees rustled lazily in the wind. The air was a swirl of the smells of salt and seaweed blowing in from offshore, and flowers and rotting plant life wafting out from onshore.

He knew he was dreaming, but he was so glad to not be having a nightmare, and the sensations were all so vivid that he smiled, sighed hugely and took it all in. He started to walk ashore and noticed that his legs dragged through seagrass on the lagoon bottom. The gentle slithering resistance of the grass around his bare legs was tantalizing.

When he looked down at the grass, he saw that the water all around him was cloudy reddish brown. He quickly checked his body to see if he was bleeding, but his skin was intact. On the other hand, his cutoff jeans, the only clothes he wore, were blood smeared. He frowned in confusion, and continued to shore.

As he walked, he smelled something out of place. He sniffed again and identified it as burning wood. He looked down the beach and saw the smoldering remains of a thatched hut village. The buildings looked familiar, but he couldn't pin down from where. He thought he had been here before. Had that been in real life, or was it in a previous dream? He looked around and the impression grew by the moment that he had been on this beach before.

An inhuman howl far off in the jungle shattered his musings. He turned reflexively to place it better. It sounded again, this time closer, and clearly coming from down the beach. He slogged up onto the beach as quickly as the seaweed would allow, watching the shore for any signs of the sound's origin.

He glanced back toward the village site, wondering if he would need this escape route, and he saw a little girl staggering out of the ruins coming down the beach. Her white dress, torn and dirty though it was, still shone brightly in the sun and contrasted starkly with her dark brown skin.

The howl pealed again, this time close enough and loud enough to drown out the wind in the leaves and the din of insects in the jungle.

Charles shot one last look down the beach toward the sound, and made up his mind. He ran to the girl, scooped her up in his arms, and fled into the village. Her pigtails bounced wildly as he loped through the sand.

Once off the beach, he had to watch his step with his bare feet, as the pathways were strewn with shattered bamboo and smoldering thatch. The pungent smell of burning wood was tainted with the stench of burning flesh. He came across a wounded old man who was being tended by his wife, and the two recoiled from him at his approach.

"You have to leave!" he insisted in Haitian Creole. "Something terrible is coming and you must go."

But they wouldn't listen, and only scuttled back into the shell that was what remained of their house, eyeing him fearfully. Why did they fear him?

The little girl had been crying the whole time, but now she began to scream. He looked over his shoulder, afraid that she would attract whatever was approaching. Then he noticed the blood. Her white dress was covered in huge bright red blotches, some of them hand shaped — his hand shaped. He looked at his hands to see if he was bleeding, but he wasn't. Then he realized to his horror that she was bleeding where he touched her.

"Put her down."

The voice was too deep to be human. It was as if a lion were speaking with its roar and it was right behind him.

Charles whirled and stopped cold. Joseph, as he had always appeared in Charles' dreams, stood muscularly hunched over, threateningly flexing his clawed hands and his leathery wings. His body was covered in steel gray scales, with two long curving horns protruding from his forehead, and hooves instead of feet. His whip-like tail lashed behind him. Across the bridge of his boar snout sat his ever-present wraparound semi-mirrored sunglasses.

Charles twisted around to hold the girl away from him, insisting, "You can't have her."

Pointing accusingly, the demon fired back, "You're the one killing her." Then with a sweep of his hand he added, "And all of these people."

Charles set the girl down behind him and she ran deeper into the village. While he was bent over, he snatched up a length of lumber. He spun back around and broke the makeshift bat across Joseph's ribs, screaming, "I have repented for my sins!" As Joseph doubled over from the blow, Charles spotted another suitable piece of wood behind his enemy. As he ran around to grab it, he insisted, "I don't need the likes of you to make me pay any further."

He planned on driving home his point with another swing, but he didn't get the chance. Joseph recovered quicker than Charles planned, and the demon caught him full in the chest with an uppercut that sent Charles up over the burned-out huts, through the fronds of the jungle canopy, out over the beach, and into the ocean.

Charles was so overcome by the searing pain in his chest, the sensation of his ribcage having been squashed like a pumpkin, that he was only barely aware of the air whistling past him, or that he was indeed airborne. Just as he realized he was falling back down, he impacted the surface of the water with such stunning force that he lost track of up or down, and floated limply under the surface. Even if his chest could function, which he doubted, Joseph's blow had driven all the air out of him, and now he was underwater. As his daze from the splashdown cleared, it was replaced by panicked realization. He was quite sure he was about to die, but he couldn't make his body respond to do anything about it.

When he felt someone grab him by the arm and start to haul him up, he was sure it was Joseph coming to deliver the coup de grace. He managed to open his eyes and saw a rope looped around his arm. He looked up and saw the bottom of a boat. As he neared the surface, he saw a fishing net hanging over the side and he clawed his way up it. He was pleasantly surprised that his lungs still worked when he broke the surface. Encouraged to find that his arms still had strength, he dragged himself up into the boat.

It was a sailing sloop, but larger than he had ever seen. He started to take in the size and details of the rigging, when he was utterly distracted by the boat's only occupant.

Standing at the stern with the rudder in her hand, stood Madame Erzulie herself. Towering over seven feet tall, she was dressed in a gossamer white floor-length sarong, wrapped up around her long torso and full bosom halter style. Her hair was a column wound of impossibly long thick braids that mirrored the shape of a high turban. The height of her hair and the arm-lengthening appearance of her bare shoulders made her look even taller and more regal. Her skin was the color and smoothness of melted dark chocolate, and although her nose and lips were broad, her features were long and aquiline. She turned her head to look down upon him and smiled. The pain in his chest dissolved away in the gaze of her solid black eyes.

Charles didn't want to insult her by staring, but he was rapt and couldn't take his eyes off of her. He bent down to prostrate himself, when he caught sight of Joseph flying up out of the jungle toward the boat. Charles was taken by the sharp contrast between the grace of the goddess' form and movements and the lurching of Joseph's bat-like flight. Charles grabbed an oar and met the demon at the prow where he landed.

"I've been saved by my goddess. I have no reason to fear you any longer," he snarled.

"I don't care who fishes your carcass out of the sea," Joseph roared back. "I've got a job to do, and you're it!"

Joseph sprang on him so fast that he barely had time to get the oar up to defend himself. Joseph swatted past the oar and slashed him painfully down the outside of the arm with his claws, but Charles managed to swing the butt end around and jab Joseph sharply in the face. Joseph hammered down with the elbow of a wing and broke the oar in half in Charles' hands. Charles stepped back, feeling suddenly utterly outmatched, when he heard a whipping sound behind him like a sail flapping in a strong wind. He instinctively ducked, and the anchor that Erzulie hurled sailed over his shoulder and caught Joseph square in the stomach.

Charles watched Joseph tumble backward, impaled and broken, over the rail. But Charles stood up too soon, and the anchor rope that still flew by caught him around the neck. As Joseph fell overboard, Charles was snatched after him. Charles clutched vainly at the rope as he was whipped off his feet. As he flipped over the railing, he caught a glimpse of Erzulie at the stern, her hands over her heart, and her face filled with compassion and sadness.

The anchor dragged him down faster than he expected. By the time he managed to twist around and get the rope off, he was impossibly far below the surface. Joseph's body plunged away from him and vanished from sight almost immediately. He told himself not to panic, and found it remarkably easy. It was as if the cold water had drained all worry, anger and anxiety from of him. He was inexplicably, almost ecstatically calm, floating weightlessly in the deep blue expanse. He wondered why he wasn't worried about running out of air, but it just didn't seem to matter.

He was considering that maybe he had already drowned when he sensed something uncomfortably bunched up behind him. He reached around and found a hard surface supporting him. He opened his eyes and realized that his clothes had rumpled in the airliner seat when he had slouched in his sleep.

As bizarre as the dream had been, it had all been so vivid, he had a hard time believing it had only been a dream. He had to feel his clothes before he could accept that he wasn't wet from the ocean. He also checked his hands for blood. The static interior of the plane seemed a continuation of his dream state. The lights were dimmed in the small crew lounge of the cargo plane as it flew through the night. The only sound was the quiet drone of the engines out on the 747's wings.

He was still quite calm. In fact, this was the first time he had awoken from one of his nightmares stress-free. He wondered why. To have faced Joseph in real life and survived was surely evidence of the hand of the goddess. In the dream she had killed Joseph, but had been unable to save Charles from being swept overboard. He turned this over in his mind and concluded that he could take great comfort in knowing Erzulie was there for him, but that he shouldn't rely on her to save him.

He looked across the aisle at Sanantha curled up under a blanket, asleep across two seats. He was genuinely sorry to have dragged her into this. He was also really glad to have someone he trusted by his side. The shadows across her high cheekbones reminded him of the proud visage of Erzulie in his dream. There would only be so much Sanantha could do for him on this trip, so he had to remember not to rely on her too much either.

He revisited his decision to go to Haiti. He had sworn he would never go back there. On the other hand, his chances of keeping anonymous were much better than his chances of surviving another encounter with the demon.

As they got off the plane in Miami, Sanantha noticed how much more at peace Charles seemed. He was calmer, smiled more and seemed more confident. She assumed it was because they were finally making progress.

After Charles met with his contact and got Sanantha's counterfeit passport, they walked back through the Miami airport to catch their final leg to Port Au Prince.

They never thought to look behind them at the middle aged, balding, clean shaven white man who glanced casually around the corner after them. Joseph returned to leaning against the wall just out of their view, pushed his mirrored sunglasses up into place and grinned.

10

MEROE

"I HOPE YOU GOT ALL YOUR PERMITS IN ORDER," Jaffa, the black
pilot of the four-seat Piper Warrior said loudly to his sole
passenger over the propeller's roar. "These soldiers are a real
nuisance about such things."

Silas, in the seat to the pilot's right, blinked his bright blue eyes
and fought to not let his alarm show. "Soldiers?"

"Oh, yes," the man continued in his thick Sudanese accent. "Last
week, when the pyramids were defaced, they sent troops in and
closed the place up. The government is very protective of Meroe," he
explained. Then, with some surprise he added, "Didn't you know
that before you hired me?"

"Yes, of course," the old man lied. "I just didn't think they'd
divert troops," he covered casually, "what with the ongoing civil war
with the southern Christians. You don't happen to know if they
caught the vandals?"

"No sir. I haven't heard."

Silas fell silent and stared into space, deep in subdued rage.

"So you have the permits?"

"Yes, yes," he dismissed as he looked out over the arid wasteland. "How much longer is it?"

"About forty minutes."

"Good," Silas said checking his Audemars Piguetin watch. "I'm going to make some notes," he explained as he reached around behind him and pulled a small notebook out of his black bag. "If I doze off, wake me when we arrive. May Allah guide your hand," he added and checked the pilot's reaction.

Jaffa smiled and nodded appreciatively, saying, "Thank you."

The magician shifted into a deceptively relaxed posture and forced himself to abandon his anger and frustration at not having foreseen such an obvious interference. With this defacing, Faen-ka may have revealed that his seal was indeed at Meroe, but now Silas needed to get into the site by guerrilla means. He considered his options, but with only forty minutes to set a plan in motion, he didn't have many. He glanced at the pilot and regretfully realized that none of his options boded well for poor Jaffa.

Tucked inside the cover of the notebook were two fountain pens. He held the book in his left hand and withdrew the pen filled with clear yellow liquid. As soon as he pulled off the cap, the cockpit flooded with the flowery herbal odor of the "ink". Jaffa tilted a questioning eyebrow.

"A cologne bottle broke in my luggage and spilled on this notebook," Silas offered smoothly." I hope it doesn't bother you."

"No, no. It's fine," the pilot said, looking back out the windshield.

Silas held the notebook in his fingers so that it looked as though he were writing on the paper, when in fact he was writing on his palm. As he drew the hieroglyphic symbols, each over the last, he infused the condenser fluid with the meaning of the symbols, and with his will that they gain function in the material world.

One after another, the figures detailed the story of how the ancient Egyptian god Seth murdered his brother Osiris. It was the darkest and most disturbing of all the Neter tales, and it brought with its telling the very nature of death.

When he finished the recounting, his left palm was dripping wet, but he didn't notice. He focused on the power the story fed him and slowly drew a long breath, not only through his lungs, but through all the pores of his body. He closed his eyes and allowed his head to fall to one side, totally relaxing his body as his mind bridged the gap between this world and the higher planes of spiritual power.

He stored the accumulated sense of death in his heart chakra, the very center of his being. He took another breath of cosmic power, and another, gathering more and more of what the inscribed story had shown to him. At the end of the seventh breath, he mentally moved the dark boiling ball of death out into his left arm and down into his hand.

He opened his eyes. Not being able to spare any concentration or energy, he stared intensely, silently ahead and waited for the village of Begarawiya they would pass over before arriving at the monuments. As he remembered from the maps, it came into view only a moment later. Silas flashed his left hand out with the swiftness of a cobra strike and touched the pilot's right temple. The condenser fluid acted as a conductor and the accumulated psychic energy leapt from his flesh and invaded the black man's head chakra, inundating it, overwhelming it, annihilating it. Jaffa's whole body flinched once as his brain despaired and died in a massive stroke.

Unhitching his own seatbelt, Silas held the pilot's body back with his left arm while he seized the dual control wheel on his own side with his leather gloved steel right hand to take control of the plane. The African's dead feet rested steadily on the wing elevator pedals on the floor, so the old man had little difficulty aiming the plane down in a level descent at the village. He brought it in low over a field next to the huts and cut the engine. Just before the wheels hit the dirt, Silas shifted back into his own seat, buckled his safety belts, and jammed the floor pedal aileron control down to the right.

The plane barrel-rolled and drove its right wingtip into the ground, setting the craft spinning on its belly, sheering off the fixed landing gear, to a bouncing, skidding halt.

Silas tried to open his door, but it was wedged fast in its warped frame. He tried again, but his neck and right shoulder seized up in a spasm of pain, wrenched badly by the violent twisting motion of the crash. He also noticed a long scrape on his right forearm where he'd braced himself against the door handle on impact. He also noticed the face of his watch on his left wrist was cracked and the sweep second hand was still. He looked at Jaffa but did not find the comically exaggerated arrangement of the dead body at all funny. He smelled for smoke but found none.

Looking out the window at the onrushing villagers, Silas recognized them as Masaka tribesmen by their brightly colored handmade clothing. He felt reassured as to the correctness of his decision to ditch the plane here.

The first to reach him was a well-muscled young man whom Silas noticed wasn't even breathing hard after sprinting two hundred yards. He hopped up onto the crumpled right wing, but his confusion stopped him short when faced with the flush fitted door.

Silas pointed at the fold-down handle grip on the outside and pantomimed the way it opened. The youth tried it, flashed a proud grin when it worked, and yanked so hard the door popped open on the first try.

"Thank you very much," Silas told him in the Semitic dialect of Arabic he expected them to speak.

The answer he got and the conversation between the other men who arrived surprised him. He did not know this Nilotic tongue. Just the same, he had no problem communicating to them that he was hurt, and that they needed to empty and retreat from the potentially dangerous plane.

Despite his injuries, Silas insisted on carrying his black bag himself. When the men looked upset and asked Silas about the dead black pilot, Silas indicated that he did not know what happened. As they hoisted Jaffa and the luggage, he could see through the openings in their loose-fitting clothing that these men bore traditional curved rows of ritual scars around their torsos.

They led him into their village, past several flimsy shacks made of rusting corrugated metal siding, to a large, beautifully crafted thatched hut. Their wizened old medicine man was waiting by his door. Upon seeing the dead black man being carried behind Silas, a tiny, brief, but telling frown passed over his face.

Silas was surprised to see the small, simple, but plainly displayed gold cross that hung around the man's neck, dangling onto his traditional ornate feather collar. This village was apparently even more isolated than Silas had expected, for its leader to be openly Christian, when everyone for hundreds of miles around the village was Muslim, and locked in a protracted civil war with the Christians in the southern part of the country.

Silas promptly introduced himself as a Christian priest, which dissolved any outsider suspicion the tribal elder may have had. He cheerfully introduced himself as "Ixpon" and generously led Silas into his home.

As they sat in backless armchairs of vaguely ancient Egyptian design, the magician experimented with several languages and was pleased to find the old man did speak a Sudanese dialect that Silas could passably use.

"The man who died was the driver of the airplane," he explained. "I don't know why he collapsed. It happened all at once."

"I will examine the body after we treat your injuries," Ixpon decided. He then called into the back of the house an expression Silas took to mean, "little wife".

When an enormous rotund woman appeared, Silas realized he had misinterpreted a term of endearment. Clearly, he could not trust what little he knew of their language.

The doctor gave her an unintelligible instruction upon which she left. He stepped behind his patient and began squeezing and pulling on Silas's neck and shoulder muscles. Each time he probed, he asked Silas if it hurt, and every time it did.

A moment later the doctor's wife returned, accompanied by a girl of maybe fifteen years who carried a bowl of water, a bottle of clear liquid, and a wad of soft cloth. Whereas the older woman wore an open-sided, loose-fitting tunic dress of clearly ancient design, the girl wore cutoff jeans and a short cropped, bare-midriff blouse.

When Silas removed his shirt so they could treat the scrape on his forearm, everyone audibly noticed the shiny form-fitting metal bracelet which protruded from the top of the peculiar, bulbous glove on his right hand.

He quickly explained, as best he could, "My hand was hurt in a fire. I have to wear this ... this," he searched for the right word, "... support, and this glove."

Ixpon smiled and nodded, then translated for the others. As they resumed cleaning his scraped arm, the girl seemed particularly taken with the prosthesis, as she kept glancing back at it as she worked.

The doctor's wife, on the other hand, seemed, from the subtle expressions on her rubbery face, impressed with the white man's resistance to pain as she applied alcohol from the bottle and he did not flinch.

Through an open side slit in her dress, Silas noticed numerous rows of shiny scars girdling the large woman's waist. These contrasted with the single row of ornamental scarring on the girl that peeked over the waistband of her jeans. Since he knew about the use of scarring among East African peoples, he satisfied himself that this meant she had reached puberty but was not yet married.

The magician marveled at how these people had survived wave after wave of conquerors, and assimilated the best of each invading culture into their own: the Egyptian furniture, the European religion, the modern hygiene and medicine. Yet they remained the same people, with the same lifestyle. This girl looked exactly like the Nubian dancing girls he had seen, and in his previous life painted, on Egyptian tomb walls. How elegant. Truly fate had finally turned back his way in providing him with this wonderful specimen, a direct, identical descendant and link to the past he was determined to restore.

"No broken bones, no joints sprained," Ixpon diagnosed. "Just don't lift anything for a couple of days and your muscles will heal fine."

"Thank you very much for your kindness," Silas told him as he began dressing.

The girl stepped up and helped him with the shirt when she saw his difficulty in moving his shoulder. He smiled his appreciation and she returned it with one of utter innocence.

He only knew of one way out of this isolated spot in the desert, and that was a bus that ran once a day from Atbara to Khartoum. As it was already late in the afternoon, he would have until tomorrow to do his work.

To keep up his ruse of being stranded on his way to Khartoum, he acted ignorant and asked the doctor, "What is the fastest way I can get to Khartoum? I need to be there as soon as possible."

"Ah, you are in luck! The train is coming through the valley tonight. There are soldiers a half an hour away at Shendi, on the Nile. I can send a runner to fetch them, and they can take you to the train."

Silas was well aware of the Nile Valley Express, but it only ran once every three weeks, and irregularly at that. He refused to consider this turn as a setback.

"Soldiers?" he asked innocently. "But you are Christians. Are not the soldiers of the Muslim central government, which is at war with Christians?"

Ixpon smiled and nodded at his guest's concern. "We are not political, and the conflict in the South is all politics, not religion. We deal with the soldiers regularly."

Silas glanced at the girl and considered, with some trepidation, how quickly he would have to work. "Then that would be wonderful," he beamed at his host. "I don't know how I can thank you enough. If I might ask, is there somewhere I can lie down. This accident has left me quite tired."

"Yes, of course. There's a cot in the next room."

Ixpon pointed to Silas's bag and addressed the girl. The only things the white man understood were his own name and that the girl's name was Nali.

As she picked it up from the woven grass mat floor, Silas commented to the doctor, "You have a fine daughter."

"Oh, she isn't mine. She just helps my little wife."

Ixpon's wife stepped outside and was speaking with the two men who had Jaffa's body. Ixpon noticed this and headed for the door.

"Thank you again for your hospitality," Silas concluded, without showing his relief at hearing that the girl was not related to this man who has shown him such kindness.

Nali set the bag down by a bench-like cot. Except for it being made of woven grass stretched over a wooden frame, the cot looked uncannily like the divans of the pharaohs. She sidestepped Silas as he entered the small room and started to leave when he called her by name and motioned for her to stay. Sitting on one end of the bed, he smiled warmly and patted the other end for her to join him. She stood in the doorway and frowned in her confusion, but when he reached down and opened his bag, her curiosity got the better of her.

He rooted around and extracted a few items, pretending that they were in his way, setting them down on the bed between them. She did not seem interested in the black leather-bound book or the bottle of clear liquid. When he set down the serpentine-bladed dagger, though, she audibly sucked in a breath of amazement. Silas pretended not to notice and continued searching through his bag.

Her fascination was so complete she touched it gently, almost as if to see if it were real. She was most drawn to the handle, which was a copper sculpture of a nude man and woman embracing each other on their knees, with their calves and feet forming the handguard, and their pressed-together bodies forming the grip.

When he was sure Nali was quite taken with the weapon, he acted surprised at her touching it and snatched it up admonishingly. As he took it, he swung its tip around and nicked her on the back of the hand, seemingly by accident. Before she could raise the wound to instinctively lick it, the old man pulled a white linen handkerchief from his pocket and pressed it to the cut. He put her other hand over the cloth for her to hold it in place.

Silas then distracted her by showing her the object of his rummaging: a tiny, exquisite, gold seven-petaled flower on a fine gold chain, the rose of Thoth. He held it up enticingly in front of her and she studied it with beaming eyes.

When he slipped it around her neck, she let the handkerchief fall as she looked down and fingered the rose, examining it while he fastened the clasp. She was so absorbed that she didn't notice him clip a lock of her hair from the back of her head with a miniature pair of scissors he had palmed from his bag.

Silas tilted her head up from looking at the flower and smiled at her with his kind blue eyes. He pantomimed that she should give him something in return. She readily agreed, and slipped off a bracelet of stone beads woven together with dried grass. He used one of the few words he had picked up of her language, and thanked her for the bracelet. She thanked him enthusiastically for the necklace, and left the room examining it.

•   •   •

Vishkek, the spirit of smoldering embers, liked the way the worn upholstery of the wood paneled railcar stank of stale cigarette smoke. It looked around approvingly from inside Silas' yellow chalk drawn containment triangle before returning its gaze to the old man who had summoned it. The red heat glow that showed through its cracked, bark-like skin glowed brighter as the two-foot tall monster bobbed up and down on its stubby legs, unable to nod since it had no neck.

"I thought you'd like it," Silas acknowledged.

"Can I burn it when you're done? Can I?" it cheerfully pleaded.

"No, you may not," he told it calmly, without reprimand. "I do want you to exterminate anyone or anything that tries to disturb my body while I'm gone."

"Thank you, Your Divinity." Vishkek grinned from shoulder to shoulder.

A light knock on the door interrupted them and the little fire spirit got quite excited at a chance to do the magician's bidding. Silas held up a restraining hand before turning to answer the knock.

"Who is it?" he called out in Arabic.

"It is I, Louis, the Porter, Father Alverado. I need to see your ticket."

Silas removed his crown, opened the door a crack, and blocked the conductor's view inconspicuously with his robed body. "Here it is," he said handing over the slip. "How did you know my name?"

"The soldiers who brought you to the station told me," the buck-toothed black man answered cheerfully. Then, more confidentially, he added, "They also said you were a generous man. If there is anything I can do for you, anything at all, just let me know."

"The only thing I want on this trip is to be left absolutely alone," he stated flatly. "I paid a small fortune to get a private room on this overcrowded, rundown relic of a train. My God, there are more people crammed on the roof than there are inside. I paid for privacy, and that's what I expect. Any further disturbance, by anyone, and I'll hold you personally responsible." Silas snatched the ticket out of the man's hand and declared intently, "Good night," before sliding the door shut in his face.

"If that greedy fool comes back," he instructed Vishkek, "he's yours."

The eager little elemental again grinned enormously and bowed from the hips.

Silas started to check his watch and remembered he lost it in the plane crash. The approximately two hours left to Khartoum should be plenty of time. He knelt down on the wooden floor, inside his red chalk circle, and took from his bag the lock of hair, the bracelet, his dagger, the bloodied handkerchief, a piece of hard red wax, and large, round, hollow silver bead.

Silas held up the wax to Vishkek and told it to, "Breathe on this." The spirit did, and the man said, "Thank you," without looking away from the melted blob in his hand.

His voice was barely a whisper as he began his incantations, but its clarity and power was obvious from the grin of rapture on the guardian spirit's face. Reciting continuously as he worked, Silas pushed the silver ball into the center of the melted wax, then pressed the hair onto its surface, then wrapped the handkerchief around it all. He looped the bracelet over the dagger blade which he held in his metal-gloved right hand. He gripped the wax fetish tightly in his left hand so as to stretch his thumb's web over the ball. He rested the point of the weapon on the exposed flap of flesh, took one last breath, and finished the spell.

"As my blade enters this, her likeness, so shall my will now enter her body." He pressed the knife tip through his flesh and into the center of the ball, piercing the silver bead within. "As my blood fills this vessel, so my soul shall drive hers from her body."

The jostling railcar vanished from his view as his mind fled his body and flew with the speed of thought across the African countryside. In an instant he was standing by Nali's sleeping form. He floated down into her consciousness and appeared to her in a dream.

He stood before her, resplendent in his ceremonial garb, glowing warmly with white, holy light. He spread his arms to her and she happily embraced him. His touch filled her with a great sense of security and belonging. He stroked her hair gently and smiled down at her with kind blue eyes. Gripping her under her arms, he swept her up off her feet and swung her playfully around him, making her laugh and laugh. He delighted her further by stooping down and hoisting her aloft over his head by her hips. She arched her back and spread her arms like some great bird. She felt him push hard as if to toss her into the air, and suddenly she no longer felt his touch. She looked down and saw she was flying.

Her initial shock dissolved in the sheer joy of the moment. She noticed that the little gold rose around her neck glowed brightly, which only made her feel more confident about what was happening. She reached up and flew higher and higher toward the sun. She looked back to the white-haired priest and saw something that confused her, but for some reason she couldn't understand, did not alarm her. He was still holding her body in his arms. She saw a glint of light off what she recognized as his fascinating knife as he swept it over her body and severed a long silvery thread that she traced all the way up to her bodiless self. All at once she felt free, freer than she ever imagined possible.

Back on the train to Khartoum, the grass bracelet cleaved over the dagger's edge and fell to the floor.

Nali's dream body in his arms dissipated to nothing while Silas looked up and watched her soul fly away into the light of the spheres.

"Go in peace, little one. May the Neters reward your innocence with eternal bliss."

The black girl's eyes opened and surveyed her surroundings with the sage scrutiny of one many times her age. Silas allowed him/herself a small triumphant grin. He was now so close to success, he could taste it. Once he snuck out of her family's shack, he flexed and stretched, getting a feel for this young, lithe body. A quick look around the village by the starlight of a moonless night, and he was off.

After over an hour jogging across the barren desert, the terrain swelled into low hills, and the ground became littered with tiny shards of broken pottery. Remembering the maps, he slowed to a walk to catch his breath, and proceeded very quietly. He had no idea how many soldiers were on guard, or where they might be. Finally, he crawled up a ridge that overlooked his objective, the pyramids of Meroe.

Miniature in comparison to their cousins in Egypt, the largest of these monuments stood only a dozen yards on a side. They were also taller, thinner, and centuries younger than the Egyptians, with their flush cut facing stones still intact.

Silas allowed himself a moment to muse over a question that had perplexed archaeologists for decades, the answer to which was obvious, now that he could see the pyramids for himself. Of all the gems of the Kushite civilization that once lined the Nile along this valley between the Fifth Cataract and the Sixth, of all the palaces, temples and marketplaces of ancient Naga and Musawarat, the only structures not reduced to rubble by the ravages of time were the burial pyramids at Meroe. Of the pyramids, most leaned crookedly on subsided ground, or bore cracked facing stones that marred their symmetric beauty. All but one. The largest and oldest of the eight structures stood straight and unblemished, seemingly unaffected by the centuries.

Now he understood why. In the centuries that followed Faen-ka's stay here, the Kushites had adopted enough Egyptian culture to begin burying their royalty in pyramids. The largest was for their greatest leader, Queen Shakdakhete, around 200 B.C. Her priests had apparently kept Faen-ka's teachings alive for the thousand years after his visit. Given the pyramid's invulnerability, Silas was now even more convinced that the Kushite priests had placed Faen-ka's seal in the pyramid.

From his high ground vantage, Silas studied the soldiers' encampment. He counted six, four asleep near their truck and two on guard duty at opposite ends of the site. The largest pyramid was near one end, so the magician would have to contend with at least one of the guards. He glanced down at his young, taut flesh and gave himself credit for having planned well.

Seducing the man away from his post was easier than Silas had expected. In fact, the man was too eager. He was so forceful, Silas found he had almost no control over the physical situation. In no time the man had painfully ripped open the girl's virginal tissues with his wild, selfish thrashing. Yet the magician maintained the appearance of enthusiastic insatiability. He had to wear out this soldier.

Finally, after his second climax, the soldier released the girl's pinned arms and rolled off of her onto the ground. Silas acted immediately. The black man never saw the girl snatch up his knife from the belt he had tossed carelessly aside, and he only felt an icy twinge as she plunged it with blinding speed into his exposed throat, through the back of his tongue and into the base of his brain.

As he let go of the blade, he quietly said a prayer for the man. "May the Gods have mercy on your soul. Know that your life is taken that millions may live in a better world."

Silas stood up and made sure all was still silent. He looked down at the soldier's half-naked corpse, and also noticed the blood and semen that ran out of the girl's body and down her thighs. He was very glad Nali was not here to witness this. The magician picked up the soldier's machine gun and flashlight, and advanced on the large pyramid.

The structure was just big enough to include the classic Egyptian floor plan and engineering. The first level had a treasure annex, no doubt looted shortly after the Kushite queen was laid to rest here. Down a sloping passage of walls painted with scenes and text, and under the center of the pyramid's mass was the sarcophagus chamber. As Silas made his way by flashlight to the sanctum, he noticed that whatever vandalism had brought the soldiers, there was none on this particular tomb. Again Silas was amused.

As he had hoped and expected, the roof of the burial chamber was a flat slab that rested on the stone walls. Above it would be the triangular, prism-shaped hollow space below the angled slabs of the stress vaulting. This would be where the seal was placed. His prize was now at hand. Silas smiled.

•   •   •

Back on the train to Khartoum, the fire elemental Vishkek was surprised to hear the compartment door lock click open. Without a knock or warning of any kind, Louis the conductor flung open the door, pass key still in hand. The black man seemed surprised but strangely not alarmed at seeing the small glowing monster.

The diminutive spirit considered getting an explanation for this suicidal outburst, when it noticed Louis's aura was no longer that of a human being. His eyes now glinted purple. "You're possessed by a demon!" the elemental spat in disgust.

The black man hissed an animal growl at Vishkek and took a menacing step toward the motionless, seated magician.

"Think again, maggot!" Vishkek chuckled as it raised one tiny hand. A cone of white-hot destruction blasted forth, enveloping and annihilating Louis. The blast also ripped out the doors and the outside wall of the train behind what had been the possessed porter.

•   •   •

Silas scouted around for the archaeologists' tunnels into the vaulting crawlspace, but couldn't find any. With precious little time before his train arrived in Khartoum, he had to take his most drastic option. Standing in the burial chamber, he decided there was no safe place to hide for this job. He would just have to look as quickly as he could while he still had eyes in the room. He got a good grip on the flashlight with one hand and braced the M-16 into his other shoulder.

In the four seconds that it took for the gun to empty the fifty-round clip, Silas cleaved a line across the least supported length of the ceiling slab. Each bullet shattered the 2,200-year old stonework into a hail of fragments, which were immediately followed by huge crashing blocks as the slab first broke in half, then collapsed. Dodging what he could of the cave-in, Silas danced the lamp's beam around the exposed superstructure, desperately seeking what his Tarot and all his spirit guides had told him would be here.

A block struck him from behind and crushed the girl's legs. *Only one more face to examine,* he thought though the excruciating pain.

He twisted around and, just before he was buried completely, he saw the seal. Surely the Kushite High Priest had painted it out of deepest respect for Faen-ka, in spite of Faen-ka's wishes a thousand years before. Surely the High Priest assumed Faen-ka would never know. Surely the High Priest was certain no one would ever see it. But now, Faen-ka's true written name belonged to Silas Alverado.

11

PARADISE

THE PUERTO RICAN AIRPORT BAGGAGE HANDLER hummed along to the reggae music playing on his Walkman while he sorted the suitcases coming down the conveyor belt onto flatbed carts. Umberto Valdez had been working this job for almost a year, in which time the routine had become completely automatic. It gave him time to think, and he was glad for that. He had a lot to think about these days, now that his wife, Consuelo, was carrying their first child.

The song ended and he noticed the sound of long, even, high heeled steps in the corridor behind him. He turned instinctively but was in no way prepared for what he saw. Six-foot tall not counting her three inch heels, with thick, almost white, straight blond hair flowing down to the middle of her back, the woman wore a thin white muslin sundress that did nothing to hide her lean, high breasted, long legged form, or the fact that she wasn't wearing any underwear. In fact, the only detail of her physique left to the imagination was her eyes, which hid mysteriously behind her large, round, jet black sunglasses. Umberto couldn't help but whistle in amazement as she strutted past him and down the hall.

Despite his fascination with her form, when she reached the end of the corridor and opened the door on the left, he realized something was very wrong. That door lead to the airfield.

Taking only enough time to turn off the conveyor belt, he ran after her, calling in his broken English, "Hey lady! Come back here! You not go out there!"

Unnoticed by Umberto, when he stopped the moving track, a large trunk on wheels rolled forward under its own momentum and drove the suitcase in front of it off the belt. It fell down behind the conveyor platform, completely out of view.

When he burst through the door in pursuit, the Puerto Rican was met by two of his coworkers walking the other way. He looked past them but saw no trace of the woman.

"What's with you?" one of the men asked Umberto.

"Didn't you just see this blonde *chicita fantastica* go by here?"

"No way, man."

"Are you sure?" Umberto demanded.

"Hey look, I think I woulda noticed."

"You all right?" the other man asked, half-jokingly.

"I don't know," Umberto wondered, shaking his head and looking at the empty hallway and its single exit to the airfield.

•   •   •

Joseph stepped out onto the sidewalk in front of Miami International Airport and took a deep lung full of the warm, humid midday air. He patted his restored face and ran his fingers back through his thinning hair. Even with the exhaust from the endless stream of taxis and busses, the air smelt a lot better here than where he had spent the last three millennia, a place to where he would thankfully never return. He looked at his watch and was pleased to realize he had a couple of hours with no obligations. He smiled a small but indulgent, self-satisfied smile, turned around and went back into the airport lobby.

The big Lincoln Town Car didn't have the animal gratification of the Ferrari he had been driving in Washington, but then, this time was his to pamper himself, to take it easy, to appreciate the lack of pressure. Fashionable Brickell Avenue was very glamorous; the old resort hotels and small shops of Miami Beach were, as expected, quaint; but nowhere in his driving did he quite find the peace for which he longed. Finally, up the Atlantic coast, he found a stretch of beach called Haulover, away from any buildings or landmarks that tied it to the city. There were plenty of people, mostly vacationing families, but everyone was there only to relax. Joseph smelled this aura in the air and parked. He walked to the water's edge and began strolling down the beach. Before long, his shoes were in his hand, his jacket was slung over his shoulder, and his sleeves were rolled up.

•   •   •

Umberto Valdez was finishing a cup of coffee in the employee break room when he heard the familiar clicking of heels on concrete. He whipped his feet off the card table and spun around in the flimsy chrome and plastic chair just in time to see the blonde strut by.

"Hey *mamacita!*" he called out as he dashed to the door. When he got to the hall, though, she was much farther away than her gait should have taken her. This enigma, and the fact that he was again seeing her with no witnesses, gave him pause.

When he hesitated, she stopped too, in front of a door. She twisted around on those tanned muscular legs, placed one hand impatiently on her hip, gave him a playful, magazine perfect smile, and tilted her sunglasses down with her other hand to look at him over their tops with her bright violet eyes. She then jerked the door open and went in.

He was running to her in a second, because that room was for storage, and it had no other exits.

He whipped the door open and found her leaning up against the back wall of the little room, fondling a perfect breast in one hand while running her other hand up her thigh, dragging her dress hem with it. He took a deep breath and boldly advanced to her.

She was the last thing Umberto ever saw. The storeroom exploded in a maelstrom of flames, wood splinters and plaster fragments. Fire Department inspectors would later find evidence of a bomb in a suitcase, fallen down behind the unmanned conveyor belt, up against the back wall of the storeroom. The only body found was Umberto's.

•　　　•　　　•

"Please take your seats and fasten your safety belts. The captain advises we are now beginning our final approach to Port Au Prince."

Charles and Sanantha were seated in the First Class section of the aged 727. When Charles caught her smiling to herself, he raised a curious eyebrow.

She pointed up, indicating the overhead speakers. "I hadn't realized how much I missed that accent. I was just thinking about the last time I flew along this path. I was a scared teenager, headed off to University. The hundred dollars and change I had on me was my life's savings after buying the airfare. It was a plane not unlike this one. Except it was a lot newer back then. And I was not sitting in First Class."

"Maybe it's the same airplane," he joked.

Her smile broadened. "*That* would be funny."

The young black flight attendant continued over the P.A. "We picked up an unusually good tailwind, so we've made very good time. In fact, we'll be arriving a half hour sooner than planned. Enjoy your stay in beautiful Haiti."

"A half an hour?" Charles commented with some amazement while looking at his watch. "That's some tailwind. We've only been in the air two hours."

The plane lurched upward with neck wrenching violence and a tremendous cracking sound echoed from the plane's underbelly. Before anyone could react, the nose dropped sharply, and the engines began screaming ominously.

"Please remain seated!" the stewardess's strained voice entreated. "Do not panic! We believe something has struck the plane! Pull your seat belts as tight as they'll go and brace yourself against the seat in front of you! We'll be landing in the water, so as soon as we stop, remember to grab your seat cushion!"

People started screaming all around. Charles sized up the cabin and tried to wrap his mind around how sturdy this plane's fuselage was. He tried to focus on contingencies and not think about being trapped in a sinking metal box in the middle of the ocean.

Sanantha gave him a wide-eyed, pressed-lip frown. He held his hand out to her and she clasped onto it tightly. Through clenched teeth, she muttered a single word. "Joseph."

As much as he wished otherwise, he had to agree.

●   ●   ●

Joseph looked at his watch and smiled. Stretching out his arms he sighed hugely. At long last he was back in control of his mission. His master had warned him of interference, but he had encountered none. He had, just to be sure, planted two suitcase bombs. He strolled back to the car confident of his master's pleasure at this news. As he pulled out onto the highway, he turned on the radio. To his mild annoyance the station was giving the news.

"… terrorist bomb exploded on a passenger railroad in the Sudan near Khartoum. Damage was extensive and one man, a train porter, was reported killed. The Revolutionary Popular Solidarity organization claimed credit for the attack. This group has only previously struck in the Mediterranean, particularly in Greece.

"Another bombing story just in. A bomb exploded just minutes ago at Miami International Airport. Details are still coming in, but initial reports say the blast, in a baggage area, killed one. We'll keep you up to the minute as more details become available."

Joseph was livid. He stared at the radio in aghast fury. Had both of his bombs been left behind? He had to know. Careening off the road to a screeching halt, he sent several cars around him swerving and attracted the attention of a nearby policeman. Ignoring the squad car with its lights and siren as it pulled in behind him, Joseph whipped off his glasses to expose his bright yellow eyes.

The policeman found the car mysteriously empty and smelling repulsively of sulfur.

•   •   •

Drawn by the howling of the wounded jetliner overhead, Jack McKinney, the First Mate of the *Purgatory*, ran up the ladder onto the forward deck of the hundred and thirty-foot Westport yacht. The 727 was only a couple of miles away, and it was low enough and dropping fast enough, that he could see it was not going to make it to shore. The barrel-chested redhead cupped his hands to shield his eyes from the morning sun, and questioned how morbid his curiosity was to watch the actual impact. The pilot had the nose up and the speed slowing in an obvious attempt to set the plane down flat on the surface. The tail dragged a rooster-tail, but then caught in the water and the wings came down in a belly flop that sent out a huge splashing wave in front of the plane. It landed maybe a mile offshore and a mile down the coast from where the *Purgatory* was anchored.

As soon as Jack saw the plane had hung together and was floating on the surface, he grabbed the whistle around his neck and blew a general alarm. Half a dozen crewmen rushed up on deck where Jack directed them to pull up the anchors and secure the ship for travel. He ran up the stairs to the wheelhouse and fired up the huge twin marine diesel engines. As soon as he saw the anchors were clear, he opened up the throttle and, with agility that belied the ship's size, it sped out to sea.

In the couple of minutes it took for the *Purgatory* to arrive, the plane had begun to sink. The wings were submerged, and only the upper half of the fuselage was still above water. Most of the hundred or so passengers were scattered out, starting to swim for shore. The crew had an inflatable raft with which they were fishing the remaining passengers out of the water. Upon the approach of the luxury yacht, many of the people who had begun to swim for shore turned around.

•   •   •

Sanantha pulled up to tread water when she heard the engines of the approaching yacht. "Charles!" she called ahead to get his attention. He stopped, turned and saw the ship. "What do you think?" she asked, nodding toward the ship.

He looked back and forth, comparing the distances to shore and back to the boat. They were about a third of the way to shore. She swam over to him while he frowned at the boat.

"I say let's keep swimming."

She made no effort to hide her surprise. "Why?"

He blinked at her and said flatly, "You asked my opinion."

She shook her head at his suddenly strange behavior. "Yes, I did. Now I'm asking for an explanation before I follow you into an unknown jungle rather than swim back onto a ship with dry towels and get a ride to civilization."

"And get hung up for the rest of the day filling out paperwork, making ourselves easy targets for Joseph."

She was disappointed that paranoia was turning out to be so useful. She looked longingly at the ship one last time. "Your right. Let's go."

After several more minutes of swimming, Sanantha noticed there were no other passengers swimming with them to shore. "Charles," she said between strokes.

"Yeah?"

"Are there sharks in these waters?"

"Oh, no doubt."

She stopped swimming and glared at him in shock. "What do you mean, 'No doubt'?"

"The splash that plane made must've attracted every shark for miles around. But you don't have to worry about being attacked. They only feed at dawn and dusk."

"Really?"

"Yeah," he dismissed.

"So where are they now?"

"Oh, all around us, checking us out. They're just curious, not hungry. But you've got to keep an even, quiet stroke. You splash around and you'll piss them off. They'll attack if they're pissed."

He took off swimming again and she found herself staring wide-eyed at the surface of the water all around them. Despite the warm water, she felt a chill run through her body. The shore suddenly looked a lot further away. "Papa Legba," she prayed. Realizing they would present a less inviting target together, she hastened to catch up to Charles, without splashing more than absolutely necessary.

She was glad when the shallow bottom rose to standing height some thirty yards from shore. She turned and saw the plane was submerged. There was much activity on board the large white yacht. She staggered exhausted up onto the beach, and only stopped long enough to pull her yellow suit skirt back down from around her hips before collapsing onto her back in the warm sand. She didn't care that the fine white grains stuck to every surface, her arms, legs, skirt, blouse and hair. She had discarded her shoes, jacket and turban when they dove from the plane. She lay there breathing hard, waiting for her heart to slow from its racing, averting her eyes from the bright sun overhead. She let the warmth of the beach bake into her tired muscles, and marveled at how the sand muffled the sounds of the surf.

Charles explored the edge of the jungle behind the narrow strip of beach. He returned and squatted down next to her. "That swim was further than it looked, huh? You gonna make it?"

She sat up but didn't bother to brush off the sand that stuck to her. "Yeah, I'll be fine. Did you see anything?"

"Just very dense jungle. Which could work to our advantage. Joseph obviously had no trouble following us from DC. Maybe a jungle will provide better cover."

"If we can avoid getting bitten by Bushmasters," she added sarcastically. She noted the cell phone still clipped to Charles' belt. "Does that thing still work?"

"Oh, wow, I'd completely forgotten about this." He unclipped it, opened it, pushed a few buttons, and sighed. "No way. He smirked and flung it into the jungle. "Besides, it would probably attract Joseph right to us."

She agreed with a sigh and a nod as she got to her feet. She looked out at the crash site. The white yacht was pulling away. She mentally drew a line inland, and gave Charles an inquisitive squint. "If the plane was headed straight at Port au Prince, then Jean Rabel shouldn't be far from here."

He looked over the jungle, seeming to scan for landmarks, but then shrugged in a little too exaggerated manner. "I'll have to take your word for that."

She fought back the temptation to press him for why he wanted her to think he didn't know this place, when clearly he did. She covered her pause by starting to shake out her graying hair and brush the sand off her clothes. "If we can find a stream, that will lead us to a village. We'll have to take it slow, since we're both barefoot. Just watch for any suspicious movement in the carpet of fallen leaves. I remember that from being a barefoot child here."

Charles smirked. "If it's a choice between Joseph and the snakes, I'll take my chances with the snakes."

•   •   •

Jack handed the wheel over to a crewman and hustled down to the main salon to check on the rescued airline passengers. As he stepped from the stairwell into the dark wood paneled room, he was surprised by their number. The leather couches and armchairs were all full, and another thirty people were left standing. They spilled out onto the forward deck and all down the side walkways. They were all still wet and most of them had towels or blankets wrapped around them, though no one seemed cold in the hot mid-morning air. Some were quiet and seemed quite upset, yet most were smiling and seemed glad to have survived unharmed.

While he surveyed the room, Jack heard the telltale soft hiss and pop at the bottom of the stairwell next to him that signaled the opening of the sealed door of Mister Alverado's private quarters. As he expected, the door swung open and up climbed Joseph.

Jack turned and called out to the other two crewmen present who were helping the victims, "Captain on deck!" He then turned and greeted Joseph at the top of the stairs. "Good morning, Sir."

Joseph took in the scene with a calm aplomb that made Jack even more nervous than he usually was around Joseph. The only expression that showed behind the semi-mirrored sunglasses was a slight furrowing of one eyebrow. After surveying the room, the shorter balding man fixed his gaze on the tall, broad shouldered redhead and the eyebrow furrowed deeper.

Jack realized how odd it would look to explain the situation anew when the passengers had been on board for some time. He motioned up to the wheelhouse and invited, "If you'll come with me, Sir, I'll fill you in."

Joseph looked back across the crowd one last time as he stepped to the hallway stairwell. "Good, you do that," he said with clear restraint.

Jack escorted Joseph into the map room behind the wheel room and closed the door behind himself. "A commercial airliner crashed within clear sight of the ship, about a mile from shore. Naturally I made the ship available for their aide. We are now headed to Jean Rabel."

As he explained the situation, Joseph's expression rapidly changed from stern to surprised to introspective to excited. He cut Jack off and asked, "Was there a well- dressed black couple, with the man in his early thirties and the woman in her forties, and wearing a tall, Haitian style turban?"

Jack didn't think he would ever get used to Joseph's logical leaps, but he answered without question since it was clear that Joseph was onto something. "I don't know, Sir. I was busy maneuvering the ship. I can have the men check."

Joseph was brimming with impatience. "No, that will take too long." He stepped purposefully to the ladder that led to the roof, climbed it and opened the topmost hatch. "Stay here," he ordered as he disappeared up onto the roof.

Every now and again, Jack wondered why he ever took this job. This was one of those moments.

After only a few seconds, Joseph came back down the ladder. He smoothed his thin hair back from the wind and muttered to himself, "This is too great a coincidence." Looking up at Jack, he asked insistently, "Did you pick up everyone? Were there any bodies you left behind?"

"No, as far as I know, there were injuries but no deaths. And we … wait a minute. Someone said there were some people who swam to shore."

Joseph lit up at the news. "Do you know exactly where they went ashore?"

"Sure," he said with a nod. "I could take you right to the spot. But we're going to be tied up for a while in port with these survivors," he pointed out cautiously.

Again, Joseph's expressions reflected a storm of internal conflict. Then his face went calm and he nodded. He looked up at Jack with a pleased smile, and said, "That will be fine. Jack, you've done me a great service by picking up these people. I'm proud of you." With that, he slapped the barrel-chested man on the shoulder and left.

"Thank you, Sir," was all the befuddled First Mate could answer.

•   •   •

Sanantha was the first to step from the shadowed jungle into the clearing and the bright afternoon sun. "Ah, civilization. I told you it wouldn't be far."

Striding up beside her, Charles wasn't convinced. "It's just a field."

"No, all those barren clearings we've been passing are fields. This is a farm. Look at how it's all sorghum, and they're all the same size," she pointed out with a hand sweep at their four-and-a-half-foot height.

"Yeah, and there are rows, sort of. There are as many weeds as there are plants. Hold on," he interrupted himself. "Something moved out there."

"Where?" Sanantha stained to see.

"There!" Charles declared with a flashed-out hand. "It's a woman working the field. We can go around this way and then down a row," he directed while starting off along the jungle's edge.

153

After carefully picking through the weed-choked crops in their bare feet, they came upon the woman, who looked up at the approaching strangers with eyebrow raised curiosity. She was a sinewy thin black woman in her forties dressed in tattered clothes that looked like they had once been gaily colored but had long since faded. The only bright item in her attire was her yellow headband, which, like most of her clothes, was clearly wet with perspiration. More noticeable than the bandana, though, was the unlit corncob pipe clamped between her teeth. Her shoes were made from slabs of old tires.

Sanantha held Charles back by his arm as they approached. "So, the truth," she said quietly to him. "Do you know this language or not?"

A grin tugged at the corner of his mouth. "Only a little. You'd best do the talking."

"Hello. We're sorry to disturb you," Sanantha began in Haitian patois. "We are lost and need to find a village. We were washed ashore after a wreck. Can you help us?"

"How many others were washed ashore?" the woman asked suspiciously.

"Oh, just the two of us."

The woman eyed Sanantha and then Charles. When she looked back at Sanantha, her frown grew more leery yet.

"She's wondering why you're doing the talking," Charles suggested. "Tell her we're Americans."

Sanantha looked at Charles. He may not have known the language well, but he seemed to understand the culture. "We are Americans. My friend does not speak much Creole. I used to live here when I was a little girl."

At this the woman's expression finally cracked into a snaggle-toothed smile.

Moving to take advantage, Sanantha extended her hand in greeting and introduced herself. "I call myself Sanantha Mauwad. This is my friend who calls himself Charles Redmond."

The woman shifted her corn cob pipe around to the side of her mouth and extended her own hand. "I call myself Aminta Bouchier. What village was yours when you were a child?"

"Seranada. It is on the north side of Haiti, near Cap Haiten.

"My village calls itself Papilia." Aminta looked up at the scorching sun. "I need a break anyway," she said with a wry grin. "Let me take you into town."

Centered in a natural clearing but extending out under the surrounding sparse jungle canopy, the village was filled with the happy bustle of women and children at mid-afternoon that one might expect in any rural village. As the strangers approached, though, they saw how poverty stricken these people were. The walls of the thatched roof cottages were repaired with salvaged, rusting metal siding. Handcarts were made of recycled wood. The clotheslines strung between houses were frayed jute rope. Everyone was very thin and clearly undernourished. Very few people wore shoes despite the rocky soil. Yet the women still sang as they took in their handmade laundry and the children still chased each other playfully around the ramshackle houses. Sanantha smiled at the familiar dichotomy. Charles, on the other hand, seemed quite put off. Sanantha couldn't tell why.

One by one, everyone who saw them stopped what they were doing and stared, frowning at the strangers. The fact that Aminta escorted them surely made them more acceptable than they would have been otherwise.

Their guide led them down the hamlet's central dirt footpath. It was then that they saw the men. Peering suspiciously from doorways and windows which had neither doors nor glass, easily two dozen men of various ages watched the strangers walk by.

"Why aren't these men working, or out in the fields?" Charles muttered, almost to himself.

"That's kind of a long story," she answered somewhat embarrassed for them.

Charles squinted at her and hesitated. Sanantha could have sworn he was going to dismiss her, but then said, "I'm a businessman, try me."

"It goes back to when the island was first settled. The French killed all the indigenous Indians, and then overworked the soil for cash crops for over a hundred years. That jungle out there should be a lot thicker and the land should support a lot more farming. All those barren fields we crossed? Nothing can grow there.

And on top of that, ever since they won their independence from Napoleon back in the eighteen hundreds, they've culturally shunned manual labor as slaves' work. They would rather be unemployed free men than be seen as doing the work of a slave."

Charles frowned again. Clearly he had never heard this explanation, and was having a hard time accepting it. "Without pride in work, their collapsed economy will never recover."

"You're right. Other than subsistence farmers, like Aminta, no one really does anything outside of the cities. The land can barely feed them."

"What about Santo Domingo on the other half of this island?"

"No help there. That was settled by the Spanish and was never a slave colony. They treat Haitians like thieves. Remember also, Haiti was run by corrupt dictators for several generations. Things have gotten a little better since democracy was restored, but it will take time for national pride to turn into a work ethic."

"What a waste," he muttered again.

"It's a cultural difference," she said a little defensively. "You know from being here that nothing in Haiti is what you'd expect."

As they neared the center of the town, the gathering crowd of curious onlookers split in front of them. The reason was startlingly obvious. The Voodou *houngan* priest who stepped from his shack stood up straight to a height of nearly seven feet. He was extremely thin, like a black-stained skeleton. His spooky countenance was further enhanced by his large, deep-socketed eyes that, due to the boniness of his skull, fixed in an intense stare. His short cut black hair gave no clue as to his age. His clothing was very much like that of the other men they had seen: oversized, brightly colored, short sleeve shirt, with dingy white linen cutoff trousers. The normalness of his dress only accented his extraordinary features.

He nodded and smiled politely to the visitors during Aminta's retelling of their meeting. When Sanantha started to introduce herself in Haitian Creole, the priest perked up and, much to the visitors' pleasant surprise, he asked her in English, "You are Haitian?"

"Yes," she said with a big smile.

He held out his enormous, emaciated hand. "My name is Father Henri Gorvil," he said slowly through a syrupy thick accent.

"I am Sanantha Mauwad," she said shaking his hand. I am very pleased to meet you. This is my friend Charles Redmond."

Gorvil hesitated slightly as he reached for Charles' hand. He tilted his bony head slightly, a skeptical squint colored his smile, but then he shook his hand.

He turned back to Sanantha and made a sweeping motion toward his front door. "Please come into my home. You must be tired."

As they entered, the priest neither thanked nor dismissed Aminta, who stayed outside. The hut had three rooms and bare wood plank floors raised two feet above the ground to avoid rainfall flooding. Grass mats were spread out before a large, throne-like chair made of sugar cane rattan and woven vines, decorated with red, black and white painted designs and adorned with rodent jaws, snakeskins and feathers. The *houngan* handed Sanantha a gourd jug of water as everyone sat down.

"From what part of Haiti did such a flower as you spring?"

Sanantha took Gorvil's flattery in stride. "I grew up in a village called Seranada, outside of Cap Haiten."

"Ah, I have been to Cap Haiten many times. It is fifty kilometers down the road."

"How far is the road from here?" she asked.

"Less than an hour's walk. If you are looking for a city, Jean Rabel is about three hours walk west, and Port de Paix is about three hours walk east. You've already been walking all day to get here from the coast. You should stay with us the night."

He turned his attention to Charles. "Mister Redmond, are you in Haiti seeking spiritual guidance?"

Charles was caught completely unprepared and bristled defensively. "Excuse me. I'm not seeking any spiritual guidance."

The priest looked at him long and hard, then quietly commented, "You should be. The Loas around you are very upset, and your soul is unsettled. Are you under attack?"

Sanantha, similarly shocked, managed to come to Charles' aide. "Father Gorvil, we are in fact here in Haiti to talk to a *houngan*, but ours is a very personal matter, and we wouldn't want to get you involved."

Gorvil looked curiously at Sanantha. "You know that all *houngan* speak with the Divine Horsemen. Did you not belong to an *oumphor* in your village?"

"Yes. I was the Head Flag Mistress under Emil Vosaux. It is Father Vosaux that we are here to see."

Sanantha noticed that Charles seemed glad to no longer be the center of Gorvil's questions, but he didn't seem very happy with her forthrightness about their business.

"I knew Father Vosaux. He was a great and gifted *houngan*," Gorvil commented reverently.

"You said you knew him," Sanantha asked cautiously. "Do you mean he is dead?"

"Yes, five or six years now."

Sanantha made no effort to hide her surprise and disappointment.

"You wanted his help to protect your friend Mister Redmond here, yes?"

Sanantha looked to Charles, who looked away, sighed and shook his head.

"Yes," she answered soberly.

He turned to Charles and his tone grew grave. "You have seen evil. You are running from someone. Is this not so?"

"Yes," Charles answered cautiously, obviously taken aback at the man's amazing insight. "We are being pursued by a powerful enemy. Now that you have given us our bearings, we will go now and not endanger you any longer. We thank you very much for your help."

The *houngan* ignored his attempt to cut off his line of questioning. "This enemy, he is not of this Earth, is he?"

Wide-eyed astonishment held Charles dumbfounded for several seconds. "No, he isn't. He's a demon straight out of hell. How do you know that?"

The *houngan*'s answer came too quickly for comfort. "You have the aura of a touched man. I saw it when we first met. I do not know how you have so displeased the gods, but they are very angry with you. Will you tell me your crime and why this demon chases you?"

Sanantha couldn't let this go on. "Charles hasn't done anything to attract this demon. We accidentally discovered it, and now it wants to kill us simply to protect its human identity."

The *houngan*'s eyebrows went up on his high bony forehead at Sanantha's explanation. The tall black man then leaned forward in his chair and frowned, looking so deeply at Charles that it made him squirm on the grass mat. But instead of putting up an argument, the priest smiled ever so slightly and nodded once. He relaxed and declared, "I insist you stay here. Since Father Vosaux cannot help you, and the Loas have seen fit that you have come to my village, then I will help you find what you seek. At the very least, a Flag Mistress of Emil Vosaux's teaching shall have my protection if there is a demon pursuing you."

•   •   •

Joseph stood on the forward deck of the *Purgatory* looking out over the black water of Jean Rabel harbor as he listened absently to his men batten down the ship for the night in port. His thoughts were filled with formulating the call he had been dreading all evening. Although he had done everything he could, he still did not know how his master would take this news.

The black leather-bound door at the bottom of its own staircase bore no markings and had no lock. The handle consisted of two silvery metal sconces, each in the form of a life-sized human hand, holding vertically between them a smooth round bar of flawless quartz. Joseph grasped the bar and waited for his master's implanted spell to recognize him by his aura. A second later a distinct click signaled the opening of Silas' private quarters.

He walked through Silas' sleeping area, past the four-posted bed and the bookshelves that lined the walls of the near half of the long room. As he stepped to the laboratory center portion of the quarters, he couldn't help but glance up at the raised altar area at the far end, with its four, different colored, floor-to-ceiling stone pillars around the evocational patterns inlaid in the black slate floor. A wry smile pulled at the corners of his mouth as he spied the triangle which was his entry point into this plane of existence. The smile disappeared when he considered that it could also be his exit location if he didn't handle this call correctly.

Sitting down at a worktable strewn with incense burners, crystals, animal skulls and other magical implements, Joseph selected a free standing, elaborately framed mirror and a tall thin flask of yellow liquid. He opened the bottle and, ignoring the pungent odor of flowers and herbs, dribbled an even line of the fluid across the top of the mirror. As it flowed down, the rivulets spread out and formed a rippling sheet across the reflective surface. As he held the frame with both hands and concentrated, his reflection distorted even more until it was a swirling pool of colors. He took his sunglasses off and slipped them into his shirt pocket.

"Master," he said quietly, not wanting to cause trouble if Silas were in a public place. "Master, I need to speak with you urgently." Silas didn't carry a cell phone or pager because such devices could be traced. The use of magic mirrors created a link that could not be tracked or tapped, even by magical means. Joseph knew that by using Silas' own mirror, the magician would get the summons even if he were separated from his portable magic mirrors.

A short but anxiety-filled moment later, the shimmering image clarified into the white-haired visage of the mage. "Yes Joseph, what is it?" he asked calmly.

"I am faced with a worst-case scenario. Nearly everything that could go wrong has."

Silas cut him off by unhurriedly listing, "Mister Redmond and his psychiatrist have discovered you are not human, you tried to kill them and failed, and now they have come straight to us in Haiti, all despite your best efforts."

The yellow eyed demon couldn't help the shocked silence into which he fell. He frowned deeply and confirmed cautiously, "Yes, sir. Precisely."

The old man's kind blue eyes frowned as he explained with paternal forgiveness, "I did a reading. It's not your fault. I need to restructure my plan midstream. My adversary is now opposing me openly. We are at war," he declared conclusively.

Joseph turned this over in his mind once and concluded, "If Redmond got this far with assistance from our enemy, does that mean our enemy knows we are in Haiti? Should I take action to protect the village?"

"No. I am certain my plan is still safe. In fact, I have achieved my goal here on the road. It seems to be no more than an unfortunate coincidence that Mister Redmond has connections to Haiti."

Joseph frowned at the quandary he was left with. "If Redmond and our enemy do not know we are based in Haiti, then maybe I should just watch his movements. If I kill him now, that might signal our enemy that Redmond is close to us."

"True, but if he does come close to us and you kill him, that would send an even clearer signal that we are prepared to fight. I suggest you find him, learn why he came to Haiti, and then act accordingly. I am in Khartoum, about to catch a flight to New York. I'll be there late tomorrow."

"That is a great relief, Master," he admitted solemnly.

"Oh, and Joseph?" he added with a sarcastic smile. "What is my name?"

Before he could apologize for his chronic oversight, Silas' image dissolved, and Joseph was left looking at his own embarrassed reflection.

12

INNOCENCE

S HORTLY AFTER DAWN, Sanantha walked up the village's central
path to the shack at the edge of the jungle where Father Gorvil
had put up her and Charles. She had spent most of the night working
with the priest on a plan to get to the bottom of Joseph's designs on
Charles, while still defending her and Charles should the demon find
them here in the jungle.

Having ruined her Armani suit in the sea, she now wore the same
wrap skirt, tied-up white shirt, and tall bright yellow turban as many of
the other women here. These too were gifts from Father Gorvil.

The droning buzz of insects in the jungle all around the village
had begun with the rising sun, and was now fully up to its usual
incessant volume. The warming air stirred the fragrances of the
jungle as well, both sweet and sour.

As she walked barefoot on the dirt path, dressed as a native, she
reflected on how she had felt about this lifestyle when she left Haiti all

those years ago. She marveled at how much clearer now her understanding was of the fears and motivations of her people. With her training in psychology, religion and its role in people's lives made sense. Gone was the cloud of mystery that had left her with distrust and disbelief. As she watched the villagers starting their morning routines, she understood them and felt for them as she never had before.

As she approached the two-room wood plank shack, she was surprised to see Charles on the front porch talking with three village men. Charles, too, was now dressed as a local. She mused at how well he blended in despite his skin being several shades lighter than the almost black villagers. How was it that he was having such an animated conversation with his supposedly limited knowledge of this language?

When the local men saw her coming towards them, they quickly wrapped up their discussion and started to make their good-byes to Charles.

Sanantha caught the attention of one of them as they stepped off the porch. "It's all right," she said with a smile. "I can go inside if you want to keep talking."

The gaunt, graying man who was clearly the leader of the group nodded graciously without stopping and said, "Thank you, ma'am, but we should be going anyway."

She watched their retreating figures walk into the village, then turned to Charles, who seemed just as surprised at their sudden departure. "So what manly topic did I interrupt?" she asked him in mock indignation.

"Nothing that secretive," he said with an eyebrow raised in thought. "I mean, they know you're a native and I'm not, yet they were willing to share with me. Probably because I'm a man," he concluded with a nod.

"Clearly." She stepped up onto the porch and leaned against a post. "So you were managing to keep up even with your scant language?"

He smiled and wagged his finger at her. "Nice try. Atienne, the gray-haired fellow, speaks pretty good English. We were talking about that work ethic you and I touched on yesterday, and they had a slightly different take on it. They seemed pretty forthcoming when they introduced themselves, so I asked them right out. They said they don't work because they are supposed to be poor. That their fate is to be poor to make penance for some wrong they did to the gods back in the war with France. They agreed with you on the Napoleon history, but they didn't say it was the slave thing you talked about."

Sanantha raised her eyebrows and sighed. "Very religious folks. What you got is the spiritual explanation, which runs pretty deep. The story is the Haitian slaves summoned the help of the gods to defeat the French, in exchange for promises to the gods, that the people then did not keep. Ever since then, Haitians have lived with the guilt of that broken promise. They have accepted their poverty as the gods' punishment. Which is why they are so devout, always trying to win back the favor of the gods."

Charles thought long and hard before commenting. "Does everything around here have to be so spiritual?"

She blinked at him. "How do you mean?"

"Well, they don't have a mayor, their priest pretty much runs the town. From what I've seen, he doesn't even answer to any kind of church hierarchy."

"That's true. Villages are so spread out and communications are so lacking, that *houngans* are trusted with direct contact with the gods. Each one is a final decision-making authority. It gives them a lot of power, but it also makes them totally responsible. I believe you find that all across the rural third world."

"Maybe," he conceded, but still was appearing to struggle. "I realize the mountains and the jungle cut them off from the world, but it's like they don't even care what's beyond these trees. As poor and as miserable as they are, they seem perfectly willing to just accept this cut-off, narrow little life. They even build religious excuses to justify it."

She nodded. "It's the only life they've ever known. Not that I want to add any more fuel to that fire you've got going there, but I brought you something spiritual from Father Gorvil. We are here to get mystical help, right?"

He swallowed hard. "That's true."

She retrieved a folded piece of paper from her waistband. "It's a spell to use if you run into Joseph." She held it up so they could both look at it as she read it aloud.

"Papa Legba man hounfor moin. Ou minm' qui pote drapeau, ce' ou minm' qu'a marvais pou moin. Tout ca qui marvais ce' pour sorti!

'God the Father, who is in my heart. You who carry the banner of victory, it is you who protect me from evil. All that is evil, depart!'

If the Creole is too hard to memorize, then use the translation."

He grinned slyly. "I think I can manage. Is this copy for me?"

"Yeah, I've already memorized it."

He looked it over again. "So multiple, point blank gunshot wounds won't stop him, but this incantation will?"

She shrugged. "There are no guarantees, but this should certainly slow him down. The same magic that makes him bulletproof makes him vulnerable to the word of the gods."

He met her gaze squarely, and very sincerely said, "Thank you — for this, and for coming here with me, and for everything."

"You're welcome." She then added in a quiet, conspiratorial tone, "Oh, and Voodou can do more for us than that. Father Gorvil is putting together a Mass to get us answers, and he's thinking of doing it tonight!"

Charles tried to contain his apprehension, but failed. "You mean a full invitation for intervention, with summoning and mounting?"

Sanantha picked up on his caution. "You're a believer. Have you never been to a full Mass?"

He tried to cover with his easy smile. "No, actually, I never have. When I contacted Madame Erzulie back in DC, it frankly scared the hell out of me."

"Let me assure you, as loud and as wild as the goings-on may seem, the actual magic is very tightly controlled by the *houngan* and his attendants. I've participated in many summonings, and I've never seen anything get away from the priest in charge. I'll be right next to you the whole time. Father Gorvil won't let a Loa mount you. You're the one posing the questions, not the one answering them."

"So I'll just be watching from a safe distance?"

"No, you'll be right there, but you will be quite safe."

He looked out into the jungle and considered that as frightening as this all was, it was the reason they had come to Haiti. He looked back to her and grinned half-heartedly. "You know I'm doing all of this on no meds."

"Believe me, I haven't forgotten."

He folded up the paper and put it in his shirt pocket. "You said the Mass is tonight? Do we just hang low today?"

"I'll be busy helping set up for tonight. But yeah, you should try to unwind. We're making good progress toward our goals here. Take some comfort in that. And memorize that spell, just in case."

"Unwind. There's a concept. I'm afraid that ugly realization you had back in Washington about Joseph being the real deal is starting to catch up to me. I don't mind admitting that incarnate demons, manifested gods and a people who see everything from a mystical angle all leaves me feeling quite out of my depth. Maybe I'll go work off some of this nervous energy helping Aminta weed her sorghum."

"That's a great idea," she said breaking out her face filling smile. "I'm sure she'll be thrilled to get the help. If you need me for anything, I'll be at Father Gorvil's. We won't need you until later this afternoon."

"Until this afternoon then."

"Ati Wedo keep watch over you," she said over her shoulder.

As he watched her walk back into town, he wondered at their chances of not only getting rid of Joseph, but of getting their original lives back. He began walking out the path towards Aminta's farm.

Charles soon left the path. His long strides quickly covered the jungle undergrowth even though he was in no hurry as he ambled aimlessly, absorbed in his own thoughts. The morning mist still cowered in the numerous shadows, trying to avoid the warming sun that streamed through the canopy at low angles. The throbbing drone of unseen insects and the occasional call of a faraway bird punctuated the serenity without interrupting it. However, not even this nearly supernatural beauty and peace could calm the storm of questions and emotions that tossed within him.

He found a stream and walked along its bank. The scrunching sound of the water-worn, smooth stones under his car-tire-soled sandals created a rhythm that helped him measure his thoughts.

Who was Joseph's master? Probably someone who tracked him down from his misadventures the last time he was in Haiti. That was assuming Joseph was originally sent after Charles. If Joseph was only after them now because they had accidentally discovered Joseph's cover, then Joseph would have no connection to Charles. Could Gorvil learn anything about Joseph if there was no connection?

An unmistakable sound shook him from his quandary. The heavy breathing and repetitive moaning of passionate lovemaking snapped him instantly back into reality. After his walk through the humid dreamland of the jungle, his head filled with the smells of flowers and the sounds of insects, reality wasn't as clear-cut as he was accustomed. Rather than modestly turning back, as he normally would, he hunched down and crept into the bushes to spy the enticing sound's source.

In a small clearing some twenty feet away, two naked teenagers were writhing about in the throes of ecstasy, sweat running off their dark bodies as hands groped and hips slapped together faster and faster. Charles found he could see better if he looked over the top of a wall of shrubs. When he stood up he discovered his curiosity had taken physical form in his growing erection. Rather than resist the voyeuristic impulse, he gave into this jungle delirium and became completely absorbed in the spectacle before him.

He marveled at their complete, reckless abandon. They were clearly so swept away by the moment that any thoughts of getting caught, of getting pregnant, of spreading disease, or frankly any thoughts at all were left scattered in the bushes with their clothes. What Charles wouldn't give for that kind of escape. He felt his growing member squirm against his trousers, and he let himself reach for it.

"Let me help you with that," the young female voice said seductively in near-French behind him.

He snapped around to see who had sneaked up on him while trying to jam his swollen manhood back in through the now too-small fly. With no way to deny she had caught him and no way to cover his embarrassment, he was paralyzed for a moment, not knowing what to do.

A moment was all it took for his eyes and hormones to assess the situation for him. She couldn't have been a day over seventeen. She was nude, having tossed her blue flowered dress over a nearby branch as she had approached him. Her dark chocolate skin glowed moistly in the sun which showed every firm, creaseless curve. It was as if Eve herself had met him at the edge of the Garden of Eden. Before he could even move, she stepped up, wrapped her arms around his shoulders and pulled his face down to a long, deep, sweet tasting kiss. His mind reeled in lightheaded bliss.

He pulled away from her lips and held her head in his hands. Was she a demon sent to seduce him? He looked deeply into her dark brown eyes and saw an entirely innocent, albeit horny, young woman.

For a moment he thought how lucky he was, what an opportunity. Clearly she saw him as the American ticket to better things, so why shouldn't he use her for the stress relief he so desperately needed?

The thought only lasted a moment. He recalled all too clearly how he had treated these people as nothing more than opportunities for self-advancement when he was last here. How many houses had he burned, how many fathers had he executed, how many children's lives had he ruined under orders from the monsters he blindly followed? He dropped his hands to her shoulders and held her at arm's length. He looked at her again and realized she wasn't there for his taking. He was stunned at how easily he almost had taken her. However, he had come back to this place he had once forsaken, and it certainly wasn't to pick up the raping and pillaging where he had left off.

"No, I can't do this," he said in perfect Haitian patois as he stepped back and closed his trousers. She stepped close to him again with an eager, plaintive look on her face, and he had to push her back. "No, I really mean it. I'm over twice your age, you don't want me, believe me."

His raised voice interrupted the lovers on the other side of the hedge. They looked over at him with the fear and shame of having been caught clear on their faces.

"Such innocence," he muttered to himself. He looked back into his would-be lover's eyes, and could only repeat, "Such innocence." He shook his head, turned and ran into the jungle.

•   •   •

For the second day in a row, a commotion at the north end of his village prompted Henri Gorvil to investigate. Unlike the entrance the two black Americans had made, though, the sounds he heard were not curious whispers but the cries of frightened children. He snatched up his holy spear as he headed for the door.

Seven white men in jungle khakis and openly carrying guns were walking down the central path, looking around as if daring anyone to speak to them. They weren't government troops, something his people were all too used to seeing. Nor were they the usual variety of mercenaries, which had also become commonplace since the half-hearted American invasion some years before.

The *houngan* stepped to the middle of the path and faced the strangers with the spear at his side, planted butt down. Then he noticed the man in front only *looked* like a man. He hadn't thought it necessary to bring his Baka amulet with him but now he wished he had. He visualized touching the flower-shaped stone back on his private altar and drew strength from it.

The demon in the silver sunglasses who lead the pack held up a hand to his men to hold them back, then stepped forward to do the talking. Not at all to Henri's surprise, he spoke fluent Haitian Creole. "We're looking for two black Americans, a man and a woman, he in his thirties and she in her forties. Have you seen such a couple?"

The *houngan* allowed no expression whatsoever to appear on his face. Suddenly Sanantha's explanation that the demon was after them because they had discovered the demon's identity made sense. The demonic forces Henri had seen around Charles were not the sort left by an incarnate *l'alouby* like this one. Yet, here was the enemy himself.

"What sort of dark angel pretends to be a man and limits himself to earthly weapons?"

An eyebrow climbed behind the sunglasses. "I have no limits on my ability to get an answer to my question."

"Then you must tell me your business with the two newest members of my flock."

A tiny grin pulled at the corner of the demon's mouth for a long tense moment. "So they are now under your protection? Their objective in coming here was to find a protector."

"You must deal with me. Now state your business."

The stocky, balding, Caucasian creature squinted and took a deep breath. "Tell them that I was prepared to chase them from Washington, but that I am not prepared to fight a Master Priest. Tell them that they were right to seek shelter here. Tell them they are safe … for now."

"You still have not told me who summoned you and why you pursue them."

The demon stepped up to Henri, and although he had to crane his neck back to meet the tall priest's gaze, the threat was plenty clear. He tilted his sunglasses down to reveal bright yellow eyes, and he said in a very quiet, very controlled tone, "You can only demand that if I attack."

The creature then turned and walked back through his men, waving for them to follow. One of the men protested, saying in English, "So we just walk away?"

The demon told him flatly, "Yes."

Once they were all leaving, Henri slowly breathed out the extra air he had been holding in case he needed to blurt out a spell.

•   •   •

Sanantha heard a peculiar sound out in the peristyle sanctuary courtyard behind Father Gorvil's house and went to investigate. As she crossed the rectangular dirt yard she heard someone speaking quietly inside the large, high ceilinged, open, three-sided wooden shed that was the *oumphor* temple itself. As she approached, she recognized the voice as Charles', and he was speaking in Haitian. She stepped passed the painted central roof-supporting post and peeked around the room partition to the inner *ghuevo* sanctum at the back to see him kneeling down in front of the stone altar.

He apparently heard her approach and turned his gaze to meet hers. His face was covered in tear streaks and his eyes were bloodshot. "I'm not supposed to be in here, am I?" he asked feebly.

"This is the priest's sanctum," she affirmed gently. "People usually pray out in front of the partition."

"I'm not familiar with the Haitian way of doing these things," he said with a nervous chuckle. "I figured this is the altar."

She stepped over and sat down cross-legged next to him on the dirt floor. "Yes, this is Legba's altar. The Voodoun vision of Christ." She looked around and realized how all of the pictures on the walls of the sanctum, and the candles, rattles, dolls, bottles, and other implements on the shelves in the back of the little room were probably unfamiliar to him as well. She frowned in particular at the phallic shaped gourd sitting on the altar. "Although some of the source-of-life symbols may seem a little literal," she added with a smile.

She waited for a reaction but got none. His clasped hands were trembling in front of him.

"As your psychiatrist, I'd like to know why you suddenly feel this need to pray. An hour ago you were off to relax your mind with weeding."

He lowered his head and looked at his fingernails. "Out in the jungle, I saw something. Actually, I saw it in myself. It just took the jungle to show it to me."

"You want to tell me about it?"

He looked up at her. "Sanantha, I'd love to get this off my chest. I just can't see any productive reason to tell anyone, especially people I care about. It would just tear apart what little I have left."

She pressed her full lips together and squinted at him. "This is about your past here isn't it?"

He nodded and looked back at his hands in his lap. "I guess I've been dropping hints, hoping you'd figure it out for yourself so I wouldn't have to come right out and tell you. Pretty juvenile, huh?"

"When something is eating us inside, we often don't have a lot of control over how we show ourselves to others. Yes, it has been growing clearer that you've been here before, and it wasn't a pleasant experience."

He wheezed a laugh through his tear congested nose. "There's the understatement of a lifetime."

"Yet you can't see, what did you say, a 'productive' reason to talk about it? Do you think I'll walk away from you if I find out you've got some dark past? Remember, I help people with dark pasts for a living." She waited a moment to see if she had gotten through to him. "What did you see in the jungle?"

"I saw the path I'd taken before. The path to ruin. The path to selfishness and abuse. It still looked good." He looked up at her and his tears flowed anew. "How could it still look good after all this time?"

Grasping for a starting place, she said, "Temptation is always a problem, even when we know better. You've been having a hard time with how these people are so spiritual and so impractical. Is that view something left over from your past here?"

"Yes. We were told they were scheming malcontents, that we should never give them an inch, or they'd take a mile. We were told not to trust anyone who wasn't a known friend, to expect subversion and sabotage from everyone, especially villagers."

As his words spilled out, she started to realize the scope of his confession. She furtively looked around, and was very glad they were alone, and he was speaking English.

"How long ago were you last here?"

"Nine years ago."

"So you were what, in your twenties?"

"I left when I was twenty-five. I came to realize how wrong it all was, but I never knew how simple, how innocent, and pious these people were." He was almost pleading at this point. "I never saw that side of them before now. We were told not to think of them as people. They were just missions, just targets."

"Keep your voice down," she cautioned. "I think I understand what you're telling me. In the time you've been stateside, have you not reconciled yourself that you were lied to by your superiors?"

"Yes, I realize that. When the CIA approached me to testify against my commanders in the FRAPH, I jumped at the chance to get out. They took me stateside, gave me a new identity, got me an education, and set me up in business. You wondered why the CIA was always hanging around. They were just keeping an eye on their investment."

"Their investment?" she let slip.

He looked her square in the eye. "Sanantha, I was a goon for 'Toto' Comfort until the U.S. decided to back Aristide. My name is really Charles Montrouge. I grew up on the Voodoun back streets of New Orleans where I was recruited by the Duvaliers at the tender age of sixteen. My entire past is either street fighting, jungle fighting, or being shuttled around by sinister governments. So how am I supposed to 'reconcile' anything when I find that I wasn't just committing murder and mayhem, but I was doing it to a people who totally believe, who eat, breath and sleep the faith that has carried me through my darkest times? These people are everything I ever wanted to be when I was a kid: pious and at peace with their world."

"You saw this in the jungle today?"

"I saw how easy it would be to go back to my old ways."

She thought for a moment about her role as his doctor and as his friend. "May I suggest an alternate interpretation?"

"Sure."

"I think you saw a fork in the road, and you decided to take the other path. You should be proud of yourself for having done so."

He stared at her for a moment, intently considering her words, but then his bloodshot gaze wandered, and his head drooped again. "I don't know what to think."

"You've obviously done something to deal with the guilt for the last nine years. You said the Americans gave you an education?"

"The CIA paid for it."

"Did you get a broader, clearer world view?"

He thought about this for a moment. "Yes."

"I appreciate that you've been suffering from depression of one sort or another for most of that time. But now you're repentant. You've got to let that count for something."

"When I originally realized how evil I had been, I committed myself to Madame Erzulie. I begged her forgiveness, I began donating huge sums to Haitian relief efforts, I even gave big breaks in my business to Haitian brokers."

"You don't think this penance has been enough?"

"Obviously it isn't. Someone from my past here has sent Joseph after me."

"We don't know that, at least not yet. That's something I'm hoping we'll learn tonight. Now that you've seen the full scale of your actions in a more complete context, what do you think you could do that would let you forgive yourself?"

He held his face in his hands. "Forgive myself? I have a feeling that's a long way off." He fell silent for a moment mulling the thought. "I can tell you this. I will spend my life doing whatever I can to make it up to these people."

She let her face-filling smile unfurl like a victory banner. "Good. You can start by helping Aminta on her farm the way you said you would."

He grinned back at her. "And get off my ass and stop feeling sorry for myself?"

She got up off the dirt and extended her hand to help him up. "I didn't say that."

He took her hand and stood up as well. "That's because you are an excellent shrink." He paused and gave her a long, tight bear hug. "And a good friend. Thank you."

She squeezed him back. "You're very welcome."

•　　•　　•

Aminta was overjoyed to see Charles when he came calling at her farmhouse. She tried to treat him like a guest, and couldn't understand why he wanted to do manual labor. After she insisted on feeding him lunch, he insisted on paying her back by pulling weeds in her sorghum field. As Sanantha suggested, it felt good to busy his hands and distract himself from the horrors he found when he looked inside.

About an hour before sundown he noticed the drums. He hadn't noticed when they had first started. The sound seemed to emerge from the constant background buzz of insects in the jungle. Once he did hear them, though, there was no way to ignore them. The field was backed by a ridge and was high enough to overlook the village's valley below. They were rapid, deep drumbeats that echoed off the mountainous terrain and seemed to come from everywhere at once. He knew the drumbeats were the call to the faithful to come into town for the mass Father Gorvil would be conducting that evening. As he stood up straight and listened, they drew him into his past.

He had been taught to use the drums to track subversives. His job had been to find meetings of the leaders of the resistance held before religious services. The drums were not just a call to worship, but also a call to these meetings. He bit down hard when he recalled how he had rounded people up, and how guilt by association had been his guiding principal.

Then he stepped back from those dark times, and let the drums penetrate him in the present. He looked at himself, standing in a field, covered in sweat and dirt, weeds in his hands, and his head filled with the relentless sound of those drums. It was as if the sound were coming from the earth itself, and he were part of nature, part of the grand sweep.

He dropped the weeds and looked at his hands. For the first time in as long as he could remember, he didn't see blood on them, just dirt. He looked out over the valley, shining dark green under the bright sun in the clear blue sky. He was overwhelmed by the sensation that he was exactly where he was supposed to be, that he belonged. His eyes welled up, but the tears that ran down his cheeks were no longer the tears of regret, but tears of joy and resolve.

•   •   •

When Charles walked back into town just before sunset, he was met in the street by Father Gorvil and a band of five angry men. Clearly the priest was the only thing holding them back. The men included Atienne and the other fellows Charles had spoken so casually with earlier that morning.

"Father Gorvil," he greeted in patois, "what is the matter?"

"One of these men overheard you talking to Sanantha about your past. Do you have anything you would like to tell me?"

Charles wasn't sure what he could say that would turn the men's minds, for clearly they meant to see his blood. He looked the priest square in the eye and said, "I confess. I admit I was a killer for hire for the Duvaliers. I offer no excuses. I will say, by all that is holy, I have seen the error of my ways, and I repent. If I have come all this way to die for my sins, then I hand myself over to your judgment."

Father Gorvil tilted his head down and raised an eyebrow. "I told you the gods were angry with you the moment you walked into this village."

"I came here seeking refuge from a demon. Yes, I did plenty to warrant someone sending the demon for revenge. I have never forgiven myself for what I did. That has been my curse for nine years. I can give you no reason to forgive me. Please know that since I came here, I feel like I have finally found home. I have come to love this place and these people."

Father Gorvil squared his shoulders and brought himself up to his full towering height. "Do you confess?"

"I do."

"Do you repent?"

"I do."

"Do you expect no forgiveness in return?"

"That's right, Father."

The priest tilted his head down and gazed into Charles' eyes with such penetration that it was all Charles could do not to collapse in tears. Finally, Father Gorvil declared, "I believe you." He turned to face the angry men behind him, and repeated in Creole, "I believe him."

The men did not take the news well, backing up, grumbling with clenched fists.

"This man has changed. He knows what he did was wrong, and he has bared his soul to us. The very least we can do is forgive him. Judgment is for the gods to make, not us. Papa Legba brought this man to us, so we could do for him what Papa Legba does for us all, forgive him."

Charles dropped to his knees and grabbed up the priest's hand and kissed it.

Father Gorvil turned is hand over and took Charles' chin, lifting his head up to face him. "I wish you had told me earlier. Now to our original business. You are still being hunted by a *l'alouby*."

•   •   •

Stepping through the side gate, Charles could hardly recognize the rectangular dirt courtyard behind the priest's house. In just the few hours since he had been there, the quiet retreat had become a gaily-decorated festival site. The palm-frond thatch walls around the yard had been decorated with brightly colored banners. Flags with intricate designs covered entirely in spangles were leaned up in the corners of the yard. The ground outside the *oumphor* temple had been covered in elaborate curlicue patterns made of white flour, the *veve* symbols of the Loa gods.

There were twenty men and women along the side walls with drums and rattles and percussive sticks, all working together to build an impossibly complex rhythm. There were another fifty people dancing around in the middle of the courtyard. Everyone accented their clothing with some brightly colored sash or turban or scarf. Many of the men had their shirts off as they swayed their bodies to the music. Everyone was singing.

He stood there for a moment and took in the spectacle. The sheer joy of the place rekindled the flame in his heart that had been set in the fields. He spotted Sanantha up at the front of the congregation, talking with some men and women who were dressed entirely in white. He made his way around the dancers to Sanantha.

"Charles! Welcome!" she greeted him with her big open smile. She blinked and stared at him upon his approach. "You look like you don't know whether to laugh or cry."

"I am rather overwhelmed. It's been a helluva day."

"Anything you want to talk about?"

Charles chuckled and looked away. He shook his head and turned back to her. "Sure. They say confession is good for the soul." He walked her over to the fence away from the dancers. He took a deep breath to steady himself. "Well, I just confessed to Father Gorvil, publicly. Some of the village men overheard me telling you about my past here. Thankfully they went to him and didn't just kill me in the jungle."

"What did he say?"

He blinked, trying to come to grips with it himself. "He absolved me."

Sanantha's frown of concern smoothed and stretched into a triumphant grin. "That's wonderful!"

Charles took another deep breath. "It's a big step, all at once."

She put her hand on his arm. "I understand it's going to take you a while to forgive yourself. But this should show you that you are worth forgiving." She nodded at the ground. "Father Gorvil is really coming through for us."

"I'll say."

"No, you don't know the half of it. Joseph came into the village this afternoon looking for us. Father Gorvil sent him packing, but it seems the conversation was very strange."

Charles' grin vanished in his shock. "How so?"

"When Father Gorvil told him that we were under his protection, Joseph backed down and said he wasn't prepared to fight a *houngan*. He told Father Gorvil to tell us that he had chased us from Washington, but that we were safe here. I can't believe he would just back down like that. I mean, he blew up an airplane to try to kill us."

Charles compared this sudden change in tactics to the other sudden changes he had seen in Joseph. "Actually, that kind of mercurial twist is not that unusual for him. Maybe he just wanted me out of Washington so he can continue with his plans there. Maybe he came here to make sure we weren't going anywhere." Then he gave it another thought and concluded, "Maybe I'm grasping at straws here."

"Maybe he wants us to feel safe so we don't ask too many questions at this mass. I don't trust him for a second."

"Neither do I, believe me."

"Look, we are just about ready to start here. You and I will be seated inside the shelter, right over here on Father Gorvil's right," she said pointing at a couple of chairs. "Go ahead and sit down. I've got a few more things to do, and then I'll join you." She clutched his shoulder. "That's so great that Father Gorvil has forgiven you. All this can move ahead with a clean slate."

Charles took his chair and Sanantha disappeared around the partition into the sanctum. He was so nervous he could barely stay seated. He was torn between his growing sense of community with these people and his growing anxiety about participating in a summoning. The dancing and music was something he wanted to be a part of, yet he couldn't help but think of all this excitement as playing with fire. Now that Joseph had found them, what if they did something that really angered Joseph? What if the gods were on Joseph's side in exacting revenge for Charles' past deeds? Did these people that he was coming to care about, who were throwing themselves so enthusiastically into this effort, realize the dangers at hand?

The first thing he noticed when he sat down was the large *veve* design of Madame Erzulie on the ground next to him. It was three feet across and built around the shape of a heart. Like the other *veves*, the interior cross bars and curling branches that projected from the heart looked like an elaborate wrought iron window, only drawn with carefully-poured flour on the dark hard soil. He took comfort that it was pointed at him.

The most conspicuous feature of the temple was how the roof was held up by a central sturdy, square wooden pillar set in a stepped stone seat. The ground around the stone seat was decorated with more *veve* drawings and the steps were piled with offerings of corn, bowls of food, and open bottles of liquor. The pillar itself was painted with two intertwining serpent spirals that ran from the ground all the way up to the rafters that it supported.

He smiled at seeing the familiar pillar, just like the one in his personal altar at home. He had been surprised earlier at how differently the temple was laid out compared to temples he had seen in New Orleans. Now that everything was fully decorated, the differences and the similarities to his own practice became clearer.

He had no idea why there was a whip hanging on a hook halfway up the pillar. On the other hand, the wooden model of a ship hung near the top made him think of Erzulie's ship in his dream. The courtyard was really an extension of the temple floor, since there was no wall on that side of the temple. He then realized that the stone pillar seat was the altar for the villagers, since one couldn't even see the stone altar in the sanctum behind the partition screen.

As he watched the villagers dancing and singing and drumming, he noticed there were very few children present. He assumed they were left alone at home, since this crowd could easily be the entire adult population of the village and surrounds.

The men were dancing in circles with other men, and the women danced among themselves. Some of the villagers worked themselves into a frenzy, dancing in double-time to the drumbeats and singing. The music was also comfortingly familiar. He focused on the stomping bare feet of a nearby group of women. He glanced up and saw that a young woman in a blue flowered dress smiled coyly at him while she danced. It was the girl who had caught him in the jungle that morning. He blushed and looked away.

He was glad that Sanantha came out of the temple and sat down next to him.

"We'll start when Father Gorvil comes out," she informed him.

"Is there anything I need to know ahead of time? I mean, will I be performing any function in the ceremonies? We're sitting right up front here."

She smiled and shook her head. "No, I don't think you'll have to do anything. Father Gorvil will run everything personally. He wants you up here since he'll be seeking answers to your questions."

Charles leaned in close and took a sober tone. "Before the ceremony starts, I want to go on the record that I'm really quite worried that these people don't appreciate how much danger they're taking on, and for a stranger's problems at that. I mean, what do my problems have to do with them?"

181

"Oh, they want to be here anytime the gods speak. It's an important part of their community. The gods could choose to speak through any one of them."

Just as the sun winked out over the horizon, Father Gorvil emerged from the *ghuevo* sanctum. The drummers and singers went silent, and everyone sat down where they were. Only the drone of insects persisted. A couple of the men and women in white made their way along the walls of the peristyle, lighting torches as they went. Father Gorvil was dressed in a long white robe that struck Charles as curiously plain for someone of the priest's position. He was attended by two men and a woman, again all in white, who held various long implements for him.

Father Gorvil carried a bucket in one hand and a leafy branch in the other. He began chanting prayers as he stepped up to the central post of the temple, dipped the branch in the bucket and shook a spray of water from the branch all up the length of the pillar. Then he walked out into the crowd and continued to shake water out over the congregation. Each time he called out a prayer, the assembly would call back a response.

When Father Gorvil came back into the temple he handed the bucket and branch to one of his attendants, and took instead a black iron bar with a large disk at one end and a hook at the other. Charles understood this bar gathered spirits and made communication with them easier. He also took an elaborately beaded, long handled rattle in his other hand. Charles immediately recognized the primary tool in dealing with spirits, the *Asson* rattle wand of command. Each time Father Gorvil handed something to or took something from one of his assistants, the helper would kiss the object.

He held the iron bar up to the crowd and the drummers started a simple, consistent rhythm. Father Gorvil began a different chant that listed the names of gods, including many Catholic saints. When he was done, the crowd sang a few choruses of a joyous song that Charles did not understand.

Father Gorvil then traded the iron bar for a long, notched, wooden pole with a mirror attached to one end, which Charles remembered was the *Joukoujou*, the tree of life and the balance beam of the gods. Father Gorvil kept the long-handled rattle in his left hand. When he held the pole up, the drummers changed to a different rhythm. Again, Father Gorvil ran through a litany of gods' names, again including saints. Again the crowd sang a song when he was done.

When Father Gorvil traded the mirror pole for a sword, Charles surmised that the priest was done preparing and was now moving toward an actual summoning. Father Gorvil held the sword up and began another round of names. The drummers began yet another set of rhythms, when suddenly a man stood up and cried out from back in the crowd. The men on either side of him stepped up to steady him, and the seated crowd parted to give him room to come to the front.

The man's face was contorted in pain and he was stooped over holding his back. Charles noticed that many of the congregation paid him only passing attention, as if what was happening was nothing unexpected. He seemed weak, almost unable to hold himself up as he staggered toward the temple. He let out another cry of pain and fell to his knees, as if he had been struck in the back, but there was no one there. He reached around behind himself frantically, as if to fight off whatever was striking him. The men at his sides did nothing to assist him. Again he cried out and again he staggered under an unseen blow, this one knocking him to the ground.

Charles was horrified and thrilled at the same time. He had never witnessed a possession first-hand. He glanced at Sanantha who nodded that this is what was supposed to happen. That these people had come for the chance to be chosen for such a punishing ordeal made Charles wonder how badly they needed this spiritual contact.

As the man lie on the ground and moaned, Father Gorvil, still holding the sword and the *Asson*, stepped up and began reciting prayers over him. He stopped moaning and slowly sat up. He looked around with a contorted frown on his face. Gorvil brandished the rattle and the man looked up at him and blinked, as if seeing the tall, thin priest for the first time. The man abruptly stood up and saluted the priest in a military fashion. Gorvil planted the sword in the ground between them and saluted him back. He then called an order to his attendants who brought forth a chair which they sat down in front of the central pillar. The man grabbed up the sword, marched over and sat down in the chair, crossing one leg broadly over the other in an imperious pose. One of the attendants stepped up and draped a large red cape over his shoulders.

Father Gorvil continued to recite prayers at the man while he sat surveying the crowd. Maybe it was his expression or maybe his body language, but Charles couldn't help but feel that this wasn't just a villager putting on an act. Could this really be a personal visitation of a god? Charles was astonished. He leaned over to Sanantha and asked, "Is this Ogou?"

She raised her eyebrows and nodded. "Probably Ogou Fer, the god of wartime strategy."

"Will the man be all right after this?"

"Oh, yeah. His soul is just set aside, subjugated, is ridden by the god. That's why the Loas are called the Divine Horsemen. The people are the horses."

Suddenly the possessed man stood up and began speaking. The drummers kept up their rhythm but did so quietly as everyone strained to hear the god's words. Even Father Gorvil stepped back to give him room as he started pacing back and forth across the width of the peristyle. He held the sword rigidly up against his shoulder as he strutted, the red cape flowing behind him. "So enemies pursue you, and you don't know why. So you come to me to figure it out!"

On his return trip he turned on Charles. He strutted over to the seated man and berated him. "You're too stupid to see why enemies chase you, so you come to me to figure it out?"

Charles was terrified. He pressed back into his chair and kept an eye on the sword.

Thankfully Father Gorvil interceded. "The enemy is a *l'alouby* of some cunning. We need to know who sent this demon." Gorvil stepped over to the stone base of the central pillar and grabbed up a pot from among the offerings. Much to Charles' surprise, Gorvil reached in and pulled out a handful of corn mash paste, which he smeared onto Charles' head. "This man is vexed, not stupid," the priest declared.

184

This seemed to satisfy the possessed man, and he planted the sword in the ground in front of him and stood up straight with one fist on his hip. He then thrust out his other hand holding up his index finger and smiled hugely.

Father Gorvil held the *Asson* rattle a little higher and demanded, "Who sent the demon?"

The man stepped up to Charles, leaned forward, grinned and hissed a single word right into his face. "Sssiillaasss."

Charles recoiled and frowned at Gorvil for an explanation.

The *houngan* frowned intensely and pursed his lips at the possessed man. He demanded, "Nothing more?"

The man stood up, folded his arms over his chest and looked away without answering.

Father Gorvil looked at Charles and said, "The name of your enemy."

13

THE APPLE

S HARIR HUSSEIN WAS DESPERATE WITH DOUBT. The young
Palestinian cleric clasped his hands together in front of his blue
hassock robes and kept his eyes down, but spoke up with a force
driven by his nervousness. "I know it is not my place to question my
elders, and I mean no disrespect. It is the highest honor of my life to
be included in these discussions with your esteemed selves. But given
what we have seen before, I have to ask, before we commit ourselves.
Are you certain this will not just lead to more deaths of our people?"

As one, the five senior clerics standing in the upstairs meeting
room of the East Jerusalem mosque turned their bearded faces to
scowl at the lone dissenter. The one nearest, a man in his fifties with
a particularly unkempt graying beard, stepped toward him
threateningly and insisted, "We are already committed. Aren't you?"

"Of course I am," the young man said, retreating a step. He
touched the prayer shawl around his shoulders with both hands and

said, "I am every bit as sworn to our cause as anyone. I only ask this one last time since we will never again have the chance to examine this question."

"But we have examined it, time and again," the gray bearded priest hammered back.

A frail old priest with an enormous white beard standing toward the front of the small terra cotta tiled meeting room intervened, asking Sharir, "Can't you see how it is different this time? We have been waiting for a sign, and finally we have it."

He had no answer in the face of such reasoning.

"Do not be so hard on him," came the authoritarian voice from the front of the room. The five senior priests stepped aside so everyone could see the speaker. Seated on cushions was a rotund man wearing the same black cap and small white wrapped turban and prayer shawl as the others. But whereas the standing men wore robes of blue or gray, this man was dressed entirely in white, except for the violet blindfold that covered his eyes. The light that poured in from the high arched side windows bounced around in the tan room, but clung to this man's enormous white form. "He is right that this is a crossroads and to want us to proceed with caution. It is true that the Almighty favors a man who thinks thoroughly. On the other hand, our young comrade is forgetting that Allah favors even more so a man who listens when Allah speaks." He raised his head to address the man in the back. "Do you doubt that Allah took away my sight so that I might see more clearly His truths?"

Sharir lowered his head. "No, wise teacher. I believe you have seen the truth. I am greatly encouraged that we will, as you have said, prevail in retaking our lands." He pursed his lips as he struggled with his feelings. "I just wish there was some other way to implement the truth you have shown us."

The blind priest asked him with fatherly calm, "But you cannot think of such another way, can you?"

"No, sir. I cannot."

After a moment's silence, the nearby bearded cleric straightened his shoulders, took a deep breath of the warm, dry mid-morning air, and declared, "Then we are decided. I will go deliver the good news. The people are already assembled downstairs in the main hall."

The four older standing priests bowed slightly to him and intoned, "May Allah be with you."

He turned to the young man, who then earnestly bowed and also said, "May Allah be with you."

As the spokesman left, the remaining senior priests offered to assist the blind man, but he waved them off. He beckoned with his hand and called to the back. "Let young Hussein help me. I would have his arm and his ear for a while."

The honor of the offer did not escape Sharir. Even as his seniors frowned at the impropriety, he stepped quickly to aid the large seer. "Thank you, sir. It is my great honor."

As the two of them labored to get the big man up to his feet, the seer commented dryly, "I was counting on your back to be as strong as your love of the people." The other priests laughed at his joke, and the young man was glad for the levity. Once they were upright, the others made their salutations and left.

As the two headed for the door, Sharir looked over this shoulder and had an afterthought, "Shall I retrieve your cushions?"

"Oh no, leave them. The 'ulamas seem to enjoy having a pile of them ready wherever I might alight."

"We want to make you welcome, sir."

"Ah, now there's a fine distinction, the difference between making someone welcome, and hoping they will come."

The young priest's gaze wandered over the geometric patterns painted on the terra cotta wall tiles as he pondered the seer's riddle, but came up empty-handed. "I see that one is for the guest and the other is for the host, but one would not make a guest welcome if one did not want the guest to come."

"Exactly. So at what point do you go beyond making the guest welcome, hoping he will appear, and move on to make an open invitation?"

Again Sharir chose his words carefully. "When there is a reason you want to see the guest, beyond just for the pleasure of his company."

The blindfolded man smiled. "So the host's need must be greater. Is there any greater motivation for the guest to come?"

"One would hope the guest would understand the host's urgency and be accommodating." Sharir thought about this for a moment and then added, "Unless there is some way to make it more worth the guest's while to come."

The seer smiled very broadly. "What have you and your people done lately to make it more worth the Almighty's time to answer your invitations?"

Sharir was stunned. He stopped leading the seer's arm and stood back frowning. "How can you doubt Allah's motives? We are His people. Of course He would want to help us."

"Because you are in bondage? I would remind you the Almighty left the Jews in Egyptian bondage for hundreds of years. It wasn't until a leader emerged that any divine assistance was tendered."

Sharir was having a hard time keeping this dialogue in the theoretical. "How can you say such a thing? The entire object of Islam is to gain peace of mind by submitting to God's will. God is all-knowing, so man must follow God," he dismissed, his voice becoming strident despite his efforts.

"You've never wondered why God left the Jews in Egypt for so long?"

"We mortals cannot guess why God does anything."

"Might He have been letting the Jews ready themselves to be saved, waiting until a suitable leader emerged?"

This was getting harder, not easier. "God chose Moses as His prophet. I don't have to remind you that the *shari'ah* tells us clearly that to question God's mercy is heresy."

The seer raised his hand to calm the young priest. "It is not Allah's mercy that I question. I question how you have invited Him to help."

Sharir blinked and frowned in silence.

"I offer you a solution to the great conundrum of free will in a world where men are to follow God. In a world with free will, the Almighty does not always openly act to change the tides of man. He acts to propel those men who are of their own accord already moving in the direction God endorses."

Sharir pondered this for a long moment, then returned to a cautious choice of words. "So if we do not lead … then Allah might not support us."

The blindfolded man smiled broadly again. "Shall we continue our walk?"

Sharir hastily took his arm. "I'm sorry, of course."

The sound of men hollering rapidly swelled from the main meeting hall of the mosque below them to fill the tiled hallways of the building. Sharir initially thought a fight had broken out, but as the roar grew, he realized the hundreds of men had all raised their voices in unison. When he heard the yelling also coming from the street, he leaned out an open window and watched the angry mob pour out the front of the building. They were all carrying rocks.

Sharir then looked up the street and saw Israeli soldiers in position behind sandbags. To his further horror, he looked the other way and saw even more soldiers. There were even soldiers on rooftops all up and down the street in front of the mosque.

"No! Stop!" Sharir screamed at the top of his lungs, but the crowd was louder, and had already spotted the front line of soldiers as their target. He watched in agony as rocks flew and bullets mowed down wave after wave of onrushing men. "No! No! No!" he kept yelling, but his voice fell powerless over the carnage below.

He turned to the seer beside him, but the man had continued walking down the hall. "How could you do this?!" he screamed after the big man. "You knew this would happen!"

The man turned, and despite his blindfold, seemed to look out the arched window next to him before turning to face Sharir. He reached up and slipped off the violet kerchief to reveal bright violet eyes. He shrugged lightly, gave Sharir a melancholy smile, and said something that took a second for Sharir to understand. Sharir thought it was in Hebrew, but not completely. He did make out the words 'taking', 'candy' and 'baby."

It was the last thing Sharir Hussein ever heard, for at that instant an Israeli rocket struck the wall next to him and reduced him and the entire section of hallway to flames and blood-spattered tile fragments.

The fat man in white smirked and shook his head. He turned and strode to the end of the hallway, growing taller and more slender with each step. His fat, round face drew taut over rising cheek bones and his fist-length beard sprouted longer and curly black below his lengthening nose. When he reached the tiled end wall, he pulled off the black and white headdress and let his long curly black hair fall down around his shoulders. He looked at the colorful mosaic that faced him depicting the Garden of Eden, complete with Adam, Eve, the apple tree and the snake Iblis. He smiled wryly, then stepped like a shadow through the wall.

He stepped out onto a flat expanse of smooth gray floor that stretched endlessly in all directions. There was no horizon, as the gray floor merged seamlessly with the gray fog that obscured anything that might be in the distance. There was no actual light source, yet diffuse light came from everywhere at once. He smiled at the comfortable familiarity of this place between time and space. From here he could access anything he wanted, or nothing if he so pleased.

He strode out across the plain listening and sniffing. His high leather sandals made no sound against the textureless floor. He caught whiffs of gunpowder and heard snatches of sobbing mothers, but none of these stood out as more than mediocre turmoil. He continued walking.

At last he found something interesting. The sound of ritual drums and the smell of familiar sweat drew him off to one side. The sweat was not only familiar, but it had that hot, acrid quality of sweat borne in sleep. Troubled sleep. He quickened his pace.

Soon the smooth floor gave way to dirt, and then the dirt gave way to grass. The further he walked, the closer he came to a specific reality, and the more features appeared out of the mist in front of him. The grass ahead was thicker and taller, with bushes and trees appearing out of the gray. All the while, the sound of the drums grew louder and was joined by the chanting of prayers that he recognized as Voodou. He also recognized the perspiration as that of Charles Montrouge.

He walked into a thicket of tall broad-leafed bushes, pushed them open with his arms, and stepped through into a clearing that contained a two room, tin sided shack. The shack was at the edge of a small village. It was nighttime, with a clear starry sky and first quarter moon. The surrounding jungle was still, with only intermittent insect chirping. But he could still clearly hear the drums and chants in Charles' dream.

He stepped silently into the shack and found a black woman in her forties sleeping in one room, while Charles slept in the other. The woman struck him as an urban sophisticate, yet at the same time he could tell that she was a native Haitian. As interesting as she was, he was still drawn by Charles' troubled dream.

He was glad to see that his intervention in Miami had allowed Charles to escape his pursuer. Luggage bombs were so déclassé. He had wanted to find out more about this Egyptian demon Charles was running from. Maybe a good nightmare would provide some answers.

He gingerly wet the tip of his finger from a drop of sweat on Charles' brow and savored the smell of it under his nose like a fine wine. He smiled at the sleeping man, the way a viper smiles at an unsuspecting field mouse.

He spread his hand out over Charles' face and teased up the edges of the rainbow-colored fabric of his dream. Once he had a hold, he drew the dream up from Charles like a flowing, scintillating cloak being pulled up out of a box, and draped it around himself, enveloping himself in the dream, while being sure not to pull it free from Charles's sleeping form. As it settled around his shoulders, the dream flooded with green.

Charles was running frantically through the jungle at midday. The humidity and the heat from the sun that poured through the leafy canopy were stifling. Ritual drums pounded and voices chanted insistently from everywhere at once. Charles was wearing military fatigues with a machine gun slung over his shoulder. He carried a machete in his hand with which he occasionally chopped away vegetation in his way. The bearded observer watched quietly from behind a tree.

Charles came upon an especially thick group of tall broad-leafed bushes, and hacked straight into them with the blade. Fronds fell away to reveal a hut hidden within. When he uncovered the entrance, Charles disappeared inside.

Not wanting to miss anything, the bearded observer stretched himself out of his human form. Like some muscular, writhing taffy, he elongated into the form of a large yellow snake and slithered in through the bushes. He climbed up the hut's thatched walls and poked his broad triangular head down through the roof.

There he found Charles rummaging through boxes of files. He would seize a handful of papers and spread them out on a table, searching with his eyes and his hands, but clearly not finding what he was looking for. Then he would exasperatedly shove the useless papers onto the floor and grab another handful out of the many boxes that were stacked up along the inside walls of the hut.

After several minutes of watching this, the snake realized this could turn into a frustration dream that goes nowhere. He slithered down a support pole in the wall and coiled up at eye level. "Might I help you find whatever it is you're looking for?" he asked matter-of-factly.

Charles looked up from his papers and jumped back with a yell of fright. He stood there staring wide-eyed at the snake, sweat pouring off his face and body. His eyes flitted to the machete and gun which sat on the edge of the table, but then he stared more intently at the snake. "Who are you?"

The snake blinked his violet eyes and cocked his head to one side. "I've come back to continue helping you. You asked for my protection back in Washington, so here I am."

Charles' eyes went wide again, but this time with a face-filling smile. He dropped to his knees. "Great Maitresse Erzulie! Thank you for coming back to me."

The snake tried not to show his impatience. "What do you seek?"

As if obsessed, Charles got up and returned to rummaging through the papers on the table while continuing to talk. "I know it's got to be here. I mean, how could I have missed something this big?" He looked up at the snake with a frown on his face. "Is it possible that I so damaged someone yet didn't even know it?"

Having considerable experience invading people's dreams, the snake realized he would have to join the dream's momentum rather than just drop in and make demands. "People sometimes take great offense even from small efforts. If you didn't know it at the time, how do you know it now?" he explored.

"Well, now that we know Joseph was sent by someone, it's pretty clear that his master has it in for me. These are the records of my exploits with the Front for the Advancement and Progress of Haiti. This guy must be someone I hurt during that time." He shook his head and insisted, "I suspected it all along."

"So the demon in Washington pursued you here," the snake tested rhetorically.

Charles looked up and frowned. "Of course. He visited the village yesterday. Didn't you … You mean you haven't …" He interrupted himself and quickly apologized. "Please forgive me. I didn't mean to presume."

"I am here for you now," he covered smoothly.

"You were there for me in my dream on the plane down here, saving me from Joseph, and for that I thank you as well."

The snake wondered what he had missed, but didn't let it show. "You are here now by choice?"

"Well, I certainly didn't choose Joseph's luggage bomb and the ensuing plane crash, but yes, I think have found the peace I came looking for."

The snake considered the thoroughness of an adversary who plants two bombs to bring down a plane. "In Washington he tried to kill you. You say he visited the village yesterday, yet you are still alive. Why?"

Charles seemed taken aback at the bluntness of the question. "We don't know exactly. He said he didn't want to fight the village priest. I don't believe that."

"You have now discovered this Joseph demon was summoned and you want to know by whom."

"Oh, I know that. Ogou told me last night at the Voodou mass." Charles looked more than a little confused, and he proceeded cautiously. "I take it you haven't spoken with Ogou recently."

"He hasn't seen fit to share," he covered. Continuing nonchalantly, he asked, "So, who did Ogou expose as this mastermind?"

Charles returned to his rummaging and answered, "Someone named Silas."

It was all the snake could do not to hiss out loud at this news. He coiled tighter around the pole and tried to contain himself, but still ended up baring his fangs.

"No last name, just Silas," Charles went on. "I cannot for the life of me remember knowing anyone with that name." Charles looked up and was startled by the snake's reaction. "What? Is it that bad?"

The snake managed to calm himself enough to continue the conversation. "You can stop scouring your memory. He is not an old enemy of yours. He is, in fact, an old enemy of mine."

Charles' eyebrows shot up. "How terrible does a man have to be, to become a personal enemy of a god? What would such a man want with me?"

"I will need to intervene. You must tell me whenever you learn anything more about this man Silas, or have any further contact with this Joseph lackey of his."

"I will be sure to stay near the *oumphor*."

"I am especially fond of burnt offerings."

Charles frowned in his confusion. "You mean incense?"

"Incense will do. Make it strong though. Tar pitch and hair are some of my favorites."

Charles continued frowning, but nodded. "Yes, Grand Madame. I will do as you say."

"Good. You will remember this dream vividly when you awake, so be sure to rethink it in the morning. You must remember to keep me informed about this, or I won't be able to intervene on your behalf."

"Yes, Grand Madame, I will. Thank you again for taking mercy on such a sinner as myself."

"Amen," the snake said with a nod, and climbed back up the pole. When he had slithered a safe distance back out into the jungle, he reconstituted himself in human form. He then peeled the edge of the dream fabric from his shoulders and unfurled it from around his body. Standing back in the shack, he scooped up the loose dream with his hands and poured it back in to Charles' sleeping form.

The sky was just beginning to glow a pre-dawn dark blue when he stepped from the two-room shack. Charles said Joseph had visited the village the day before, presumably to verify that Charles was safely out of the way of Joseph's activities in Washington. Now to find Joseph. Of the impressions to follow, he preferred to track by smell, but even in the morning cool, the stench of the jungle was too strong a competition for the subtle nuances of a soul's odor, even a demon's soul.

He started to look into the center of the village for traces where Joseph had touched the ground when he saw the path right in front of the shack was littered with the demon's ethereal imprint, both coming and going. Since he could see these "footprints" from a distance, he considered his options and decided on flight. He took two bounding steps, transformed himself into an enormous raven, and took wing out over the jungle.

Tracking the demon's path was not difficult. It appeared that Joseph had systematically visited villages in a sweep out from the coast. Once Joseph had located Charles, he had headed straight back to the shore. Clearly there had been a boat involved. About a mile offshore he found the sunken airliner. The raven was disappointed with how long a search of the coastline would take. He was glad that by now he had a clear grasp of Joseph's essence visually, since the seashore was every bit as pungent a cover of scents as the jungle had been.

He was pleased and surprised at how quickly he picked up the trail. Just ten miles up the coast in the harbor of Port de Paix, he found Joseph's essence fresh in a variety of shops. He was intrigued that there was no trace of Joseph heading inland from the port area of town. If the docks were where he visited, then the docks would have to do. He swooped in low and verified that Joseph was not on the waterfront.

He realized that if Joseph was any kind of demon worth his salt, he would be able to see right through any outward disguise. No, this situation called for a bolder tact. He landed on a wharf behind a ramshackle storage warehouse and emerged as a doppelganger of Charles, wearing island whites and dark sunglasses.

Walking down the weathered planks of the wharf front, he saw a lot of contact trace at the Harbor Master's office, but this didn't really suit his purposes. The main road into town, though, with its provisions and marine supply stores, yielded pay dirt immediately. Clearly here were the people with whom Joseph did regular business.

Christof's Maritime Mercantile had enough inventory to fill a space twice the size of its small, rickety warehouse building. Racks of boat parts and piles of gear were stacked eight feet high or higher all throughout the store, forming narrow aisles that often were mere spaces to slip between stacks. The three bare light bulbs that hung from the rafters did little to illuminate these canyons of merchandise. "Charles" kept his sunglasses on just the same.

Both of the men behind the counter had recent contact trace on them, and they both looked like either could be the proprietor. The muscular, gray haired black man was loading a roll of receipt paper into the very well-worn cash register, while the fine featured, bearded white man was checking a list on a clipboard.

"Have either of you gentlemen seen Joseph around today?" he asked casually while stepping up to the counter.

The two men looked up with a tell-tale flicker of recognition, and then glanced at each other. The big black man stood up straight and asked bluntly, "Who wants to know?"

"Charles Redmond," he said with a friendly smile, and held his hand out.

Although the big man's handshake was forthcoming, the look of mild suspicion did not leave his face. "Hank Marquez."

"Pleased to meet you. I was told Joseph does a lot of business in these parts. I happened to be in town this morning and I was hoping I might cross paths with him."

Hank shook his head and shrugged. "Customers come and go. He's not been in today, and he might not be for a while."

"Although he does have a shipment in," the white man interjected in his crisp prep school accent.

Hank shot him an angry look over his shoulder that Charles spotted without reacting. Hank turned back to Charles stone faced and commented off-handedly, "He might be in soon."

Charles shrugged and asked, "In that case, might I leave a message for him? I really have no other way of reaching him, and it is rather urgent," he added, directing his comments to the less resistant white man.

The man glanced to see his partner's reaction before answering. "If he comes in, and if I see him when he does."

Charles smiled. "Good enough for me. The message is really quite simple. Please tell him that Charles Redmond came looking for him, that our business is not over after all, and that I know about Silas' plans and I'm not happy about them."

The two men exchanged nods, and Hank turned back to Charles. "Simple enough."

Charles held his hand out again and smiled warmly. "Thank you so much." When Hank had shaken it, he held his hand out to the white man, who shook it as well. "You've been a great help to me."

As he stepped back out onto the street, Charles scanned the other store fronts for similar targets to drop his bait.

•   •   •

Sanantha shifted nervously as she and Charles sat on the front stair of their shack. "So you want to stay here, lay low, and what, wait for a sign?"

Charles could see that she was trying to be reasonable and remain calm, but he could also see her growing impatience with his inaction. They spoke in English in case they were overheard, which was unlikely given the din of insect and bird noises all around them in the jungle. "I don't see much other choice," he explained. "I mean, I don't know who this Silas guy is. Erzulie has been there for me all along. I am convinced I would not be alive today if not for her help. If she says she is going to intervene against this enemy, even if it was in a dream, then who am I to argue?"

She scratched her temple under the edge of her tall yellow turban. "In the meantime, you do nothing to find out who this Silas is?"

"In the meantime, I stay within the only protection that I have against Joseph, and that's here under Father Gorvil's watchful eye.

Besides, what could I do for research? I'm not very well going to walk into the Ministry of Defense and say, 'Hello, I'm Charles Montrouge, a wanted criminal. Do you mind if I look through your records of my exploits?' I really don't have anywhere to search."

"I could go into a city and start checking phonebooks or newspapers. Better yet, I might even find Internet access."

"That's a great idea," he said genuinely. "I would really appreciate that kind of effort."

"But you're staying here."

"Joseph as much as said that if I leave, I'm a dead man. It's not like I want to just sit here. You know me better than that. Getting caught up with Joseph was bad enough. I can't tell you how thrilled I am to find out now I'm a pawn in some battle between gods and their enemies."

Sanantha paused in thought. "Erzulie gave you no hint as to how she would intervene?"

"None."

She stood up and brushed off the seat of her long skirt. "Then it's off to the big city for me. Father Gorvil said the road to Jean Rabel is about an hour's walk."

"Yeah, and then it's another three hours walk along that road into town."

"Assuming I don't get a lift. At the outside, that will get me there right around nightfall." She was suddenly distracted and looked intently into the bushes on the other side of the path. "What the *merde* is that?"

Charles turned to see a cloud of yellow mist condense spontaneously from the air. It grew denser and swirled into a man-sized, dark yellow tornado which in the space of two seconds coalesced into the all-too-familiar form of Joseph.

"Shit!" was all Charles could blurt before grabbing Sanantha's hand and dashing toward the village center.

Joseph was quick on his feet and cut them off. Joseph had a machine pistol, but he let it dangle on a strap over his shoulder. Holding his hands up in front of him, he said, "Not so fast. Right now, my men are surrounding this village. You either come quietly or a lot of people are going to die needlessly."

"*Tout ca qui marvais ce pour sorti!*" Charles yelled.

Joseph winced. "That is *so* offensive. You keep that up and I will shoot you right here."

Charles wasn't sure what to do next, given that was the only countermeasure he had.

Sanantha turned fear into anger. "You can't hold an entire village of innocents hostage like that!"

Joseph remained chillingly calm. "That depends on how many of them know about 'Silas'."

Despite wanting to hide the truth from Joseph, Charles and Sanantha couldn't help but glance tellingly at one another.

"Oh, they all do. Well, too bad for them."

"No wait," Charles pleaded. "It's just a name. No one knows what it means."

"You do, and you've been blabbing it all over the island. I don't know what you were trying to do by calling me out, but you shouldn't be so surprised that I'd accept your little invitation."

Sanantha looked at Charles who could only frown in confusion. "What are you talking about?" he demanded of the demon.

"Don't play stupid with me. We both know the only reason you're still drawing breath is I don't know how much you know or who you've told. But we're going to solve that little deficit in private," he added with a wry grin. He pointed down the path behind them. "Now move it."

Charles' heart was pounding so hard from the adrenaline rush that he could barely contain the urge to dash off into the jungle. The only thing that stayed his feet was the thought of harm coming to the villagers he had come to care for.

He and Sanantha exchanged doubtful looks and were about to go with Joseph when a burst of gunfire rang out from the far side of the village. Joseph grabbed the field phone off his belt and demanded, "What was that?"

"It's the damn villagers, Sir!" came the easily overheard man's voice on the phone. "They're armed and ready for us. We're held up on the north side of town."

"Well, blast your way out of there if you have to, but meet me on the west side immediately!" Joseph barked. He then turned to Charles and Sanantha. "So much for your innocent villagers."

It was all Charles needed to hear. He knew he'd have to make this up to Sanantha somehow, but with Joseph's weapon dangling at his side, and the villagers apparently no longer in danger, this seemed his only chance to get back to Father Gorvil. Without so much hint as a blink, he dashed full speed into the jungle. Much to his surprise, he actually made it into the thick cover without Joseph shooting him. In fact, he heard no gunfire and no one following him. He realized that running from someone who can teleport at will could be a new height of folly, but he had to try.

Heading south, he didn't want to get too far away from the village on his left. He kept running as fast as the rocky, vegetation strewn terrain would allow, knowing that he had never explored the jungle on this side of the village.

He smashed his way through a stand of leafy bushes and nearly tumbled over the edge of a deep, wide ravine. Having run out of ground while still not knowing where Joseph was made his heart race so fast he could hardly think. He spotted a tree that had fallen across the ravine some twenty yards to his right. As flimsy as the bridge looked, it was his only escape route.

As he clamored along the edge of the ravine, he heard running footfalls coming up rapidly behind him. The tree was too narrow, too slippery with vines and rot to walk across, so he had to swing under it and cross hand over hand. His grip was tenuous at best on the moldering wood, but with one unsure grasp after another he slowly made his way out over the chasm. At about the midpoint, the slender tree began to sag under Charles' weight. One of his tire tread sandals fell off and spun lazily into the green depths. Only then did he notice how easy a target he made in his white shirt and khaki pants against the green lined ravine. He imagined Joseph standing at the edge with his gun aimed. He didn't want to look back, but he had to. No Joseph. Yet. He sighed his relief and pressed on.

As he climbed up into the jungle, he turned around only long enough to dislodge the tree from his side and send it crashing down into the bushes below. No sense in making it easier for his pursuers.

Just as he made his way back under cover, Joseph broke through to the edge of the ravine. Charles was sure he would simply teleport across, but the demon stopped and assessed the chasm, then glanced back over his shoulder. Joseph selected a tree and opened fire with his machine gun to saw it down. The fleshy pulp exploded with the bullet impacts, but the damage did not sever the stringy, fibrous timber. Charles watched with horrified fascination as Joseph then removed his sunglasses. A bright flash of white light lanced out from his eyes and cleanly sliced the tree from its roots with the sound of a thunderclap. He stood back as it wavered and then fell across the ravine, forming a much sturdier bridge than Charles had used. When Joseph spoke into his field phone and started to run across the bridge, Charles' fascination turned into fleetness of foot.

Charles found a path leading to the village and turned onto it. Just as the outermost shacks came into view, Joseph stepped out of the bushes right in front of him. Figuring he had little left to lose, Charles hoped to take advantage of his speed and tried to barrel into Joseph. The shorter man deftly sidestepped him and scooped Charles under an armpit which sent him flipping over backwards to land spread eagled, painfully onto his face in the hard pack of the path. Whatever of his light-colored clothes wasn't already covered in green plant stains was now smeared with dirt. Charles tried to turn over and found himself pinned by Joseph's knee in his back.

The sound of multiple rifle bolts being cocked made the both of them look up. Ten village men stood at the ready with their weapons aimed at Joseph. Charles looked up at Joseph and saw him grin that wry self-assured grin that always gave Charles the creeps. A moment later, a commotion from behind them in the jungle produced half a dozen of Joseph's men, also with weapons drawn and ready.

Behind the villagers walked the looming figure of Father Gorvil. "Joseph," he called out in Haitian loud enough for all to hear. "You have come to collect one of my flock, but you must first face the shepherd."

Joseph answered him in Haitian without letting Charles up. "I told you he was safe as he was. But you couldn't leave well enough alone. This is the price of your curiosity."

"But my curiosity persists. Why does your master seek this man?"

"He does not. This man is insignificant except for the trouble he has caused me. The harm he is about to cause you is further proof of his troublesome nature. I suggest you step away from this vexing man, lest he drag you down as well." With that Joseph seized Charles by the back of his shirt and hauled him to his feet. "You might note that my men are wearing Kevlar and your men are not. I am leaving with this man. Any bloodshed will be on your hands."

Charles couldn't help but notice the stench of nervous sweat that covered everyone except Joseph. Gorvil took a moment, clearly sizing up his options. While he did, the sound of a vehicle wending its way through the jungle grew louder behind Joseph's men. Charles despaired that it was probably reinforcements for Joseph. Apparently Gorvil came to the same conclusion, because at that point he gave up. "You may have won the day, Unclean One. But I cannot allow this to go unanswered. We will hunt you down."

The vehicle stopped just out of sight, and a man stepped from the bushes. "You won't have to do that," he announced calmly in Haitian with a gravelly voice that carried despite the open jungle. The tall white man was dressed in island whites and had a shock of pure white hair, heavy jowls and piercing blue eyes. He walked up between Joseph's men, past Joseph and Charles, ignored the villagers and the weapons they trained on him, and reached between them to extend his hand to Gorvil. "I am Father Silas Alverado. I apologize for my servant's enthusiasm. I assure you, as one *houngan* to another, that no harm will come to this man."

Gorvil looked at this newcomer with unabashed skepticism, but then seemed to have some kind of revelation. "Father Alverado? I have heard of you." He went to shake the white man's hand and noticed that he had offered his left. Charles craned his neck to see why, but could not see what was happening. Gorvil shook his hand, although still tentatively. "I did not know your first name was Silas."

"I'm glad my reputation precedes me," he chuckled. "We need to ask Mister Redmond some questions, and then we will release him back to your care."

"You run a village where it is said people have strange customs. It is a day's walk from here, yes?"

"Yes. It's called Terre Noir, and it is about twenty miles east of Port de Paix. You are welcome to come and see it for yourself."

Gorvil eyed Joseph and told Alverado, "*Houngans* do not employ demons, sorcerers do."

The white man, nearly as tall as Gorvil, pointed at the flower shaped stone amulet the black priest had around his neck. "Consult your Baka Stone. Joseph is not a demon, but an archangel of the Guedes, the gods of order and ritual."

The village men all sucked in an amazed breath. Many of them touched their privates. Gorvil's lean face squinted into a tight frown.

Charles couldn't take this any longer. "Don't believe him!" Pointing at Joseph he insisted, "I've seen the heartless destruction this monster can do."

Joseph started to restrain him, but then smiled when he had finished his outburst. The balding white man in sunglasses commented quietly to him in English, "Thank you for proving our point. Archangels are known for their heartless destruction."

Charles sighed and shook his head.

Alverado continued in Haitian. "You should also know that this man is not the innocent victim he would have you believe he is. He had considerable contact years ago with previous oppressive regimes here in Haiti. My grievance with him is largely due to his involvement with the American CIA in Washington. I will let him explain himself to you when I return him."

Charles was speechless. Who was this guy and how did he know so much? He looked at the villagers and saw how effective this seed of doubt was. These people hated the CIA even more than they feared demons. Obviously Alverado knew that too. "I came to you for help," Charles pleaded with Gorvil. "You said you would protect me. You can't let these evil people take me like this."

The tall black priest looked from Charles to Alverado, to Joseph, to Joseph's armed men, and back to Charles. "I still have many questions, but there does not appear to be much I can do to stop them."

Alverado looked Gorvil in the eye and said earnestly, "All of your questions will be answered."

He then turned around and led his men, and Charles, away into the jungle.

As they left the village clearing, Charles felt his chest heavy with dread. Had he really run out of options? He happened to look up and spot something in the branches of a tree overhead. A large black snake was coiled up defensively and was looking straight at him. When it opened its mouth and hissed, Charles thought he caught a glint of violet in its eyes.

14

PURGATORY

SANANTHA AWOKE TO THE SOUND OF AN OUTBOARD MOTOR and the jostle of moving at high speed in a small boat. As she surfaced from unconsciousness, she struggled to put a context on how she was suddenly at sea. She cracked open an eye and found herself strapped into an upholstered seat, propped up against a rolled blanket. Then she noticed the smell of the sea and the wind blowing through her hair. She turned her head tentatively and saw Charles sitting next to her. She raised her head and saw she was on a six-passenger speed boat headed out to sea. The passenger in the front seat was Joseph, who was turned around facing her.

He gave her a remarkably compassionate smile. "How's your head?" he asked, voice raised over the sounds of the wind, the motor and the water rushing under the boat.

Charles hadn't seen her awake until then. He started to put a hand on her shoulder, but couldn't since he was handcuffed to the side rail of the boat.

"A bit fuzzy, but not bad," she answered with a sarcastically raised eyebrow. "What the hell did you do to me? The last thing I remember is standing with you on the path in front of the shack. Charles had just run into the bushes and I turned back to you … wait a minute. You reached for your sunglasses."

Joseph grinned boyishly. "Believe it or not, the best thing for your head right now is a cold beer. I'll have our cook bring you one as soon as we dock."

Sanantha looked out in front of them and was stunned by recognition. The huge white yacht they were approaching was clearly the same one they had seen at the plane crash. She made out the name on the prow: *Purgatory*. She turned to Charles with her mouth open.

He smirked weakly. "Yeah, I know. Once again, paranoia is our friend."

She sat quietly the remaining minutes of the trip, reflecting on how swimming back from the plane crash to be picked up would have certainly gotten them killed. As it was, they had learned enough in the meantime to make Joseph curious enough to spare them, at least for the time being.

Given that he was covered in mud and plant stains, and was now in handcuffs, Charles had obviously put up a good chase. Obviously not good enough. When he saw her looking over his condition, Charles shrugged and shook his head. She gave him as reassuring a smile as she could.

On board, she was shown to her own spacious, richly appointed stateroom, with clean clothes, a shower, a cold beer as promised, a locked door and a non-opening window. She wondered if the beer was poisoned, but then realized how pointless that would be. To her mild surprise, it really did clear her head. She took advantage of the shower and the clothes, a Middle Eastern looking embroidered yellow caftan, and then sat wondering what would come next.

A few minutes later a dull rumble sounded through the walls, and she felt the ship accelerate. She looked out the window but could only see open ocean, therefore no landmark by which to measure motion.

Half an hour later, just as the sun was setting, someone knocked on her door. "Ms. Mauwad, are you decent? May I come in?" asked the large-sounding man's voice.

"Yes to both," she said, without getting up from the nest of pillows she had made on the bed.

The door opened and a tall muscular redheaded man in a blue polo shirt and white slacks came in. "Evenin' ma'am. I'm the First Mate, Jack McKinney. Mister Alverado will see you now."

"Oh, is it Mister Alverado, now?" she asked dryly, continuing to sit on the bed. "I thought Joseph and I were on a first name basis."

Jack looked surprised at her response. "No ma'am. I meant Mister Silas Alverado. This is his boat."

The mysterious 'Silas' after all. She raised her eyebrows and pursed her full lips for a moment, then hopped off the bed. She breezed past the redhead and out into the wood paneled hall. "Well, we mustn't keep him waiting. So, where are we headed?"

"I'm not supposed to talk to you, ma'am, just deliver you."

"Ah, the strong, silent type."

As Jack escorted her forward, heated words filtered through the closed salon door. She recognized one of the voices as Joseph's and had to assume the other belonged to Silas. Her escort seemed surprised enough at the argument that he didn't immediately think to lead her away.

"How am I supposed to continue serving you at this point if you don't tell me what your objective is?" Joseph asked, frustration tightening his voice.

"By following my orders to the letter," Silas demanded indignantly.

"But Master," he pleaded, "you said we only have three more days. Will you not tell me what happens in three days?"

"No," came the calm, flat answer. "That's the last I want to hear of it. Or do I really need to remind you that I'm still the one wearing this ring?"

"No, Master," he said quickly in a much-subdued voice.

Sanantha wondered how much the crew knew of Silas' hold over Joseph. Jack suddenly grasped the situation and turned her back. "Afraid I'll hear something I shouldn't?" she asked him coyly.

"We can wait in the Mess next door," he said without answering her.

The conversation inside had stopped anyway. When they heard footsteps coming toward them, Sanantha quickly reached around the big man and knocked sharply on the door.

Jack was caught flat-footed. She flashed him her big face-filling smile, just as Joseph answered the door. He looked at the two of them without expression, then wordlessly stepped past them as he left.

"Ah, Doctor Mauwad."

The old man inside warmly greeted her, with no trace of being upset from the previous conversation. He stood well over six feet tall, with a mane of pure white hair over piercingly blue eyes. The bags under his eyes and the jowls that hung off the square jaw softened his look, making him look more like someone's grandfather than a demon-commanding sorcerer. The heavily-embroidered dark blue caftan he wore was the only thing exotic or mysterious-looking about him.

"Please come in. Thank you, Jack. Close the door on your way out." As Jack did this, Silas crossed the room and extended his left hand to her. "I am Silas Alverado."

She instinctively started to hold out her right, but corrected herself as smoothly as she could. She noted that his right hand was deformed and in a glove. She shook his hand and found it warm and strong. At close range, his eyes were intense.

"I apologize if my bringing you on board under these circumstances has left you ill at ease. In fact, your freedom is precisely what I would like to talk about. Please have a seat, make yourself comfortable." He stepped to the door and traced a pattern on it with one finger. Moving toward the bar, he asked, "Can I get you a drink?"

Sanantha walked across the club-like room with its wood shuttered windows and dark wood end tables and sat down on one of the cream-colored leather sofas. She did not lean back or relax. "You can drop the act."

The white-haired man went ahead and poured two snifters of cognac anyway. "I have every intention of telling you what you want to know, Doctor. You are understandably under a lot of stress and this will help you cope."

The psychiatrist took the offered glass but did not drink.

Sipping his own and taking a facing armchair, Silas asked simply, "Where would you like me to begin?"

Sanantha leaned forward and eyed him suspiciously. "Did you send Joseph to exact vengeance on Charles for something he did when he was last in Haiti?"

Silas leaned back and put his sandaled feet up on an ottoman. "No. Charles was simply a business contact of Joseph's, until Charles unfortunately became aware of Joseph's non-human nature. I had suspicions that Charles may have been acting on behalf of my enemies, so I had Joseph investigate further and restrict Charles' ability to interfere."

"You do know that he blew up an airliner full of innocent people?"

"Yes I do. Fortunately I had the advantage of knowing in advance that no harm would befall any of the passengers. In fact, that incident led directly to this meeting we are having, which alone is worth such a sacrifice."

His matter-of-fact tone left her not knowing where to go next. "You're telling me you knew no one would be hurt *before* the plane went down?"

"I'm telling you that fate drew you and me together, and I am not going to criticize anyone who acted to expedite that. I would never have brought you here if this had only been about Charles and Joseph crossing swords. When I discovered that Charles had brought you to Haiti, I had to make sure we would meet."

She frowned at him, looking for some sign of deception. He looked back at her with no telltale eye shift or blink. "Why me?"

"You are the one piece my plan has always been missing. You know the people of Haiti and you know Voodou. You know psychology and you understand why people believe the things they do. You are articulate so you can put that knowledge to work.

"To risk being immodest, I am in the middle of ushering in a new Age of Mankind. My first steps are here, in Haiti. My progress has been slow because I have had to split my efforts between my work here and the rest of my plan. I need a lieutenant to assist me here.

"This weekend I am going to capture a powerful demon and extract from him a set of keys that will allow me access to tremendous scientific knowledge. I will need a scientist to interpret this knowledge so that it can be used by mankind. In addition to a practicing psychologist, you are also an accomplished scientist, with many published papers. With so many of your qualifications matching my needs, the question becomes, who else but you?"

She mulled this over for a moment and decided to have a sip of the brandy after all. "Why should I help you?"

"My plan will proceed with or without you. I'm offering you a chance to be part of a turning point in history, the sort of thing that only happens once in a hundred lifetimes. I don't know how to make it any more attractive to you."

"You said this weekend. Today is Wednesday. Where are we headed?"

"The world's largest stone obelisk."

"The Washington Monument? Do I have to sign up before you tell me the details?"

Silas raised his bushy white eyebrows and laughed. "No, no, it's not like that. As I said, this all goes down in a few days, one way or the other. Let me try to encapsulate the scope of my plan.

"My magic is that of ancient Egypt. I am, in fact, the reincarnation of a High Priest of Amun who lived in the twelfth century BCE, exactly one hundred generations ago. In that previous life, I saw this demon use these keys. I was probably the only one who actually saw them, but I did, so I know they exist. The demon used these keys to betray Egypt. I was the priest appointed to try to rectify the betrayal, but that was not possible at the time. This betrayal was the beginning of the eventual decay and fall of Egypt as a world power. My quest is to reverse that course.

"My plan starts here in Haiti because the Voodoun faith is the direct descendant of the religion of the ancient Egyptians. With remarkably small changes to ceremony, Voodou summons the gods of Egypt, who are alive and well. My research shows that whatever magical effect is possible with Voodou is in fact derived from accessing the power of the Egyptian gods. I'm sure you have noticed the obvious similarity between the *Joukoujou* balance beam and the staff of Thoth. The *houngan*'s source of power, his Baka stone, is a crude version of the Rose of Thoth that was worn by high adepts in the Egyptian temple. Even the word Baka comes from Ba and Ka, the Egyptian names of the soul in heaven and here on Earth. The list goes on and on."

Sanantha caught herself being drawn into his calm confidence. She retrieved her skepticism. "Wait a minute. I can see where African Voodoun inherited rituals and terms from ancient African sources, including ancient Egypt. But you're saying Voodoun practitioners today are actually, accidentally, addressing those old gods?"

"Precisely. The details have become diluted over time, but the results one gets from praying to Erzulie come from Isis. Similarly, Legba is actually Horus, and Danbhalah is Amun-Ra. The pantheons line up god for god because they are different names for the same beings."

"Wait a minute. I believe in these gods. I know these gods. These gods have helped me all my life."

"I'm not denying their existence — quite the opposite. I'm offering proof of their power. I'm just clarifying their identities. Doesn't it strike you as unlikely that your patient would get tangled up with Joseph, and the two of you would come here for help, directly to me? You believe in Erzulie. I believe in Isis. She's the same deity. She drew us together."

Sanantha had to blink; she had wondered at the coincidence. "So you want to, what, convert the Haitians?"

"Yes. I've already converted a sizable village," he added with evident pride. "My villagers immediately saw the improvement in their lives once they began addressing their gods by their rightful, original names. All the old fears and guilt from the French war have been wiped away."

"You're saying one of my jobs would be to expand this conversion? I think you called it a lieutenancy."

"Correct."

"Let's say you accomplish your three-thousand-year-old revenge on this demon, and you get his 'keys,' as you called them. What could you do?"

Silas shook his head and shrugged. "Anything." After a second's thought, he smiled. "Everything. What do you know of the Tarot?"

Sanantha frowned, not sure if he had changed the subject. "You mean fortune telling cards? Almost nothing," she admitted frankly.

"How well do you know the Old Testament Book of *Exodus*?"

Sanantha's frown deepened. "There is no demon in the story of Moses," she asserted cautiously.

Silas' face brightened. "Oh yes there is. No matter what miracles Moses brought down from his god, Ramses wouldn't listen to his pleas for Jewish freedom. You were raised using a Christian Bible, so I'll only cite the King James version. There, it's described that, 'Pharaoh's heart was hardened.' Why? How could an intelligent man of the world — the leader of his faith — miss the point that Moses' god needed to be reckoned with, not just dismissed? I'll tell you how. Pharaoh's High Priest performed magic to prove Moses' miracles insignificant. This reduced the conflict to a personal, ego driven one between Ramses and Moses."

"Excuse me," Sanantha commented, raising her hand. "You've lost me. Is this what happened in your previous life?"

"Yes."

"Who was the demon?"

"The High Priest," he offered patiently. "Think about it. Who was this man who could match, up to a point, Yahweh's own magic, who could alter the nature of a cosmic conflict of two religious systems, and yet remain anonymous and inconspicuous throughout?"

"You think he was a demon?"

"I know he was. I was there. In my past life, I was his pupil, his successor to the office of High Priest after he fled Egypt when Moses won. No one suspected at the time, but we should have known." Silas looked down into his drink and reflected. Looking back at Sanantha, he resumed with new vigor. "Ramses was the best Egypt had to offer. A brilliant politician, a devastating soldier, one of the greatest leaders in all of history," he insisted with obvious reverence. "Moses was trained in the most-sacred ways of the Egyptians before he was cast out. He too was a great natural leader. The two of them had grown up together in Court. To see these two clash as the champions of their respective gods was just too tempting an opportunity for subversion for this demon to pass up. What should have been a test of religions was reduced to a battle of egos. With such an 'inside man' working against him, Ramses didn't stand a chance."

"Wait a minute. You're Egyptian?"

"Yes."

"You're saying this was a Jewish demon? Masquerading as the pharaoh's High Priest? Was it working for Jehovah?"

"He was none other than Sammael, the Hebrew demon Prince of Liars. But I believe Sammael was acting on his own. I don't think Jehovah, or Yahweh as he was known then, knew what this demon was doing. In fact, Sammael's actions made Moses' job more difficult. King James' scholars gave this man the name Janus, which comes from the Roman gatekeeper god who had two faces. Two-faced, in other words, a fraud."

"Wait a minute. Sammael, as in the snake in the Garden of Eden. The Devil? You're going after the Devil?"

"He goes by many names, and he's left his black mark throughout history. In this one instance he walked the Earth as a man, and he had in his possession the physical keys to the secrets of the universe. He knew the conflict with Moses was coming. He also knew Moses would bring down divine intervention, and he needed to make it look insignificant compared to Egyptian magic. So, years earlier, Sammael, as the newly appointed High Priest of Amun, introduced new magic to the Egyptian Temple. Magic more powerful than anything that had ever been seen on Earth, or ever has been seen since. By the time Moses returned from Sinai and confronted Ramses, the High Priest could wield tremendous power without arousing suspicion.

"Remember I mentioned the Tarot. The Tarot cards we have today barely work. They work so poorly, in fact, that most people, like yourself, view them as the tools of carnival fortune tellers. The deck doesn't work because the seven most important cards have been removed. These missing seven Tarot cards were created by this demon who insinuated himself into the royal court shortly after Ramses became Pharaoh."

"This is the same man who set up Ramses with Moses," she concluded.

Silas nodded. "When Ramses failed, the priest took back the seven most powerful cards and left."

"All that power, all that magic, was from just seven Tarot cards?"

"The Tarot is a tool," he explained. "It connects the conscious mind with the subconscious. The subconscious is the spirit, with access to all the knowledge of the universe. By communicating accurately with the spirit-self, those secrets can be brought into this, the material plane. Think of it, all the knowledge that ever was or ever will be."

However bizarre and frightening his scenario was, she had to hear him out. The black psychiatrist's gaze shifted around the dark blue and gold carpeted floor as she drew her conclusions. "So the cards are of Jewish origin, not Egyptian. You and Joseph are Egyptian, which is why you can't tell Joseph what you're after?"

"Yes. It really is none of his business. I therefore must demand that you not share this with anyone, at least not until I have the tablets."

"Tablets? You mean the missing seven cards?"

Silas smiled. "Yes. The missing cards are called the Tablets of Aeth. They have been the quest object of mystics for the thirty-two centuries since their one appearance. As I said, as the demon's protégé, I may have been the only man to have ever actually seen them."

"This really is a personal matter with you?"

"I am the right man for the job," he countered. "My goddess chose me at the time to be the one to come back and capture him."

Sanantha did not miss how he diverted her from focusing too closely on himself. At the same time, she realized again how seductive it was that he had answers after she had gone for so long with none. "I'm still unclear on why you need to convert the Haitians. Once you have these cards, won't you be able to go back to Egypt and perform whatever miracles you want?"

Silas' smile turned a wry edge and he took a deep, sighing breath. "This is where it all comes back, full circle. After the fall of Egypt to the Romans, the legacy of the Gods was carried on by the other nations of Africa, by those who had seen the grace of nature the way we Egyptians had. Eventually these beliefs in nature forces degraded to the animistic faiths of Western Africa.

"Meanwhile, Yahweh became Jehovah, who became the God of the Christians in Europe. The Europeans kidnapped West Africans to use as slaves in the New World. This little pocket of culture-clash spawned a new religion, synthesized from Catholicism and the old animistic religions of Africa. Haitian Voodou is the synthesis of the inheritors of two religious heritages that were originally at odds: ancient Hebrew and ancient Egyptian. What better place to pick up where that conflict left off?"

Sanantha tried not to let her dark realization show on her face. "This isn't just about getting the demon's secrets," she started cautiously. "You're talking about reinstating your faith on a world scale. In particular you're talking about unwinding the influence the Jewish faith has had over the last three thousand years."

Silas shook his head. "I am not out to eliminate Judah. I have nothing against the Jewish people. To get back to the Egyptian faith, it is simply easiest to strip the Christian influences out of Voodou."

"People are slow to change," she persisted. "Changing the world won't be easy, even with all this knowledge. People resist change. They only see their own narrow interests."

"That's why I want you. Besides, I'm willing to make those sacrifices," Silas answered dispassionately.

"You mean, you're willing to kill whoever gets in your way," she accused with some restraint.

"If you mean am I willing to force my changes on people who don't see things my way, yes. Death means nothing to me. Does that bother you? I know this doesn't fit with the Christian notions of resurrection, but it's just recycling souls," he explained with chilling sincerity. "I've killed eight people in just the last two months to get where I am, and that's not counting Joseph's exploits. I fully expect my efforts will lead to a holy war which will leave millions dead."

It was all Sanantha could do to not let her reaction to this grisly revelation show on her face. Her breathing quickened and she took a sip of her brandy. When she could unclench her teeth, she decided she just couldn't sit there dispassionately any longer. She stood up with her feet spread and her free hand in a fist at her side. Looking down at the casually seated magician she accused, "With all your abilities, with the limitless knowledge you might gain from this demon and these cards, you're still thinking in terms of conquest and destruction. This is madness."

"Is it mad to want to end disease once and for all? Is it wrong to find the elusive answers to clean fusion energy, pollution and famine?"

"You're no better than the Nazis, with their dreams of a 'better world,' which was in fact just a world of slavery with them on top."

Silas looked up at her with an earnest frankness that nearly disarmed Sanantha. "Don't talk to me about the Nazis. Joseph Goebbels was an opportunist with no vision and not a single fact to back up his manufactured mythology. The Aryan fairy tale of Atlantean supermen was hogwash, and I said so at the time. Not that anyone in their position would listen to a seventeen-year old." He looked at his drink before taking a big mouthful.

Sanantha was dumbstruck and could only look at him wide-eyed.

Silas swallowed, looked up at her, raised his bushy white eyebrows and explained patiently. "In 1936, I heard a radio broadcast of Hitler talking about his vision of a mythically inspired 'better world'. I traveled to Germany, and found that all he wanted was a propaganda excuse to move ahead with his deeply racist plans. I tried to convince him that the true path to greatness was in revisiting the ways of ancient Egypt. Even as a young scholar, I knew. But Goebbels had already manufactured this myth for him. Heinrich Himmler, the head of the SS, had always been obsessed with the occult, and he actually believed the Aryan lie. I couldn't convince them otherwise, and barely escaped with my life. I know the difference between seeking the truth and seeking unbridled power."

Sanantha was impressed but not swayed. "So why the threat of a holy war with millions dead?"

Silas swung his feet off the ottoman and leaned forward intensely in his armchair. "I didn't say I wanted a holy war. I said it is inevitable. This knowledge will mean seeing the truth about the nature of the universe. Ever since Egypt fell to the Romans, mankind has gotten further and further from the truth. A lot of misconceptions have built up since the Ptolemies fell twenty-two hundred years ago. Every now and then, someone will get a glimpse of the truth. If he's lucky, people will listen to him (or, more rarely, her) and he'll be remembered as a prophet or a philosopher. Most of them have been strung up as heretics. You yourself said people are slow to change, that they don't like to let go of their personal views, their own narrow interests. Imagine the resistance they will put up when confronted with the truth, that their long-held views are wrong."

Sanantha stared at him for a long moment as she imagined the scenario. "You're talking about biblical apocalypse."

"If you want to couch it in Christian terms, yes. I'm here to tell you that this is not necessarily a bad thing. The change will be painful," he said as his face brightened into a warm, proud grin, "but the outcome will be wonderful!"

•   •   •

Charles was incensed. Sitting in the chair of his cramped stateroom while Sanantha sat on the bed, he could hardly contain himself. "I don't know whether I'm more frightened, angry or just plain shocked. How can he turn back the clock like that? How can he expect people to just change overnight? What about the culture that has grown up around Voodou, and the other faiths that will be wiped out?"

Sanantha frowned and shook her head. "He says the truth will come out when he reveals all this knowledge he's going to uncover."

"Well, hell, he doesn't need a holy war for that. He needs a good PR firm. If he's able to perform miracles, then plenty of people will convert on their own." He stood up and nervously paced the three steps of the width of his room. "I don't buy it. There's got to be more going on here. I think he's more interested in keeping control over these discoveries. He wants to build a power structure. For that you might need a war," he nodded at the thought. "'Cause then you'd have winners and losers. In a war you can force people to convert or die."

Sanantha sighed at the possibility. "You might be right." Then she shook her head. "He doesn't want such a war. He said he wants me to deliver the discoveries to the world as scientific truths, so that people can accept them and use them without getting into the religious implications. He said he hopes that will mitigate the chances of a holy war."

Charles refocused his intensity on Sanantha. "What about you? You who understand why people believe in things. How are cultures and ways of life going to be impacted? You sound like you think this guy's on to something. Have you thought about the people?"

"Hey! Let's not get too personal here. I came to you to try to work out the details, remember? I haven't joined up with this guy. He has not convinced me of anything."

Charles backed off and sat back down. "All right. I'm sorry. It really sounded like you were arguing his side." He collected his thoughts with a deep breath and tried again. "We are in a position to defend the people who could get steamrollered by this guy. We've got to keep the people in mind."

"Of course," she agreed. "He said he's already converted a village."

"That's true," he interrupted. "Gorvil said he knows about it."

"Well, he insists the people saw immediate improvement in their lives, that the old Egyptian gods do a better job for the people than their Loas. In fact, he's not wiping out the Loas, he's showing us who they really are."

Charles couldn't keep his cool, and he returned to his feet. "That's the part that drives me nuts. How can he say that Voodou is, what? Egyptian Lite? That's like saying Christianity is just Jewish Lite, and we should all forget about Jesus and just go back to the old Jewish ways.

Religions grow with the times, and cultures grow with them. This whole thing smacks of him imposing his ego on the world."

"Except that his magic really works," she countered. "He knows things and does things that nobody can do. I mean, look at Joseph."

"Sanantha, all that means is he's powerful enough to do a lot of damage, maybe even pull off this Armageddon he's talking about."

Sanantha looked down at her hands in her lap. "Armageddon. That would make him the Antichrist. His name even means 'Bringer of the Truth.' Aren't such stories supposed to just be cautionary tales so churches can keep their flocks frightened enough to come back next Sunday? What about the rest of the world, like the Buddhists and the Hindus, who don't believe in the End of the World?"

"Well, it is a new millennium. Isn't that supposed to bring big changes?" he explored.

Sanantha squinted and nodded. "Except that date is only on the Christian calendar. The Jews, Hindus, and all the rest have their own calendars, and this year is no big deal for them. In fact, if Silas is ancient Egyptian, then this year wouldn't mean a new millennium for him either." She pressed her lips together in thought and nodded again. "Maybe this doesn't have the earmarks of Armageddon after all."

Charles was still adamant. "Regardless, it still stinks, and I see my job as trying to stop him."

She frowned at him and tilted her head. "So you see yourself as the Defender of Voodou?"

"Yes, and of the people of Haiti, your people, whom I have come to love."

Sanantha gave him a warm, proud smile. "I can see that. Even though I don't see how you or I can stop him, I see my role as trying to prevent this holy war. If he is unstoppable, then the only way I can do that is to try to influence him." She sighed. "Unfortunately, that might put us on opposite sides, with me working with him and you working against."

Charles was angry all over again. "I don't see how helping this madman kill millions of people can help anything," he accused, and stormed from the room.

He got a dozen paces down the hall before realizing he had just walked out of his own room. "Damn!" He looked over his shoulder and decided not to go back. He needed to walk. He finished the length of the corridor and scaled the stairs at the end up to the main deck level. On his way through the hallway to the outside walkway, he passed the entrance to the Mess and met the gaze of two crewmen there. They didn't seem to care that he was walking freely about the ship. Apparently Alverado didn't feel he was enough of a threat to bother with. He gritted his teeth at the thought.

It was late at night but still warm enough that the wind from the ship's movement left it only pleasantly cool on the deck walk. It was too dark, and they were too far from shore for him to be able to tell anything of their course. He paced along the rail, his gaze lost over the dark sea as he struggled internally.

What could he do to protect his faith and his adopted people? Joseph had collected his antiquities in Washington DC. Those items must be what Alverado was going to use to gain all this knowledge Sanantha had talked about. If he could get off the ship he could call the CIA and have them confiscate Joseph's collection. Maybe they were travelling to Washington now. In that case Charles could sabotage the ship. He knew so little of what Alverado was going to do next, he really had no starting place from which to plan.

But then he remembered he didn't have to plan this alone. Indeed, he had been told not to go this alone. He took a huge breath and sighed to let go of his frustration. He walked back below, nodding cordially to the crewmen along the way. He steeled himself as he approached his room, hoping that Sanantha had left.

She had. He locked his door and began rummaging through the drawers in the room until he found a shaving kit, complete with a disposable razor. He had to use his teeth as a vice to break it open, but he finally got the blade out of the plastic safety holder. He cleared off the nightstand for a work surface. He cut off several locks of his short curly hair and twisted them tightly in a piece of note paper. He was grateful that in addition to the wall mounted light, there was also a free-standing lamp. He unplugged it, cut the cord, and stripped the insulation back on the cut ends.

He tasted blood, and realized he had cut his lip on the razor when he had removed it from its holder. He touched his lip and looked at his fingertips. He chuckled when he saw the blood. How many times over the years had he compulsively checked his fingers for blood, the old blood of guilt? This was the new blood of determination.

He listened one last time at the door to be sure no one was in the hallway. When he was sure he was alone, he plugged in the cut cord, being careful to hold the bare ends apart. He knelt down in front of the nightstand and began to quietly pray.

"Great Madame Erzulie, hear my plea. I have been taken prisoner by our enemy. Great Virgin Mother of Mercy, please hear my call. It is worse than we feared. He plans to destroy Voodou and replace it with the dead religion of the ancient Egyptians. Great Mistress of the Rainbow, please hear my prayer. I need your guidance, for I do not know how to stop this madman."

While he spoke, he brushed the bare wires together on one end of the twisted paper. A blue-white spark sputtered between the ends, but did not ignite the paper.

"Please let this message reach your merciful ears." He tried again, and this time the paper caught flame. He picked up the paper and held it flame down so it would catch and spread up. When it had, he blew the fire out and gently puffed on the ember to keep it glowing. He smiled as a stream of white smoke wafted up.

It first it smelled sweetly of toasted marshmallow, but then the hair caught, and the smoke turned putrid. He fought the urge to hold his breath or turn away.

"Here is my message, Grand Maitresse. Please come to save your faithful. All will be lost if this man succeeds."

15

ARMAGEDDON

C APTAIN SIR ROGER COVENTRY HAD JUST SAT DOWN at his office
desk after his usual pre-dawn inspection of the nuclear
submarine H.M.S. Wellington. He took his cap off and brushed back
his short cut brown hair when his phone rang. Punching the speaker
button, he answered, "This is the Captain."

"Stubbs in Telecom, sir. There's a priority coded message just
come in for you. I'm putting it through to you now."

"Thank you, Stubbs," he said punching the button off as he spun
his chair around to the terminal behind his desk. As soon as the
e-mail arrival signal beeped, he typed the password sequence that
would unscramble the message. Indeed it was priority, highest
priority in fact. Top secret and from Whitehall itself. He raised one
white-streaked eyebrow.

"KNIGHT TO QUEEN'S BISHOP FIVE."

Despite the shirtsleeve warmth of his office, a chill ran across his shoulders. As he grasped the implications, his brows knit below his high forehead as his green eyes went wide. The words slipped breathlessly from his lips, "First strike."

He typed in his receipt confirmation and awaited the target coordinates and other particulars of the mission.

"COORDINATES ROUTED TO MISSILE CONTROL," came the reply.

"What?!" he shouted at the screen as he hurried to type the commands to belay the transmission. When this failed, he snatched up the phone.

"Missile Command. Armstrong here."

"This is the Captain," he began in a terse, controlled tone. "A set of mission instructions has just been sent down to you in error. Shut down all guidance and firing sequences immediately."

"Yes, sir." Captain Coventry then heard him call out, "Curtis, switch off that ... Curtis? Curtis! For Christsakes man, put that down!"

Three unmistakable staccato pops on the phone were followed by silence.

"Armstrong! Armstrong!" the captain demanded. He punched open the ship-wide intercom. "This is the Captain. We have a security breach in Missile Control. Shots fired, at least one man down. I want that room secured immediately. Seaman Curtis is your prime target. I'm on my way." Coventry then punched in another phone number.

"Systems Control, Boucher here."

"This is the Captain. Cut the connections between Missile Control and the rest of the ship."

"Lock them out, sir?"

"Yes, immediately!"

He hung up and, stopping only to grab his pistol and holster from his desk drawer, he ran from his office.

When he got to Missile Command, armed sailors had both doors covered. The ranking lieutenant, a broad-shouldered black man, briefed him. "Armstrong is still in there, Captain. I think he's dead. Traynor was hit too but he got out. I don't know what Curtis is doing. I haven't gotten a clear view of him."

"You did fine," he said without taking his green eyes from the steel doorway. "Now back me up."

He tiptoed the half dozen steps, gun muzzle leading the way. Curtis was seated at a console typing away with a twisted grin on his face. "It's over, Curtis! Stand up and put your hands behind your head!"

The typing seaman didn't even look up from the screen. "Ah, Captain," he began with unsettling calm. "Your threats mean nothing for you are, in fact, too late."

"Seaman Curtis, I ordered you to stand down," he demanded tightly. "Systems Control has already cut you off from the ordinance. Whatever you're doing there isn't leaving this room. Now get up or I'll fire."

"You are sadly mistaken, Sir. Re-routing past Systems Control is where I started," he continued, grin intact, fingers tapping at full speed. "Next you're going to tell me that only you know the firing clearance code."

By now the captain had entered and circled around behind him, only three paces away. Curtis' gun was at his right hand, between the keyboard and the missile firing switches. "That's right," the captain confirmed.

"Not true," he said calmly as his hand flashed out toward the gun.

Coventry fired, hitting him square in the right shoulder. The impact threw him forward onto the console, but failed to stop his hand from reaching its true target: the first firing switch.

As a whooshing sound rang through the hull, Curtis slumped off the console and fell to the floor. He had dragged the gun with him in his left hand.

At that instant someone hit the combat alert, alarms started blaring, and red warning lights came on in every room.

Meeting the fallen man's gaze for the first time, the captain was taken aback by the purple hue in his eyes, unmistakable even in the red glow. His hesitation was just long enough for Curtis to raise the gun to his own head and, grin still intact, pull the trigger.

One of the men behind the captain rushed forward to the terminal.

"Where is it heading and how long do we have?" the captain barked, doing his best to ignore the gory mess that had been Seaman Curtis.

"Jacksonville, Florida, Sir. It'll be there in twenty-three minutes."

"Florida?" he said, incredulous. "Well, you know what to do. Disarm it, then drop it into the sea."

"Yessir."

A moment later, though, the sailor added hesitantly while continuing to punch in commands, "Sir. I've got a problem here. It's not responding."

The captain kept his voice as calm and focused as he could. He didn't need his men panicking at a time like this. "Can you tell why not?"

"It's acting like the computer has some kind of block preventing the commands from going out to the missile."

Flashing a hot glare at Curtis' corpse, he cursed, "Bastard set up a cipher." Grabbing up the nearest phone, Coventry dialed quickly. "Systems Control, this is the Captain. I need your best people down here in Missile Control on the double. You're locked out so you'll have to work from down here."

Hanging up, he commented to the sailor at the console. "So we have twenty-two minutes to reconnect the main computer to here, have the computer solve Curtis' cipher, and bring the bird down." He took a deep breath, raised his white-shot eyebrows and sighed out loud. "I've got one helluva phone call to make."

•   •   •

Charles' first perception as he awoke was the painfully bright red of the insides of his eyelids warning him the sun was burning down on him from directly overhead. Rolling to his side before opening his eyes, he still had to blink at the reflected brilliance of the light-colored forward deck. The sun was hotter than he remembered it, even though he was sure he had nodded off only a few minutes ago. Can't trust the tropical sun; better get in and cool off.

As he got up from the lounge chair, he stumbled, lightheaded, and had to steady himself on the rail. On the other side of the forward deck, Joseph, completely unaffected by the heat in his steel gray business suit, was standing in front of Silas, who was seated, wearing much more sensible white linens like Charles, and doing a Tarot spread on his drink tray. With his back to his master, the stocky man in sunglasses was obviously there to prevent any interruptions. He watched Charles walk off the deck without shifting his position.

Something about the way Joseph was standing didn't seem right. As he was about to round the corner of the salon, Charles glanced back across the deck and was so shocked he gasped out loud. Joseph was no longer there, and Silas was now dressed like the Pope except all in black, playing cards with Satan himself. The Prince of Darkness looked at his hand of cards and threw his horned and goatee bearded head back in uproarious laughter.

Unable to accept what he saw, Charles ducked around the corner, blinked, and shook his head. He ventured a tentative look back. Not much to his surprise, but much to his relief, Joseph and Silas appeared as they had before his bizarre vision, and the devil was nowhere to be seen. Thankfully neither of them noticed Charles' startled behavior. He rolled back against the cabin's side, out of view, and clutched his hair in amazement. It was very hot. "Papa Legba," he muttered to himself. "I've fried my brain out here." He headed in without delay.

Running water over his head in the bathroom sink refreshed him greatly. As he toweled off, the sound of a woman's quiet sobbing caught his attention from down the hall. He thought it sounded like Sanantha, and when he looked around the doorway into the stateroom, he thought it was she who had her back to him. He was therefore completely unprepared when the woman standing in the middle of the room turned around and he saw it was Erzulie herself.

He dropped to his knees and averted his gaze from her solid black eyes. She put her hand on his shoulder, bidding him to stand up. When he did, he kept his head down, but he could see that she had been looking at a figure lying in the bed. She stepped aside to show him it was Joseph. His body was wrapped loosely in lengths of linen cloth, like he was in the early stages of being made into an

Egyptian mummy. He didn't appear to be breathing. Charles was initially very pleased to see his enemy in a state of demise, but Erzulie was clearly very upset, with tear tracks down her dark brown face. He looked closer. The sun shining through the half-closed shutters illuminated Joseph's placid white face in a golden halo.

By now Charles was aware that he was dreaming, but this didn't help him figure out what his goddess was trying to tell him. She took his wrist and held his hand palm up. Before he could react, she swiftly brought her other hand around to cut his palm with a long thin dagger. He started to pull his hand free, but the cut did not hurt. She then led him to Joseph's bedside and held his cut hand palm down onto Joseph's chest. The blood spread into the linen fibers and out past the edge of his hand. When she let go of his wrist, he found no cut on his palm.

He was standing there amazed at his intact palm when Erzulie brought the dagger around again, this time plunging it into Charles' stomach. He gave her a shocked look, but she was busy looking at his stomach. When he looked down, she was pulling the knife out in a twisting motion, like she was fishing something out with the tip. To his further horror, she had impaled a thick black snake and was pulling it out of his body. She had stabbed the snake just behind its head, which hissed and twisted viciously. It had bright violet eyes.

When she finished pulling its length out it writhed wildly despite the firm grip she had with her free hand. Again, Charles found he was left with no wound. She turned around to the door, which now led directly onto the forward deck, and pitched the snake out into the sun. It tumbled on the deck, turned red, and transformed into Satan, who rolled up onto his hooves facing them.

Before Charles could react, Joseph rushed past him, out the door, and dove into melee with Satan. Joseph was dressed in white leather armor that looked to Charles like that of a Roman gladiator. Joseph wielded a stout bronze sword and defended himself with a square wooden shield.

The sword recognized the enemy and burst into flames as Joseph swung it at the onrushing monster. He brought it around too slowly and Satan slipped inside his attack to rake a vicious slash across his chest. The armor held.

Joseph swung again, faster this time. Satan ducked under it and leapt against him, knocking him back against the forward bulkhead. Satan clawed at his torso and bit into his neck. As they slid down the wall and hit the deck, Joseph dragged the length of the sword's edge across Satan's red leathery back to slash open a huge gash. Satan howled and leapt up off of him, the wound burning black putrid smoke. Joseph scrambled to his feet and rushed him before he could initiate another attack. Holding the sword with both hands like a baseball bat, he swung it into Satan with all the strength he could pinion out of his legs, back and arms.

With no time to counter, Satan simply lunged into his attacker's body, apparently trying to get inside the most destructive arc of the swing. The body slam knocked them both off balance while the sword's momentum spun it around behind Satan and wrenched it out of Joseph's grasp. It spun through the air and landed at Charles' feet with a loud clang.

Satan's lunge and Joseph's spin combined to send them both into, up and over the railing, flying overboard in a mass of flailing combative limbs.

Charles started for the railing but ducked when a huge exploding fireball erupted where they splashed. Satan's burning body had set the sea aflame. Spreading out in all directions like some unstoppable spill, the carpet of fire soon surrounded the ship and moved out toward the horizon.

Shocked though he was at the scope of the destruction he had started, the sword reminded him he still had a job to do. He picked it up and turned to his true enemy.

Silas remained impassively seated at Charles' armed approach. "Look around you, Charles!" he yelled smugly over the roaring flames. "Apocalypse has arrived! Whether you or I survive is unimportant!"

The flames had now risen around the ship to form a curtain that blocked out the horizon. Everything was red. The air was so hot his lungs burned with the slightest breath. Charles paused only for an instant to take it all in, then raised his sword.

"If you kill me, you die as well!" Silas warned ominously.

Was this supposed to stay his hand? Victory and deliverance all in one stroke? He brought the weapon down so hard it cleaved through the old man's shoulder all the way into the middle of his chest.

Silas' appeal may have been misjudged but his promise was all too accurate. When the sword hit Silas' heart, his body exploded into white hot coals that blew out and seared holes right through whatever they touched, including Charles, who caught most of them in his chest.

He was thrown back onto the deck a limp, shattered, smoking shell. He was so overwhelmed by the sudden violence it took him a moment to recognize the crushing pain of having been fatally wounded. He didn't care. He opened his eyes and saw the flames roaring up into the sky all around him. He wondered fleetingly whether he would bleed to death before the fire stole all his air and he suffocated. Maybe the heat would just cook him. He could no longer distinguish one horrible, mind numbing sensation from another. He didn't want to. Silas was dead and soon he would be too. It was finally over. He smiled.

The avalanche of feelings simplified and withdrew. All he noticed was the heat and the red light everywhere. Very cautiously he opened an eye and winced it closed again as the sun overhead stabbed him in the retina. He shaded his eyes as he sat up in the lowered deck chair and waited for his eyes to acclimate to the reflected glare that surrounded him on the forward deck.

Deja vu seized him, and fear sent a chill up his spine despite the heat. He couldn't trust his senses. This deck was no more or less real than the one he was just on. But what about the horrors he had seen? He was nearly paralyzed at the prospect of what he might find if he looked around, let alone went exploring.

"You have another nightmare?" Sanantha asked from behind him.

The fact that he jumped at the sound was probably answer enough. Greatly relieved to find his friend standing there and no one else on the deck, he confided quietly, "Yeah. It was a doozy."

"You were thrashing around pretty good. I didn't know if it would be better to wake you or leave you alone. Your dreams have been remarkably prescient. Normally, the most a person can hope is for a dream to show you the subconscious mind working on unfinished business. Your visions of the supernatural are closer to what Silas described with Tarot cards and spirit contact."

Charles was amazed. His dreams were about spirit contact, and Silas had been reading Tarot cards in the dream. He covered as best he could by raising his eyebrows and nodding as if her comment were only slightly interesting. "Really?"

She pointed to his face and commented, "That's a nasty cut you've got there on your lip."

They were interrupted by a commotion up in the wheelhouse. They turned around and looked up to see several of the crew yelling and pointing out to sea on the starboard side of the ship. Most notable among them was Joseph. Charles and Sanantha looked in that direction but saw nothing. The ship's general alarm horn began blaring and the two of them decided to go in.

As they rounded the hallway corner, Silas rushed past them and up the stairs to the Bridge. Charles followed him as far as the top of the stairs where he found too many people already there for him to be able to slip in unobtrusively. Sanantha climbed up behind him to listen too.

Joseph described the situation. "I don't know what it is, but we are definitely under attack by something from out at sea. It's over the horizon right now, so I can't actually see it," he tried to explain.

"But you can sense it as a truth," Silas ventured.

"Yes, exactly. It approaches with tremendous speed and enormous destructive power. I could identify it if I could just see it." Joseph stopped short. "Wait. It just dropped into the sea, right at the horizon."

"Is it dead?"

Joseph concentrated at the spot. "No, Master, it's not."

"We're about twenty feet from the water," the magician calculated out loud. "So our eyes are twenty-five feet up, which puts the horizon twenty-five miles away. Twenty-five miles at three hundred miles an hour in shallow water, gives us about five minutes."

"Five minutes for what, Sir?" a crewman asked with obvious fear in his voice.

"Tsunami," he answered flatly. "How deep is the water here?"

"Thirty-one feet, Sir."

"We're what, two miles from shore? How far out from shore does the bottom finally drop off?"

The Wheelman answered. "The bottom has a very low slope. It stays shallow for almost a mile further out."

Silas commanded tersely, "Turn the ship and head full speed directly out to sea."

"Right at it, Sir?"

"Yes, the wave will pass under us if we can get to deep water."

Charles and Sanantha had to hang onto the stairwell railing as the engines roared and the ship turned faster than either of them expected. Charles asked Sanantha, "The wave will pass under us?"

"Yes, Mister Redmond," Silas answered to Charles' surprise. "My adversary has fired a nuclear missile at us, and it appears whoever owns it has successfully brought it down, but not disarmed it. If it goes off, it will create a compression wave that will travel through the water itself, not on the surface. It only rises into a wave when it stands up on the shallow bottom near shore." He turned to the wheelman, who happened to be the closest. "Please give me your watch."

"My watch? Ah, yessir." He peeled off a very expensive steel cased wristwatch and handed it to his boss.

"Thank you." Silas pushed passed Charles and Sanantha on the stairs. "Excuse me."

Charles and Sanantha stepped up onto the bridge to make room and watched Silas through the windows. He briskly walked out onto the forward deck, and stood up on the seats of the built-in conversation pit. He reached into his shirt and pulled out a long translucent yellow rod.

"Is he going to do what I think?" Charles asked Sanantha quietly.

"I think so."

Silas yelled out over the waves that crashed up on either side of the hurtling prow, and gestured broadly with the wand. He was not speaking anything Charles could understand. Holding the watch aloft in front of him, he then pointed the rod at it and barked one last command. He paused and waited, then turned and looked up at the wheelhouse.

Joseph lifted his sunglasses and frowned intently at the horizon. He then gave Silas a thumbs-up through the window.

Joseph took over the wheel, pulled the throttle down, and turned the ship back onto course.

As Silas walked back up the stairs, Sanantha spoke up. "You didn't tell me your enemy is on to you."

"We've been at war for some time now. I have to admit, I am surprised that he located this ship. I had thought it was untraceable. As it is, he still overplayed his hand."

"How do you mean?"

"Our enemy is clearly desperate not to have anticipated either the control the military maintains over its weapons or my knowledge of natural forces. The law of nature dictates that the bolder the action, the greater the risk of failure." He reached over and handed the shattered timepiece back to the wheelman. "Sorry about the watch."

The man frowned at it, and then tried to smile dismissively. "That's okay, Sir."

Charles couldn't help but notice Joseph standing aside giving Silas a very disappointed look. Silas turned and noticed it too.

Joseph lowered his gaze but still voiced his concern. "You told her our enemy's identity."

"Yes, Joseph, I did. She has a need to know. You don't."

Charles turned on Sanantha. "You know who's throwing nukes at us? You didn't tell me about being at war with some unseen enemy. Am I on a need-to-know basis as well?"

She looked at him sadly but answered resolutely. "We all are. Can we talk about this in private?"

"Apparently we can't talk at all," he accused, and stormed off the bridge.

He found the rear deck to be big enough to pace effectively. After several minutes, though, he realized he was so angry he couldn't collect his thoughts. Charles put on his friendliest sales face and headed for the Mess. The ship's cook was remarkably easy-going, and handed over a bottle of twelve-year-old Scotch with hardly any resistance.

Back in his room, Charles tried to piece together what he knew and what he could salvage. Despite her insistence otherwise, Sanantha had clearly joined up with Silas. The whisky stung his cut lip. He found the pain a refreshing addition to the sharp flavor in his mouth and the warmth it left in his chest. It was pretty clear they were headed to Washington to use the stuff Joseph had gathered. Amazingly, Joseph was apparently just as much in the dark as to what Silas was going to do with the stuff.

Joseph. Erzulie had focused his dream on Joseph. He had been dreaming about Silas before the goddess had changed his attention. Silas was turning out to be way too resourceful, seemingly indestructible. Another shot of liquor left him feeling relaxed and invigorated.

She had used Charles' blood to revive Joseph, only to send Joseph into a fight that ended in his fiery death. She had used a snake, her snake, to bait Joseph into that fight. He shook his head. There were too many images in the dream, and it all went by so quickly. Why was she upset that Joseph was incapacitated, just to then kill him off? Why was this dream so much harder to interpret than the ones before?

He poured himself another shot. She had cut him, twice, to accomplish what she wanted. Clearly this meant he was supposed to sacrifice of himself. No problem there. She didn't just sucker Joseph into any battle, but an impossible one against an unbeatable foe like the Devil himself. He drank the shot. The sharp flavor had subsided and it tasted smooth. His lip didn't hurt anymore.

Joseph's not knowing Silas' plans made him ineffective, like he was half dead, like he was lying ready for burial in the dream. So Charles' job would be to sacrifice of himself to revive Joseph into action, and bait him into taking on an impossible task that leads to his self-destruction. It didn't explain everything, but it felt like something Charles could do. It certainly sounded better than sitting idle and letting Silas proceed unabated.

•   •   •

As strange as life was under Joseph's command, Jack was glad to hear Joseph coming up behind him. Granted the crazy black man wasn't going anywhere while Jack had him in the sights of his nine-millimeter pistol. But the sooner he could relieve this situation to someone with authority, the better.

"Hold it right there or I drop it," Charles threatened while kneeling over the open engine room access panels in the rear deck, an open bag of sugar poised over the big marine diesels' exposed carburetors.

Stepping up beside Jack without looking away from their prisoner, Joseph asked quietly, "What about the engine room?"

Charles answered for him. "Barricaded from the inside. I started down there and climbed up over the engines to get here." Indicating the unconscious sailor sprawled on the deck in front of him, he went on to explain, "That's when I surprised him." The wrench he had obviously used was next to the angry looking red swelling on the man's temple.

From the moment he'd discovered him, Jack had noticed Charles was squatting oddly, turned sideways as if hiding something in his left hand behind him.

"So, what do you want?" Joseph asked tersely.

Jack figured Joseph must be pretty angry for his voice to tighten like that.

"Freedom."

"For yourself?" The balding man obviously didn't believe him.

"Yes. I can't compete with the brainwashing your boss did on Sanantha," he declared, his voice full of hate. "I don't want to be around when the shit hits the fan."

Joseph squinted ever so slightly behind his sunglasses before answering. "All right," he agreed calmly.

Jack couldn't believe what he was hearing.

Pointing over the rail at the barely visible shoreline, Joseph finished his thought. "That's Georgia out there. Have a nice swim."

Charles laughed sarcastically. "Not quite." Dropping the false humor, he demanded adamantly, "We're going into port or this tub's not going anywhere." A moment passed where the only sound on the deck was the hungry sucking sound of the open engine intakes, gulping air and whatever else came near.

Maintaining his usual dangerous cool, the demon asked, "You're going to sit there, holding that bag like that, the whole time it takes us to go in?"

As if to punctuate his point, two other crewmen arrived at that moment and filed in on either side of Joseph and Jack, machine guns leveled at Charles.

Matching his adversary's cool with an over-polite, saccharin manner, Charles answered, "Oh not at all. You're going to promise me safe passage. You know what Silas would do if you made me drop this bag and wreck his precious timetable. You see Joey, I figure, if you're anything like the demons where I come from, it's pretty binding when you swear by whatever ass-licking slime-god spawned you."

Jack barely restrained the shocked gasp that pushed up into his throat. Did this guy want to escape or die? In the instant it took him to turn to see Joseph's reaction, the balding man had made up his mind and was in the midst of snatching off his glasses. The sailor looked back at Charles and realized the nature of his game. The item behind his back, which he was now whipping up in front of himself, was a bathroom medicine cabinet mirror. Jack spun and dove behind Joseph with absolutely no time to spare.

The bolt of pure destructive energy was so powerful that just its corona edge annihilated the released bag of sugar in mid-air and ripped the black man's clothes to smoking shreds. The center of the shockwave bounced off the mirror, expanding as it moved. Both the sailors standing to Joseph's sides were torn limb from limb, their shattered bodies flying with the blast like shards of broken pottery.

Jack looked up from the deck and saw from the rear that Joseph's clothing was in tatters, but couldn't see the extent of his injuries. The demon was looking down at his own body, assumedly in amazement at the unexpected outcome of his attack. Charles peeked around the mirror, his eyes went wide with horror, he let out a tiny, aghast, "Shit!" and dove over the stern. Joseph walked to the back rail and just stood there.

Jack stepped up alongside him and gasped out loud. He looked away as quickly as he could, but it was no use; the image persisted in his mind. All the flesh on the front of Joseph's face and body was peeled away, ribs and skull blasted clean, with undamaged naked yellow eyes scanning the waves above grinning white teeth.

The First Mate staggered to the starboard rail and clamped onto it with both hands, trying to steady his suddenly weak knees. He breathed deep and hard, fighting against the almost uncontrollable urge to retch.

Joseph laid a hand on his shoulder and the redhead jerked reflexively. The hand squeezed with surprising warmth and reassurance. The sailor dared not look back since Joseph's glasses had obviously been destroyed. The demon didn't say anything. Maybe he couldn't. He withdrew his hand and walked away.

Jack looked back and watched him stop and shake his head at the two dead men's remains. He then walked forward, his head down and one hand up, shielding his eyes in case he encountered anyone coming to investigate the explosion.

16

JUDGMENT DAY

CHARLES KNEW THE ATLANTIC IN APRIL WOULD BE COLD, but he had not planned on the shivering and numbness that racked his body within minutes of hitting the water. He tried not to think about whether he had just thrown his life away after failing to stop Silas. He had to concentrate on moving his limbs, focusing on the shore, even though he couldn't see it at this distance.

Try as he might, after an hour the cold began to sap even his will. It didn't even matter how he got into this mess. All he could think about was how he probably wasn't going to survive it.

Something brushed his leg and he jolted with fright. Were there sharks off the Georgia coast? The numbness in his body was swept away with the pressure of the pounding of his heart. What greater ignominious end than to be eaten?

Then he felt it again, but it wasn't a brush this time, but a sinuous embrace. Something was wrapping itself around him. He reached down to pull it off and felt giant muscular coils. He pulled up to try to look down and came face to face with an enormous black anaconda.

Charles almost laughed, but he was so tired and so cold, all he could manage was a grim chuckle.

"Oh, I know who you are. You had me believing you were Madame Erzulie. But She has shown me the truth. You're the Devil." He frowned as he made a connection, and then smiled. "And you're afraid of him. He's gonna kick your ass." He frowned again. "And then turn around and destroy the world." He looked up into the snake's violet eyes. "Unless I help you. Because I know all that crap he has up in Washington that's he's going to use to capture your ass."

The snake nodded slowly.

"Mankind has dealt with you, somehow, for thousands of years, and it will go on dealing with you. But him, he is a different kind of ancient evil. You've got me stuck between the Devil and the deep blue sea, but I've already made up my mind. You are evil incarnate, but you are the enemy of my enemy. He wants to wipe out my religion and my country. He wants to turn the world against itself. He must be stopped. If I have to surrender my soul to you to stop him, then so be it. My unredeemable soul is a small price to pay. Maybe Madame Erzulie will save me in the end. If not, then that will be my just reward for my crimes against my people.

"Oh yes, I know who you are."

•   •   •

The glow of the lights from central Washington, DC at midnight was only bright enough to hint at the true form of the ominous storm clouds that loomed overhead. The sunset had been veiled by the gathering clouds as the *Purgatory* had entered Chesapeake Bay. The full moon was now fully shrouded behind the storm. Sitting in the ship's salon, Sanantha could clearly see Silas' objective out the windows only half a mile away. The tumultuous sky looked like it was about to reach down and claw at the top of the gleaming white obelisk of the Washington Monument.

The only lights on in the salon were the spots over the bar. Sipping again at her brandy, as she had almost continuously for the last two days, Sanantha sat draped sideways in the leather armchair, leaning her arms over its back, looking out the window behind it. Apropos of nothing, she chuckled sarcastically to herself.

Joseph sat on the couch behind her. The demon appeared as usual, having had two days to reconstitute himself. The ship was very quiet, empty as it was, anchored in the calm Potomac tidal lagoon. "Something funny?"

"Yeah," she started without turning from her viewing. Melancholy was clear through the drunken waiver in her voice. "I was just thinking about fate. Here I am back in Washington where I started. I've failed my patient and joined his enemy. I'm a wanted criminal without ever having done anything. I'm in a position to take advantage of everything I've ever learned, to help humanity on a huge scale, yet all I can do is get drunk and mope around worrying about whether I've sold my soul to the Antichrist." She turned around to face him. "I've been seduced, Joseph. I want to go on the record as saying I have been seduced."

"Is that humorous?"

"Irony, Joseph. It's sheer, ugly irony. Silas said something about you being able to see the truth. Is that right?"

"Yes," he said with an unusual show of pride. "I am an angel of Ptah, and so all my eyes are all seeing."

"Ptah? I'm afraid I'm not up on my Egyptian gods."

"Ptah is the Opener of the Ways." The more he talked about his god, the more emboldened he became.

Watching Joseph get excited about something was a little frightening.

"Once Amun-Ra created the universe, order was lost in chaos. Ptah brought order out of chaos with his eyes."

Sanantha moved to calm him down. "Let me put this in a context I understand. It sounds like Ptah would have ended up as a Guede in Voodou?"

Joseph blinked and relaxed, clearly having caught himself all puffed up. "Yes, I believe so. Guede L'Orage would come close."

She laughed sadly to herself again. "Then the irony is even richer than I thought. For someone who can see the truth, who can see order in chaos, an awful lot seems to have gotten past you this time."

Even in the deep shadows, she could see his only reply was to scowl.

"I'm sorry, I don't mean to pick on you. This thing is going to take everyone by surprise." She blinked and reconsidered her audience. "See, you live in a world where gods and magic are real. We humans never see proof of anything of your world. We just have to take it all on faith. Silas wants to change all that."

Joseph gave her a dubious frown. "How?"

"All over the world, Christians pray for salvation on Black Saturday, the day after Good Friday, the one day a year that Christ is symbolically dead. Until he told me what he is up to, I was sure that date would be important in Silas' calendar. But that's next Saturday, April 14th. Tomorrow, the 8th, Jews all over the world will celebrate their deliverance from Egypt. Sundown today marks the start of Passover, the anniversary of the event that Silas is out there trying to rewrite."

Joseph leaned forward and raised his eyebrows above his sunglasses, not even trying to contain his curiosity. "The conflict with the Hebrews?"

"Yeah. I know, I wasn't supposed to tell you. Frankly, the details would be way too much trouble to go into now." She scratched her scalp through her unwashed mass of hair. "In a nutshell, Silas feels the Egyptians should have won that fight. So he's going to re-visit it, and this time he hopes to win." She took another sip of brandy. "You know, he was there the first time."

"No, I didn't know that," Joseph answered quietly, deep in thought. "Do you know why he wouldn't tell me his plans?"

"He figured you would be offended by his dealing with Hebrew magic. But, I have to admit, he seems to know what he's doing. Despite all the delays he's had to deal with, and the attacks from this Hebrew demon he's fighting, he's managed to stay on calendar."

"He is a very resourceful man." He looked off at the gleaming, newly refurbished obelisk. "I just wish he would let me help him now."

Sanantha was snapped into stunned sobriety by the distant but unmistakable sound of pistol shots coming from ashore.

Joseph was on his feet instantly. Before either of them could say anything, their alarm was further heightened by a volley of automatic weapons fire. A whooshing rush of air behind her made Sanantha look back, but she only saw a cloud of yellow smoke where Joseph had been.

The initial whiff of sulfur was enough to make Sanantha hold her breath as she ran for the door. She thought about taking the water cycle but decided it would be more hassle than it was worth. It was only a couple hundred feet to shore. Pausing only to lose her sandals, she hopped the rail and landed with a resounding splash. The water was so surprisingly cold it actually hurt. But it did wonders to clear her head.

Sanantha swam to the dock of a paddle boat rental, climbed up and ran toward the giant illuminated spire. At over three-hundred feet tall, it was farther away than it looked. She had to cross several looping access roads before she got to the open-air theater that faced the monument hill.

Her impatience with the distance was aggravated when she realized that she hadn't heard any more shooting since the first exchange. What in the world could be happening?

She paused at a stand of trees at the base of the hill and assessed the fight. In the center of a sprawling lawn hundreds of feet wide sat the circular concrete park that was the base of the monument. The square column was illuminated by a ring of spotlights on the ground around its base. She saw Silas up near the obelisk, and his men were scattered about on the lawn, obviously fending off someone with weapons drawn.

She was trying to make out who they were fighting when a massive bolt of lightning lunged from the sky and struck the monument. Bypassing the point-mounted lightning rod, it fanned out over the stone surface as if driven by some unearthly passion. When the frantically groping, brilliantly bright blue-white fingers of electricity reached the base, they danced out over the ground but stopped abruptly to form a triangle around the structure, right next to where Silas was were standing. The thunderclap was so loud, Sanantha thought the ground actually heaved. Through the ringing in her ears, she could hear Silas laughing like a madman.

Out of the corner of her eye she spotted a group of thirty or so people break from the trees and rush toward the obelisk. They were dressed as ordinary citizens. Some of them had handguns which they fired at Silas' men, who returned fire with their automatic weapons. The advancing mob had no more strategy than a suicidal charge. Sanantha spotted Joseph standing among the crewmen, giving them directions. Although the crew had no more cover than the mob in the open park, they were spread out and on their stomachs. Needless to say, the exchange was essentially a massacre.

Sanantha had to look away. In doing so she took a better look at what Silas was doing. Laser beams? It took her a moment to fathom what she was seeing. Reflecting off mirrors spaced a hundred feet apart, a yellow laser enclosed the monument in an equilateral triangle an inch or two off the smooth concrete ground. This triangle was clearly where the lightning had stopped. Another set of mirrors bounced a blue laser into a ten-foot wide five-pointed star that touched the triangle in the middle of its facing side. Silas was shaved bald, and was dressed resplendently in white billowing robes, a purple belt, a metal crown, and what looked like a leopard fur draped over one shoulder. He stood inside the blue-laser pentagram. He held a clear yellow rod in one hand and a wicked looking knife in the other.

She looked back at the gunfight and saw that the charging mob was just one part of the offensive. Two dozen other people had run across the expansive lawn from surrounding angles and were running broken patterns across the lawn. Several of them made it as far as the outermost mirrors. One of them lined up a kick worthy of the NFL, but the mirror did not move. The assailant tripped and bounced off some unseen barrier and fell sprawling on the pavement.

She couldn't let the carnage continue. She didn't know who these people were, but they were clearly not acting with their own survival in mind. She stood up, spread her arms to make her yellow caftan more visible, and yelled over the gunfire and the gathering wind, "Joseph! It's Sanantha! Let me come down!"

Joseph spotted her and told his men to not shoot her. As she approached, though, the attackers moved to intercept her. Much to her added horror, the crew defended her by mowing down her would-be assailants.

When she reached Joseph, she was in tears. "Who are these people and why are they just letting themselves die like this?"

"They are citizens, bystanders, possessed by my master's enemy. They are indeed innocents, but we have no choice. Their deaths are on the enemy's hands."

"But Silas seems to have built some kind of magical wall around his equipment. Can they do anything to hurt him?"

Joseph looked askance at Silas and commented, "It is the Shield of Horus. I frankly did not think a human could wield such magic." Rather than being proud of his master, Joseph seemed deeply worried about the magnitude of what Silas was commanding. "It reflects all attacks back on the attacker. If we allowed them to shoot the shield, they would all certainly die. I've instructed my men to try to shoot to maim. We're actually doing less damage than the shield would."

At this close distance, Sanantha saw that Silas had formed something of an altar up against the face of the monument with large carved wooden boxes, statuary and urns. Various smaller items, many with colorful stone inlays, were set in the corners of the triangle and the pentagram. Sanantha realized these must be the items that Charles had imported for Joseph.

All during this time, Silas had been reciting unintelligible prayers while pointing to the objects or up at the obelisk. He stopped and the sudden silence caught everyone's attention. He turned around to survey the tableau, and Sanantha saw he wore thick black makeup lines around his expressive blue eyes. With the bald head and metal crown, he had a predatory, regal appearance.

He seemed satisfied with what he saw, for he then turned back to the monument and proceeded, this time in English. "I, Silas Alverado, stand inviolate within this, my pentagram of humanity, and project my will to embrace this, my triangular crucible of summoning."

Another group of attackers came too close and another volley of gunfire ensued. The wind rose in gusts and made it harder to hear what Silas was saying. "… in the name of the souls of those who died at your negligence. You who walked among them, you who ruled them with your wisdom, you who betrayed them." He drew a pattern in the air with his carved yellow rod. "You who once called yourself Faen-ka, High Priest of Amun, Vizier of Ramses the second, Pharaoh of all the world, hear my words and obey my commands."

A man's voice from around the side of the triangle caught everyone by surprise. "I refuse."

Everyone looked. It was Charles. Despite the bleeding bullet hole in his chest, he stood resolute with his fists at his sides. His usually light brown eyes glowed bright violet.

"You can't summon me if I am already in physical form."

Joseph snatched a machine gun from one of his men and started to aim it at Charles.

The demon within Charles cut him off. "You'll only seal Charles' fate by destroying his body. You know from your own experience that I can heal this form at will, and that no physical force can drive me from it if I don't want to leave." He turned back to Silas. "You can't use any destructive magic on me from inside that pentagram. If you step outside, you soul is mine!"

"You won't stay in that useless form forever, Sammael," Silas countered.

"Not forever. Just longer than you stay inside that pentagram." He looked away at the edge of the park. "Oh, you have company."

The sound of police sirens coming up the boulevard adjacent was quickly followed by four squad cars. Joseph ran around the side of the plaza and whipped off his sunglasses. He fired four bolts from his eyes in quick succession, one each into the front grills of the approaching police cars. The engines exploded and the cars were thrown spinning on the street below. Two of them flipped over from the impact.

Charles raised his eyebrows in mock admiration at Joseph. "Sweet." Turning back to Silas, he continued. "As I was saying, the only way out of this stalemate is for you to break the bond you have formed with my seal."

Silas looked at his long amber wand. "That would mean breaking this."

"Correct. With no more hold on my identity, there would be no justification for me to harm you. We would all just walk away."

As Joseph rejoined Sanantha and his men, she pulled him aside. "Don't get the wrong idea. I still haven't taken sides in your boss' little war. But I can't just let Charles get mowed down in the melee." She grabbed the pen out of his shirt pocket and spun him around. When he started to resist, she insisted, "Trust me, I've got an idea. Take off your jacket." He did and she quickly drew a complex curlicue *veve* pattern on the back of his white shirt, "If you're essentially a manifestation of Guede L'Orage, then this will protect you from magic that would force you out of your body."

He turned around and broadly smiled his conspiratorial understanding. He then walked away to a point thirty feet directly behind Charles as he faced Silas.

Sanantha could see that Silas saw Joseph, but the magician continued his discussion without interruption. "Walk away, indeed. As if you ever needed justification to torment a mortal. You've spent six thousand years operating with no justification whatsoever."

When Joseph started running at full speed straight at Charles, Charles turned around and only had time to comment sarcastically, "What do you think you're doing?"

Joseph picked him up under the armpits and slammed him into the Shield of Horus with such might that his own body crushed up against Charles'.

As Sanantha had hoped, Silas saw what they were trying, and made a sweeping motion with his hand to alter the Shield. As Joseph crushed Charles against the barrier, a third form was squeezed out from between them. Sanantha's line drawing on Joseph's back flared into red flames as it encountered the Shield, before Charles and Joseph fell through into heap on the other side. The ghostlike third form writhed as it pulled back from the Shield. It had a goat's head with long horns and angelic wings on a long snakelike body. It turned and hissed viciously at Silas, then vanished into thin air.

Silas smiled and nodded to Sanantha. He also smiled at Joseph as he got up. "Thank you both. Now get that body out of the pattern, and I'll do this properly."

Joseph grabbed Charles' limp form and started to drag it out, when he stopped and frowned at Silas. "No Master, that won't work!" His sudden insistence caught Silas by surprise. "Charles must have initiated contact with this demon from the *Purgatory*, which was how the demon knew to fire the missile at us." He turned to Sanantha. "Do you know how long Charles had been in this demon's thrall?"

Sanantha was stunned at the possibility. "He's been talking about contact with Voodoun gods since before we left Washington. I've even encouraged him. You think it's been this demon all along?"

Silas' tone was grave. "This creature is called the Prince of Liars for very good reason."

"That's my point," Joseph continued. "Having been in Charles' mind all this time, this demon knows exactly what items we imported. Now that he has seen how you've constructed this trap, there's no way it will hold him."

"So if I summon him," Silas concluded, "he will appear and act as if he were my prisoner, when in fact he is not."

"Knowing what he does of your plan, Master, I'm afraid you are already in great danger!"

The magician's stony expression didn't change as he considered his servant's advice. With a speed and decisiveness that left Sanantha blinking, he verified the truth of Joseph's words by telling him flatly, "Send me to my village in Haiti. I must make preparations immediately."

"Master," he hesitated reluctantly, "I don't know if I have …"

Cutting him off without impatience, Silas held out the end of his amber wand. "Take what strength you need from this."

"What about the trees?" Joseph asked sheepishly as he stepped up and gripped the rod's end.

"Then put me on the beach," Silas decided.

Joseph took a deep breath, gritted his teeth with the effort, and the old man vanished in a blinding, silent flash of light.

•   •   •

Warm waves lapping at his feet aroused Silas from unconsciousness. Rolling over in the sand and sitting up, every muscle-fiber in his body complained in stiffness and aches. He quickly surveyed the starry heavens and satisfied himself that only a few minutes had passed. He stood up slowly and carefully, tentatively stretching one muscle group at a time. Checking his gear, he was pleased to find his robe, crown, sash, fur and sword had all weathered the journey unscathed. On the other hand, the condition of his carved amber wand left him genuinely surprised. The four inches at the end where Joseph had grasped it were gone, melted away and evaporated in the ordeal. He shrugged at the unexpected side effect, shook the sand from his robe, and started walking.

Joseph's inexperience at teleporting others was apparent. Silas was about a quarter of a mile down the beach from where he had expected to be. He picked up the pace, urgent to get to his village.

As he walked toward the dock that marked the village road, Silas saw by the light of the full moon that there was someone on the pier. An old Haitian man was sitting on a couple of stacked tires, resting his elbows on a large crate as if it were a table at which he was seated. Silas didn't much care what the black man had seen, and was going to ignore him.

"Good morning, Amun *Houngan*," he called out to Silas in Haitian Creole.

This was the name his villagers had given him. "What are you doing out here in the middle of the night?" Silas asked him in his own tongue.

"Waiting for an old student of mine to come play cards with me while I wait for the new day."

Silas knew all the teachers in his village, and this man wasn't one of them. His interest aroused, he stopped at the top of the dock and asked him directly, "Are you from my village?"

"I was a long time ago, but only for a short while. You probably don't remember me. I'm easy to forget."

Silas never forgot anything in his life. The man was unremarkable, with typically very dark skin, short gray hair, dirty khaki pants and white shirt. Why would this old man lie? It hardly mattered. Silas dismissed him as lonely and turned to go.

"I know you've got a lot of work to do," the Haitian called after him. "But your preparations will go better if you stop and play a hand with me first."

Silas stopped and turned around. "Preparations?"

"Yes. For the coming storm," he offered with a yellowed smile.

There were no storms anywhere near Haiti. Maybe this old man was just a crackpot. He started to go again, when he caught a glint of odd color in the man's eyes. Where had he seen that color before?

He walked out onto the dock to question the man further, when he saw that the man had cards already spread out on his makeshift table. At first glance he assumed the spread was a form of solitaire. As he reached the man, though, he recognized it as a Tarot spread, only with regular playing cards. "Who taught you this arrangement?" he asked, curiosity getting the better of him.

"I thought it up," he announced proudly. "Do you like it?"

Quickly substituting the suits for their Tarot equivalents, Silas read the significance of the spread. It described a student coming to kill his teacher. He also remembered where he had seen that shade of purple. "Yes, it's quite ingenious. But you've left out a card," he said as calmly as he could as he reached into his robe and pulled out a card and dropped it onto the center of the spread. It depicted a chain held by two hands, one white and one black, surrounded by runic symbols.

The moment the Haitian saw it he burst out laughing. "Oh, my boy, your memory always was a marvel! After all these millennia. Congratulations!"

The magician grinned in a tight, controlled grimace. "How about this one?" he said, slapping down another, this one built around an image of a mask.

"Oh, most excellent!" he cried as his disguise was stripped away to reveal a white man with long curly black hair and beard, wearing a loose muslin robe over gold studded black leather armor. The cards on the crate also were revealed as actually being Tarot. "I guess this means we can stop using this childish pigeon language as well," he said in fluent ancient Egyptian.

Responding in the same language, Silas kept his guard up. "Before we proceed, it's only fair that I point out that I too am currently immortal."

"Oh, I know about your get-out-of-death-free deal with Osiris." He remained seated while he stroked his beard and frowned at the cards. "That hardly concerns me in my present predicament."

"I'm supposed to believe this means you are now my prisoner?"

"You know how much I hate to admit anything, but yes. I was assuming you wouldn't have much left up your sleeve after managing to squeeze me out of poor Charles' body. I figured I could chance this meeting, even in my weakened state, have a little fun tempting you with banter and clues, and then lower the boom on you, immortal or not." He smiled weakly up at Silas and shook his head. "But then you whip out not one, but two of the actual Tablets!

"I've got to tell you," he continued in his easy manner, "I always was quite impressed by you. I guess if anybody's going to put an end to my fun, it ought to be the first person who was the butt of it. Do you realize how much fun I've had tormenting scholars and mystics with these Tablets? I show them to the Egyptians once, and people spend the next three thousand years trying to figure out how to get them back. It's been a laugh riot."

Silas griped the handles of both his dagger and his wand which were tucked into his belt. "I know that you're the only creature with the audacity to reveal the essence of creation in a physical form that men could understand. Did Yahweh know what you were going to do, or did you just proceed on your own?"

The demon folded his arms, shrugged and looked aside in a dismissing gesture. "What's done is done. But you figured it out. I'm proud of you. You're the first one to do that."

Silas knew he wasn't. Cold realization gripped the magician. Indeed, everything this creature said was a lie. Could he get the true images of the Tablets of Aeth from the Prince of Liars? He recalled the spell of a 15th century Spanish Kabbalist who had once captured this demon, only to lose him to trickery. "Thy master's name is upon thee, Sammael," he spat.

"Oh relax, Royarna," he insisted breezily. "You've got me already."

Which, of course, meant exactly the opposite. Silas stood back and whipped out his sword and wand. Pointing the dagger steady at Sammael, he drew symbols in the air with his shortened wand for each of the magical words he proclaimed. "*Ik-Ku,* the thought of existence! *Mer,* the force of union!"

Sammael stood up as well, kicking the tires out of his way. He spread his arms wide, threw his head back with his mouth wide open and sucked in an impossibly large breath.

"*Sekham,* the destruction of the notion!" Silas continued with greater and greater conviction and volume. "*Kheper,* the creation of reality! *Ab-Ib,* the desire for creation!"

Sammael stretched out his fingers as if to claw at the very fabric of reality, then let loose with a thundering howl that grew in volume and depth. He leaned forward and brought his hands around in front of him as if to focus the sound straight at Silas.

"*Tekh,* the capacity for creation! *Sefekht!*" Silas screamed over his enemy's curse as he swung his dagger down on the demon's outstretched wrist. "Creation!"

The pre-dawn sky was lit from horizon to horizon by the flash of the blast. The water, sand and soil swept up in the explosion sent a mushroom cloud hundreds of feet in the air. Every bird in northern Haiti fled noisily, terrified into the night sky. Villagers all across the island nation were rocked from their beds. No one would ever understand what had happened.

17

HELL

WEARING ONLY A DRENCHED CAFTAN, Sanantha was glad the buffeting wind subsided at the base of the Washington Monument. It was the only thing she was glad about. She ran through what had a moment before been the impenetrable magical barrier and knelt down over Charles' fallen body. She felt his neck with her freezing cold hands for a pulse and found only a very faint beat. His breath too was fading fast. She scooped up his shoulders to prop him up against her chest. She looked up at the crewmen who were gathering around. "Can we get him to the boat?"

Joseph looked down at Charles and frowned. He then looked at Sanantha and shook his head sadly.

"What does that mean?" she spat.

"It means he's going to die and there's nothing we can do about it."

"But this bullet hole is over here through a lung," she insisted, pointing. "He's probably just lost a lot of blood."

Joseph knelt down and put his hand on her shoulder. "The bullet's only part of the problem. I hit him pretty hard before the demon finally let go of him."

She held the fallen man in her arms. Panic started to crack her voice. "But that can't just be the end of it."

Charles moaned and a trickle of blood ran out of his mouth.

"Charles, hang on. Can you hear me?"

He opened his eyes just far enough to see her. "Did I save ...?" he gasped quietly.

"What was that?" She put her ear down in front of his mouth.

"Is Voodou safe?"

She steeled herself and gave him the warmest, proudest smile she could muster. "Yes, Charles, Voodou is safe."

He smiled, his eyes fell shut, and he stopped breathing.

Once she was sure he could no longer see her, she let her emotions free and began to cry. "I'm so sorry, Charles," she sobbed quietly. "I'm so sorry I let this happen to you." The calming breeze stopped all together, the ominous clouds slowed their angry tumbling, and a warm, soft spring shower began to fall.

•   •   •

Silas Alverado awoke face down in dry, dusty dirt, aware of voices all around him, as if he were surrounded by onlookers. When he opened his eyes and turned over, he winced at the bright light from the sun overhead, but saw that he was indeed encircled. Hundreds of men and women were gathered around, all keeping their distance, as if they were afraid of him. The hushed silence that fell over them as he rose affirmed this impression. He was still wearing his priestly garb, but that was hardly strange enough to warrant their fear.

There were men and women of all ages. They were dressed in simple robes, sarongs, and sandals befitting the arid weather. He looked closer and saw they were all of the same ethnicity, generally short and slight of stature, olive skinned, almond eyed, with black hair. His first guess was Egyptian Coptic.

Being taller than most of them, he looked over their heads. All the way around the horizon stood an enormous vertical cliff, as if they were in some huge roughly circular depression. He was near one side of the hole, only a hundred yards from the near wall, while the far cliff appeared to be several miles away. No features were visible at the level top edge.

He still had no idea where he was. He approached a random individual, and the crowd recoiled back from him. On closer inspection, he could see they all looked very tired, haggard with dark circles under their fearful eyes.

"Where is this place?" he asked in Arabic to anyone who would answer.

Some of them muttered to one another and he caught a word or two. Silas didn't respond right away. He stood there blinking in amazement. He knew the language; he just had a hard time believing what he heard. Ancient Egyptian.

"Who are you people?" he asked in the correct language.

This generated more muttering than his first question, but not an answer.

He started to clarify himself with gestures, but he was again dumbstruck when he looked at his upraised right hand. His servo glove was gone, and his hand was tanned like his left. What had happened to him?

His reverie was interrupted when a commotion arose back in the crowd. Everyone stopped talking and turned around to see. Finally the crowd parted and a small group of men stepped into the clearing, led by one with silver streaked red hair and opulent clothes.

Silas was so stunned by what he saw, and moreover, what this meant, that he almost failed to react. He dropped to one knee, lowered his gaze, and greeted Ramses II. "Your Highness."

Pharaoh was furious. "What are you doing here!? We've waited 82 years. You were supposed to get us out! All this oxen dung about you being Chosen by the gods to change history. Was that just boasting?"

His tirade was cut short when the crowd all looked up to the near cliff top. When Ramses did as well, Silas ventured a look up too.

Two bearded men dressed as shepherds with striped blanket shawls over their shoulders stood at the edge and looked directly down at Silas. One had curly dark brown hair while the other had black hair that was almost completely replaced with white streaks. It was Moses and his brother Aaron.

Silas stood up and defiantly addressed the two onlookers in ancient Hebrew. "My goddess helped me to escape from here once, and I will do it again!"

Moses shook his head sadly side to side.

"I defeated the Prince of Liars! The world is a better place now that I've eradicated that wretched demon!" he insisted.

Moses looked surprised. He turned to Aaron and his brother raised his bushy eyebrows and nodded. Moses faced Silas again and graciously bowed to him.

"Surely that counts for something," Silas muttered to himself.

But the two men then turned and walked out of view.

Silas gritted his teeth and seethed at the empty cliff top. Then he noticed all eyes had turned on him.

•　　　•　　　•

Sammael was jolted into consciousness by the searing sting of a flail striking him across the back, despite his leather armor, as he lie on his stomach. He gritted his teeth and leapt to his feet, ready to unleash his full fury on his attacker. But when he spun around, he faced the malevolently grinning eight-foot figure of Osiris.

The demon's grimace of hatred dissolved in to a cocky, contemptuous grin. He quickly sized up the underground passage they were in, noting the wide natural stone corridor connected cavernous chambers which connected to even further passageways. From the way sound traveled, he could tell the extent of the maze was huge. From the stale smell of the air he could tell there was no exit. He looked up at the Egyptian god and sneered in ancient Hebrew, "You can't hold me here."

He noticed that a silver-white metal band, deeply engraved with Egyptian hieroglyphics, now enclosed his right wrist. He recognized it as the object Silas had created in their exchange. He snorted indignantly and stated self-assuredly, "This puny thing can't hold me either." He dashed his wrist against the stone wall, but the bracelet did not break. He glared at the resilient device for a moment before demanding of Osiris, "Just where the hell is here, anyway?"

"Nice choice of words," the god commented wryly in ancient Egyptian. "I should expect that from the Prince of Liars. Here," he gestured broadly about the tunnels and caves around them, "is what is left me of my *Duat* underworld, my Land of the Dead. It was to be but a temporary retreat for me until my champion could bring me followers, and with them, the power to take back my old realms and subjects." The vicious grin returned to his face as he added, "Now it seems it will be your prison, for the rest of time."

Sammael met him with dismissing, blatant sarcasm. "Hardly. As soon as your pathetic champion lands where I sent him, you'll have no one left on Earth to support your miserable existence, let alone keep me prisoner."

Osiris' grimace broadened into an enormous smile, and he burst out laughing. He laughed and laughed, so loud his voice echoed down passages and caverns that seemed to reach endlessly.

Sammael cocked an eyebrow and waited with folded arms for his towering jailer to finish. When the god finally settled down, he asked tightly, "What is so damned funny?"

Osiris took a deep breath and looked down upon him victoriously. "In your mad rush to exterminate my champion, you completely overlooked his servant. Joseph is free on Earth."

"He's a demon," he spat. "That hardly counts."

"If that were true, then it would create all the more delicious an irony, given how much I hate demons. No, Joseph was accused of being a demon three thousand years ago, and he served his time for that. What matters to you is that is he immortal," the god continued unabated, "and he will continue to create more believers wherever he goes."

Sammael's expression didn't change, but as minute followed silent minute, it became obvious that Osiris' words had their impact.

The god smiled again, and again began to chuckle, then laugh out loud. As his booming amusement went on and on, the demon slumped to sit on a nearby rock. For the first time in his six-thousand-year reign of terror, his glare of contempt was mixed with the resignation of genuine defeat.

·   ·   ·

A moment after Charles died, Joseph commanded his men back to the ship. Police sirens blared from all around the park as flickering blue and red lights cut through the dawn and formed a tightening ring.

Sanantha didn't care. She held Charles' body in her lap as she sat on the wet grass and rocked back and forth. Was there anything else she could have done? Charles made his choice. She had tried to save his mind. She did help him find his courage. In the end, that saved his soul.

She looked up and watched the Purgatory's crewmen running back through the trees toward the river. Joseph turned back and caught her gaze, just before he disappeared in a cloud of yellow smoke. She looked around at the dozens of wounded innocents sprawled on the lawn. They had regained consciousness, but none of them knew what had happened.

She blinked as she realized just how close they had come to Armageddon. Had Charles not given Sammael the advantage, Silas would have probably succeeded. She looked down at Charles. He wanted to save Voodou, and ended up saving the world. And no one would ever know.

When the police arrived, they treated her the same as the rest — another innocent swept up in something no one could explain.

·   ·   ·

When Joseph arrived on the beach, he initially thought he must have teleported somewhere other than where he had sent his master. The dock at the end of the village road was nowhere to be seen. In fact, the beach under where the dock should have been was now a semi-circular divot-like inlet some twenty meters in diameter. The trees around this spot were knocked down, leaning away from the shore. Then he realized what must have happened.

He reached out with his mind's eye for the sense of Silas' presence that was always there. Now it wasn't. He took off his sunglasses and scanned the area. He found a few scattered ashes of pier pilings, but that was all.

There was simply no way he could tell whether his master had succeeded in defeating the demon. Nor could he trace how it was that Silas left this plane of existence. All Joseph knew was, he was now free. He wasn't sure how he felt about that.

He scanned the area once more, and found one more item. Half buried in the sand, face down, was a card. He picked it up. It was the Three of Swords, three swords piercing a heart above a rose that had been cut to pieces, the Tarot card of lost hope. He decided not to assume that its meaning reflected on his master's fate. He did decide to keep the card.

ABOUT THE AUTHOR

Jay Hartlove is the award-winning author of the urban fantasy "Goddess Rising" trilogy (*Goddess Chosen, Goddess Daughter,* and *Goddess Rising*) and the fantasy romance *Mermaid Steel.* He is also the playwright, director and producer of *The Mirror's Revenge*, the musical sequel to the Snow White fable, which had its theatrical run in the San Francisco Bay Area in August 2018 to rave reviews.

His stories are filled with conspiracies and the supernatural, gods, dreams, angels, and hidden connections. His creative motto is "Dark Secrets Revealed". He loves to take stories where the reader does not expect, with sympathetic villains, heroes with very dark pasts, and lots of plot twists. He was selected as one of the "50 Authors You Should Be Reading" by *The Authors Show.*

Jay is a former competitive costumer, having won Best in Show at both San Diego ComicCon and WorldCon. You can read more about Jay's creative adventures, including much of the research he put into his books, at *jaywrites.com.*

YOU MIGHT ALSO ENJOY

Best Intentions

Book One of the *Glass Bottles* Series

by J Dark

When your past is left undone, it will come find you.

DUE DATE

by Nancy Wood

Surrogate mother Shelby McDougall just fell for the biggest con of all: a scam that risks her life ... and the lives of her unborn twins.

MEMORY AND METAPHOR

by Andrea Monticue

Civilization fell. It rose. At some point, people built starships.

www.ingramcontent.com/pod-product-compliance
Lightning Source LLC
Chambersburg PA
CBHW030243200626
46816CB00002BA/485